Roommates Don't Kiss & Tell

Roommates

Don't

Kiss & Tell

By Caz May

Book 1 in The Always Only You Series

First Published 2019
ISBN 978-0-6484998-0-0

Published by Caz May

© Caz May 2018

To my best friend forever Bianca, my biggest fan always

Table of Contents

Author's Preface

Hello lovely reader! I thank you for purchasing my book, your support means the world to this newbie author.

Before we get into the story it's essential for you to take note of the following information. It will ensure you understand the story and enjoy reading it as much as I enjoyed writing it.

This story is set in my current city of Melbourne, Victoria, Australia. I've been a Melbourne girl for eleven years now and absolutely love the unique city life it offers. Some of the places in the story are fictional, and some are real.

At the end of the book you will find a slang glossary which contains most of the Australian slang references you will find in the story.

This story is told in first person alternating point of views. If there is only a chapter title then the chapter is told from the main protagonists' point of view. If another name is underneath the chapter title that chapter is narrated by another character.

Lastly, I leave you with some pronunciations for my characters names.

Annika/Anni (main protagonist): Ann-ic-a & An-e

Jairus/Jai: Jye-rus & Jye

Austin/Aust: Aus-tin & Aus-t

I truly hope you enjoy the story.

Caz May

xx

A guy and a girl can be just friends, but at one point or another, they will fall for each other... maybe temporarily, maybe at the wrong time, maybe too late, or maybe forever

Dave Matthews

Prologue

Late December 2014

I was what most people would describe as a plain Jane, not beautiful, maybe cute, painfully shy and a late bloomer in every way.

It wasn't as though I didn't think about guys, or didn't want to kiss someone, but meek, petite Annika didn't register on their radars.
Instead they all went after the girls who somehow over the summer holidays grew voluptuous breasts and looked as though they'd gotten butt implants.

There was only one guy I'd wanted all through high school, watching him from afar, as he dated nearly every girl in our year level.
He had the boyish good looks every girl lusted over, his fiery red hair unruly and his dark eyes that made every girl swoon including myself.

What was odd about Austin though, was he was a certified geek; academically a science whiz and totally addicted to video games.
If he wasn't buried in a book or glued to the television screen, he was pashing his latest hussy.

It was stupid and incredibly naive to want to be
Austin Belvinz's girlfriend, as even though I was nerdy
I wasn't exactly his usual type.
He always preferred brunettes and the
aforementioned curvy girls, not little old me,
blonde haired, no curves at all and so shy I'd barely
spoken two words to anyone let alone a guy.

I spent my days in the library, my nose buried in a
book hiding down the back of the shelves where no
one would disturb me, or so I thought.
Until the biggest storm Stawell had seen rolled in
turning day into night.

The lights flicker, and every person in the library
screams like the end of the world is descending upon
us. When they cut out completely, an eerie calm
settles over the library.
Liking the darkness, I sigh, taking my phone out of my
pocket and shining the torchlight onto my page to
continue reading.
Around me, I can hear faint whispers and the sound
of lips puckering as someone is pashing nearby.

Feet shuffle along the gap between the shelves.
A tall guy who isn't thinking about where he's going
holds a torchlight up scanning the shelves to find an
item. He falls on top of me in a tangled heap when he
bumps into my feet.

Holding up my torch to see, my face is now only a whisper away from Austin's.

"Sorry, I couldn't see," he says apologetically, stating the obvious.

"Um...well..." I stammer, completely tongue tied as he stares at me, not seeming like he was going to move anytime soon.

My heart is pounding, having him so close and speaking to me.

"It's Annika yeah?" he asks, shocking me that he actually knows my name, even though I'd spent Christmas at his house for the last few years with my family.
I'd been so painfully shy, even as a sixteen-year-old that I'd stayed glued to my Mum's side and didn't engage with him at all.

"Yes," I manage to squeeze out from my pursed lips.

"Well, Annika," he states, climbing off my lap and sitting next to me stretching out his legs in front of him, crossing them at the ankles, "I'm Austin. Nice to officially meet you, even though I've known you for years," he coos, with a hint of laughter in his tone.

Caz May

Gulping, I will my mind to cooperate with my tongue
to actually say more than two words to the gorgeous
guy sitting next to me.
No doubt he looked dapper as hell like he always did,
wearing skin-tight dark jeans, a white second skin t-
shirt and his purple Nikes.

In the darkness I could feel his eyes on me, like he
had cat like night vision. His hand brushes against
mine, and he laces our fingers together, breaking the
silence when he whispers, "I always wanted to talk to
you, but didn't have the guts."

I chuckle softly, completely taken aback by his
confession, but even more taken aback when
I feel his rough hand across my cheek, his finger
grazing across my bottom lip.

He inhales a breath, and lets it out desperately,
before pressing his lips to mine.

His kiss soft, his lips warm and tingly on mine. My
heart is galloping in my chest, my mind screaming
'your first kiss, Anni, your first kiss is with Austin, you
lucky bitch'

Wanting more I gasp, and feel him smile as he pulls
away. The lights flickering back on cause everyone in
the library to hiss in appreciation.

Austin was still looking at me, and I feel my cheeks turning crimson.

"I guess you liked that," he jeers at me light-heartedly.

Not trusting myself to speak, I nod and gape when he asks, "Will you go out with me on Saturday?"

Work brain, say yes Anni, Austin is asking you out, what are you waiting for?

"Yes, Austin," I reply smiling.

"Great, meet me at Clocktower at five?"

"Ok," I reply, trying to not sound too eager, as he stands up, brushing his hands across his butt to wipe off the dirt from the floor.

"See you then Anni," he coos, making my heart skip at his use of my nickname.

Shutting my book, I hold it to my chest, hoping that finally my luck had turned and I was going to be Austin's girlfriend.

I'd most certainly dreamt about it, just as I had dreamt about kissing him and his kiss was far beyond anything I could have dreamt of.

Caz May

One I Monopoly Night

Two- and a-bit years later
May 2017

Sitting cross legged on the fluffy rug, the fireplace in our Richmond apartment is ablaze warming my back and making me feel comfortably warm enough to only be wearing three-quarter leggings and a V-neck fitted t-shirt in late May.

Across from me on the other side of the low glass coffee table, Austin is sitting with his long legs outstretched, wearing a tank top that shows his defined arms with pyjama pants that hang low on his hips, pooling at his crotch.

Gazing at his outfit I have to stop myself from licking my lips, and jumping him.
He might have been my best friend now, but I can't deny his good looks and the attraction to him I still feel.
I certainly wasn't in love with him anymore though, our breakup amicable as we both thought we were better off as friends.

For some reason, if we defined what we had together as boyfriend and girlfriend we fought like cats and dogs, never kissed and certainly never had sex.

Austin had been my first kiss, and I'd been shocked when we slept together that I was his first time too, as he was mine.

It had crossed my mind that it was maybe the reason that he couldn't now let go of being with me completely, preferring to be my best friend and partake in some bedroom action when he saw fit.

Sometimes I hated myself for giving in, but sex with Austin was good; not that I had anything to compare to.

I also knew since moving to Melbourne for University, finding the two-bedroom apartment we now called home together that I'd not been the only girl Austin had snuggled up with between the sheets.

Me on the other hand, romance wasn't really on my radar, too busy with my nursing degree and knowing that if I really did want sex, Austin would be more than willing to help me scratch the itch.

Part of me wondered if he did want us to get back together, that maybe he was in denial about how he felt about me. He'd never actually said I love you when we were together, only since we'd crossed back into the friend zone and his tone was always jovial whenever the word 'love" came out of his mouth.

I shake myself back to reality, gazing at him sitting across from me.

He bites down on his lip, concentrating as he shakes the dice in his hand, no doubt wishing in his mind to roll a six to get out of jail for the fifth time since we'd started our usual Thursday night game of Monopoly. Throwing it against the board, it teetered a little before stopping with four as the number facing up.

I laugh at his response, "Fuck a duck, I suck at this game."
"Yeah says the guy who owns half the board right now."
"You're just upset because you have to pay me big bucks when you land on my squares," he jeers taking a puff of his joint.

My eyes dart from the rolled paper to his eyes, "Why do you have to smoke that inside Aust? The place reeks of weed and we've got the inspection on Monday."

He laughs, stabbing the stubby remains in the ashtray on the edge of the coffee table, "Sorry, Mum, didn't know it was a crime to smoke a joint in my own house," he chastises me, knowing how much I hate when he calls me 'Mum'.

"Um, actually, Austin. It is a crime and something that could get us kicked out of here."

Picking up the dice for my turn, I scowl at him, knowing my comment is falling on deaf ears. The only reason I even really cared about Austin's weed habit was because I'd seen it become a gateway drug with my older brother, before he took to Meth and Cocaine. His battle with addiction partly being what led me to nursing, wanting to specialise in drug rehabilitation.

Seeing the look on my face as I throw the dice against the board Austin breaks the silence, "Babe you need to lighten up, it wouldn't kill you to take a drag once in awhile."
"Not going to happen Aust and you know why."

The dice crashes against his ashtray, with only two facing up, the expression on his face changes to a frown, "Sorry Anni, I shouldn't have said that. I miss Alex too, but it wouldn't hurt you to lighten up a little."
"I know, Aust, I'll try ok?" I promise, moving my koala pawn two spaces along the board, only to find I'd landed on the one square of the board he'd bought up big on. He had it lined with hotels, and I scoff as I count the paper money I need to hand over to him. Holding the wad of paper money in my hand out towards him, he shakes his head laughing, "Pay up babe."
"Here, take it all bitch," I laugh, quoting one of our favourite movies 'Centre Stage'.
Again, shaking his head, he taps a finger against his cheek, "Uh-uh....pay up babe.... I don't want your wad of paper cash."
"Oh, so that's how it is huh?" I tease, smirking at him.

"Tease me like that babe, and you'll pay with a proper pash."

I curse myself that my insides flip-flop at his cheeky suggestion.

"So are you paying up or not babe?" He taunts leaning across the coffee table.

Leaning forward I close my eyes, leaning closer to him to press a kiss to his cheek, but instead I feel his lips on mine.

He pulls back, "Anni, you could have just jumped me babe," he laughs.

"I...I didn't want to kiss you Aust," I protest, cursing myself for the blush that is rising up my cheeks.

"Your face says otherwise Anni," he teases, licking his lips, "so...you have two minutes to get away or I'll fuck you right here in front of the fire," he threatens with a teasing tone.

Go on Anni, you need sex girl, you've been so uptight lately

I hate that my subconscious is right, but it is, my vibrator just isn't cutting it and Austin was offering as usual, a quickie.

I toy for a moment, of letting him take me on the fluffy rug by the fireplace, but I know it's a bad idea as our new roommate is supposed to be arriving sometime today and he hasn't turned up yet.

I wasn't shy around Austin anymore, even when it came to sex but I certainly didn't want a stranger to walk in on our romp to meet me for the first time with my daks around my feet.
Giggling I get to my feet, turning to look back at him when I stand in the doorway of his bedroom, beckoning him with a finger and a smirk.

Before I even have a moment to think about the fact that I'm teasing my best friend he's in front of me, grabbing me by the waist and carrying me to his single bed.

Smashing a kiss to my lips, he moans a little. I can feel his dick straining against the front of his pyjama pants, pressing against my stomach. "God Anni, you're such a tease," he drawls.

"Really? I didn't do anything," I laugh, as he reaches over to the drawers beside the bed to grab a condom out.

At the same time, we both yank our daks to our ankles, and I giggle as he rolls the condom on. Smashing another kiss to my lips, he drives himself inside me, hissing against my lips as I rise my hips to meet his.
Hearing a banging sound, I break our kiss, my eyes locking on the door that is still slightly ajar.

Gasping at what I see in the doorway, I push Austin off my body.

Both of us struggle to pull up our daks, the voice of the figure standing in the doorway speaks, "Sorry to interrupt ya romp, but I'm your new roomie, Jairus."

My cheeks flush, as I look at the floor racing out of Austin's room to my own. Slamming the door shut I flop down on my double bed, feeling utterly humiliated and downright stupid that I'd not told Austin to shut the door.

I might as well have been naked, as my new roommate had just seen a lot more than he needed to.

How in the hell am I going to face my hot new roommate now?

Two | Spoon Me

Only a few minutes pass before I hear the scuffle of
feet on the floorboards heading to my room.
Austin doesn't bother knocking, instead barges in like
an elephant.
I'd pulled the covers over my head, not wanting to
face him.

"Go away Austin, I don't want to talk to you."
He sits on the edge of my bed, trying to pry the
cocoon of covers off me.

"Come on Anni, I'm sorry ok?"

Sticking my head out to look at him, I protest "Not ok
Aust. Our new roommate caught us fucking."
"I was just as embarrassed as you Anni, probably
more so because I had to walk out of the room, still
with a hard on."

I laugh, picturing the look on Jairus' face.
"I guess you don't want to face our new roomie
tonight then either?"
His face flushes and he bites his lip in the sweet way
he always does when he's not sure what to say.

"Aust?" I coo at him, smirking a little.
"Yeah?"

Caz May

"Can I ask you something?"
"Yeah, babe, anything."

I sit up on the bed, leaning into him a little, still with
the covers over my head.
"Do you want to be more than friends again?"
He shifts back from me, pushing the covers off my
head to look right into my eyes when he replies,
"What's made you ask that Anni? I thought you were
sweet with being fuck buddies."
"I um...I am...I just kind of miss how things used to be
before."
"Before when?" He asks giving me a quizzical look.
"We moved here, back home in Stawell."
"Really Anni? You miss having the parentals breathing
down ya neck, wanting to know your every move?"
"Ok maybe not that, but I miss the days we used to
spend together out bunny bashing in your Ute and..."
His face flushes, as though he's remembering the
same moment I am.
"You say that like I've forgotten our first time
together Annika," he muses, a serious tone in his
voice.
He hardly ever uses my full name anymore, and
when he does the conversation is always more
serious.
"I didn't mean it like that, but we hardly do anything
together now and always just fall into bed together."
"Yeah, I get you babe, and I'm sorry. How about we
go out on Saturday night?"
"Sounds like a great idea, but only if we don't go to
Risqué."

"We'll go wherever you want to go babe," he promises.

"As long as it's not Risqué and I can get blind and boogie I'll be happy."

"You're such a country girl Anni, blind and boogie...like what the fuck?"

"Yeah a country girl and proud of it," I laugh, punching his arm lightly when I jeer at him, "you're a country boy at heart too Aust."

Laughing he pushes me down on the bed, his body over mine when he sings in my ear, "You want to boogie wit m'baby?"

"Mmm, but only if you close the door this time," I laugh.

Huffing he stands up, his hands covering the front of his pyjama pants, as he tiptoes closer to the door, kicking it shut.

He dives back onto the bed, grabbing me around the waist and tickling me.

"So, bestie are we going to finish what we started?"

Rolling over to face him, I don't reply, instead kiss him.

Again, he moans against my lips, running his tongue across my bottom lip.

Gasping I let him deepen the kiss, parting my lips to let him in to take my tongue with his.

Austin's kisses were always hot and demanding, but I sometimes cursed myself for how turned on kissing him made me.

The lust between us was like fire, and it made me
wonder why things didn't work out between us out
of the bedroom.

Teasing him was all part of the friendly banter that
had always been a part of our relationship, but nine
times out of ten now teasing lead to pashing, and
pashing led to fucking.

As he continues the delicious kiss, I can feel the
arousal pooling in my undies.

Pulling back, I whisper in his ear, "Aust, fuck me
now."

"Mmmm," he moans, nibbling my earlobe before
teasingly asking, "only if I can go bareback babe?"

My mind ponders his question, thinking back to
when I'd had my last period and mentally calculating
my cycle days.

Without speaking I kiss him again, but he doesn't let
me deepen the kiss, instead breathes in deep against
my lips, "is that a yes Anni?"

"Mmm," I moan, dakking him and grabbing his dick in
my grasp.

"Fuck Annika," he moans, his eyes glazing at the
contact.

He looks down at my still clothed body, clearing his
throat to tell me to take off my leggings.

Letting go of him, I yank my leggings and undies
down together right down to my ankles.

He barely gives me a minute to think, to take a
breath before he enters my damp core.

His thrusts in and out seem more carnal than usual, more sensual and the sensation of him bareback inside me makes my desire rise even more.
I buck my hips up to his, pushing him deeper inside me.

Emotions swirl in my mind, feelings that something has changed between us and this isn't just two best friends scratching the itch.
His eyes look straight into mine, and breathlessly I demand, "Kiss me Aust, please."
"Mmm," he moans before smashing his lips against mine urgently as he thrusts harder.
Not able to control myself, I can feel the beginning of my climax taking over.
Ripping my mouth from his, I scream out, "Aust, I'm going to come!"
"Fuck, Anni..." he drawls out, his release hot and sudden inside me, as my climax overtakes my body and I bite down on my lip to stop myself from screaming out his name.
Panting he pulls out to lie next to me, "That was seriously hot babe," he taunts.

I giggle, "I love you Aust."
He gapes at my words, and I slap a hand over my mouth to not say another word.
"Huh? What?" He snaps, looking at me wide eyed.
"Not like that you goose," I laugh, even though my heart is pounding and my mind is racing, wondering if I actually mean it.

"Good I'd thought you'd gone loopy, but I love you to babe."
The way he says those words, I can tell he means it in the way I told him I do, but my pounding heart says otherwise.

I can't fall back in love with Austin again, as I'd only get hurt. I know that, but still as he sits up about to get out of my bed, I grab his arm to pull him back down.
"Spoon me?" I ask softly.

"Is that a demand?"
I nod and he settles against my back, his hand running over the sensitive skin of my hips beneath my t-shirt.
"Are you sure you're sweet just being fuck buddies, Anni?"
Turning my head back towards his, I give him a soft kiss before I reply, "Yes, why wouldn't I be?"
"Ah...no reason...just um.." he stutters, biting down on his lip.
It seems as though he is just as confused as I am, so I try to calm him with my words, "We don't work any other way."
"True," he declares, pressing a kiss against my forehead and pulling my body closer to his.
Lying in his arms, spooning feels way to comfortable but so nice and I let myself slip into a dreamless sleep.

Three | Breakfast Encounters

Rolling over in bed, much to Austin's protest I slap a fist against the snooze button of my blaring alarm clock.

He lets out a grunt, as he stretches his arms above his head, "Ahh...you have to be shitting me?"

I glare at him, snapping,"Shitting you about what Aust?"

"That it's time to get up."

"For me yes, I have an extra tute to go to."

He pouts at me, pushing the sheets back and nodding towards his crotch.

As usual with boys in the morning; in the front of his daks there is a tent.

Thankfully at some point during the night, we'd managed to both pull up our daks though.

"Really Anni? I was hoping you'd help me deal with this," he laughs teasingly.

"I can't Aust, I need to shower and eat something."

"Can I help you get clean then?" he asks, with the same teasing tone in his voice.

Playfully I slap his arm, "Aust what's gotten into you?"

"Nothing," he snaps at me, pouting again, "it's just been forever since we've had a morning quickie."

"Yes, but most mornings I'm out of here before you even roll out of bed."

He doesn't reply, instead grabs my cheeks in his palms and smashes a kiss to my lips, "Is there no convincing you babe?"

"No Aust, there's not," I reply, silencing my alarm again and flipping my legs over the edge of the bed. Turning to look back at him, I taunt, "It wouldn't hurt you to get out of bed before noon ya know. You're such a bludger."

Standing up I stretch my arms above my head, my t-shirt creeping up my torso a bit exposing my stomach.

Austin shifts in the bed, propping himself up on his elbow, "Mmm, you still look hot as under your clothes Anni."

Grabbing a discarded pair of daks from the floor I throw them at his head, "Stop it Aust, you're disgusting seriously!"

"Disgusting Anni?"

"Yes, disgusting, I hate ya face!" I chortle at him, almost doubling over in laughter.

"No, you don't! You love me! You told me so last night," he teases, beckoning me to lean in closer to the bed so he can whisper to me, "you know before I fucked your brains out!"

"Austin, you dirty boy!" I tease him.

He grabs my waist to pull me back down to the bed. I try to wriggle free from his arms, but he's wrapped them tightly around my back.

"One kiss and I'll let you go," he demands looking up at me with an odd look in his eyes, that doesn't appear to be lust.

"Aust, a question?"

"If you must," he laughs.

"Should fuck buddies kiss?" I ask, feeling like an innocent fool for asking such a stupid question.

"What kinda question is that Anni?"

"A valid one and you know what I mean."

"I don't actually."

Leaning closer to him, he grips my back tighter, "You know like in the movies they don't kiss."

"Yeah, well we aren't in a movie babe and if I want to kiss my best friend," he pauses, licking his lips, "then I will."

"Best friends don't kiss Aust," I tease.

"Yeah but fuck buddies do," he laughs, crashing his lips to mine for a kiss that again seems more than just lustful.

~~

After making out with Austin for a lot longer than I should have, I grab my dressing gown from the hook on the back of the door.

Slipping my arms in, I look back at Austin still tangled in my sheets, "Thanks to you bestie I don't have time for a fucking shower."

He laughs, "Sorry, not sorry."

My stomach has decided to grumble and food was
definitely more important than a shower, even
though I smell like sex and the intoxicating scent of
Austin's cologne mixed with my perfume.
If I didn't eat, I'd no doubt get a headache and pass
out in the practical class.

I couldn't miss anything this time, as it was all
practice for the upcoming placement in a month or
so time.

I'm about to turn the doorknob to leave, when Austin
asks, "What's this extra tute for anyway?"
"Placement practice. I missed the last one because I
passed out remember?"
"Right, the day I had to rescue the damsel in
distress."
"Ha-ha," I spit at him, sticking my tongue out
mockingly, "stay in bed if you want, bludger."
"Oh, I will," he laughs, "your bed is so much better
than mine."
"Don't get used to it, you'll be back in yours tonight,"
I reply, finally leaving my bedroom to head to the
kitchen.

Momentarily forgetting the night's event before
Austin's arrival in my bedroom, I gasp finding our
new roommate standing in the kitchen.
He's leaning against the bench by the fridge, holding
a bowl and spooning into his mouth what appears to
be Weetbix.

His only clothing item are his super tight Richmond football shorts, which accentuate the ample package beneath them.

To be honest, footy shorts barely hid any guy's package and were the only reason any girl ever watched football, myself included.

Jairus had responded to our advertisement that we stuck up on the Coles community notice board for a new roommate.

The rent for our furnished apartment, being in Richmond, so close to the CBD had been raised too high for two University students to pay.

I'd wanted a female roommate but Austin convinced me that having a male would be better because his room had two single beds and he didn't want me to give up the double bed in the main bedroom I'd claimed as mine.

It was clear that his reasons were clearly selfish though, as he liked sneaking into my room for sex in the middle of the night and he didn't want a girl to get suspicious of me sneaking out if the tables turned and we switched bedrooms.

Jairus seemed like the perfect candidate, as his new found career as a full forward for the Richmond tigers meant he was sure to be earning a pretty packet and could afford the rent as well as any utilities.

I should have thought more about that, as I clearly didn't think he'd be helping himself to our food the first morning in the house, but he was and he looked absolutely gorgeous doing so.

As he was only wearing the footy shorts, his chest was bare showing off his defined six pack abs and his arms were muscular, the veins rippling every time he lifted the spoon to his mouth.

He smirks at me, as I stand completely dumbstruck by him on the other side of the kitchen.

"Hey roomie," he sasses, "or should I say sex fiend?"
"Um...hey," I mutter, feeling the blush rise up my cheeks.

"Sorry we didn't get properly acquainted last night," he apologises, grinning, "Training ran over."
"Um yeah, um all good."
"You alright?"
"Yep, I'm...ff..fine," I stammer, stepping into the kitchen closer to him, to the fridge to grab out the milk.
"Mmm yeah...except for the stick up ya arse," he taunts, still with a devious smirk on his face.

Stepping closer to him, I have to look at him even closer and I gulp as his olive green eyes look me up and down as though he's thinking about seeing me half naked the night before.

Opening the fridge, I will my brain to cooperate with my tongue to speak, "I don't have a stick up the arse."

"Oh really sweetheart, " he drawls, "when I met you last night you had a dick up your front clacker."

Simultaneously, I blush and scoff at his complete insolence.

He was so cocky; it irritated me but also sent a rush straight to my core.

I don't respond, instead bend over to grab the milk from the bottom of the door. My dressing gown feels like it's tight against my body, showing off the curve of my butt and I can tell he's copping a good look.

"Mmm, you've definitely got a ripper arse sweetheart."

"Are you always this crass?" I ask, stepping back from the fridge and pondering how I'm going to get a coffee cup from the cupboard above his head.

"I might be, or it could just be you bringing out my best stuff."

"Me?" I scoff, clearing my throat and pointing towards the cupboard.

He turns his head to look up, "You want something from there?"

I nod, blushing as standing next to him is making my blood pump everywhere but to my brain. My mind is foggy, affected by his so sure of himself presence.

"Um...yeah a coffee mug," I stammer, licking my lips.
"Well, come and get it, I'm not going to stop you," he laughs.
"Your...um...in the way."
"Oh right, should I just move then?" he asks stepping from side to side, every time I take a step to either side. When he appears to stop the silly side step game, I stretch up on my tiptoes to open the cupboard, grabbing the first cup my fingers brush against.

With the mug in hand, I push my feet hard into the tiled floor, gasping when he shifts his body along the bench and his package brushes my thigh.

Move Anni, why are you still fucking standing there, Anni, earth to Anni

His olive green eyes drop to the front of my dressing gown, where it's fallen open when I'd stretched up to the cupboard.
My tight V-neck shirt is showing a little too much for his glance as well.
My feet however are not cooperating, not moving away from him.
I can feel the tension between us, wondering for a moment if he's going to kiss me.
Instead he leans closer, hissing in my ear, "You smell like sex, and it's damn arousing."
His words shock me; I'd only met him officially mere moments ago and he is already speaking to me as though we are far more than acquaintances. The way

his proximity is making me feel, I suddenly feel very aware of my own body.

Trying to taunt him back I reply stuttering, "Yeah.... well...well...you smell like grass."
He laughs, "Grass, really sweetheart?"
My reply caught in my throat when I hear Austin enter the room clearing his throat asking, "You didn't happen to get anymore coffee Anni did you?"
I jump back, tripping up on Jairus' foot and stumbling against the island bench in front of me.

"Um, no Aust I um didn't," I stammer, really hoping he hadn't seen the comprising situation I was just in.
"Oh I'll get some later then," he yawns, looking at Jairus nodding, "oh hey man."
Jairus nods back, walking over to Austin and shaking his hand, "Hey, ripper to officially meet you man."
"You to, and sorry ya had to see me with my daks down."
"To be honest man, I wasn't looking at you," he laughs, turning his gaze towards me.
"Oh yeah right," Austin replies, blushing.
"Are you two a couple or what?" he asks, darting his eyes between us, waiting for one of us to answer.
"Um...no...just best mates," Austin replies, trying to sound casual.
Jairus laughs cockily, "Oh its like that huh? First time you've fucked then?"
Neither Austin or I reply, instead he walks away calling out, "Dibs on the shower."

I'm running super late now, and haven't eaten anything so I grab an apple and leave my mug on the bench, next to the milk.

"Your lack of an answer tells me everything sweetheart," Jairus taunts, as I start to walk out of the kitchen to get dressed.

He is so damn infuriating and it weirdly excites and scares me at the same time. As I dress, I contemplate how shy little me is going to handle living with two hot as hell guys, who both seem to want the same thing.
Me.

Four | Caught Out

Having barely eaten all day, only scoffing down the apple I'd grabbed when escaping from Jairus' intense gaze in the kitchen this morning, my head feels like I've been hit by a bus square between the eyes.

Not even the sweet caffeine hit of my Iced Coffee I'd grabbed down the road at my local Gloria Jeans on the way home has quelled it. It makes me happy though, as walking in they made my drink before I'd even sauntered up to the counter.

Some people, Austin included thought I was mad ordering an Iced Coffee when it was like ten degrees outside, but I had my Iced Coffee every day; rain, hail, shine or icy death blast.

Unlocking the front door, I find Austin sitting knees apart on the couch, with his PlayStation controller in his hands. His gaze is locked on the Television screen, as he's biting down on the corner of his lip in concentration.

It's probably crazy to disturb him in the middle of whatever latest game he's playing, most likely 'Call of Duty' or some other shooting game, but I drop my

bag by the door, hang my keys on the hook and
proceed to make myself a wall by standing in front of
the television.

"Babe, move yeah?" he snaps at me, shifting his head
to the side to try and see around me.
"No, not until you agree to cook tonight," I taunt.

He presses a button on the controller and the sound
of his game cuts out in pause mode.

"Anni, I cooked like um..." he stops, obviously
thinking about the last time he cooked, which seems
like yonks ago; but was most likely last week.
"Last week?" I suggest.
"Yeah, so lay off..."

Arguing with Austin about household chores was
sometimes like pulling teeth, excruciating and
pointless.
 I move away from the television to sit next to him on
the couch.
"Aust, I'm dying," I muse at him.
"What? Are you serious?"
"No, you idiot," I laugh, "well maybe if dying of
starvation from only having an apple and iced coffee
counts."
"Anni, you can't keep doing that to yourself," he says
concerned, resting a hand on my knee.
"I know, but..."

"No buts Anni, I'm going to cook you something and you'll promise to eat better," he declares, giving me dagger eyes, as though he's telling me I must obey him.

"OK, Aust," I reply, leaning against his shoulder, "can you get some water and painkillers first?"

Again he shoots me the dagger eyes, "Anni, that's another thing?"

"What?" I spit.

"There's no Nurofen Plus left."

"How? I picked up the script like two weeks ago."

"Stuffed if I know Anni."

"Well, give me some Panadol then. It's shit but it'll have to do."

Before he stands up, he wraps his arms around my back, pressing a kiss to my forehead. It seems like another too weird loving gesture and makes my insides flutter a little.

"So Carbonara good with you?"

"Sounds delicious, especially if you're cooking it," I tease.

"Not funny babe, I happen to think I'm a ripper cook," he protests, as he walks to the kitchen.

Following him I sit at the table, as he goes to the fridge to grab out the ingredients.

"I'm just teasing you Aust," I inform him.

"I know babe," he smiles at me, starting to cut up the onions.

Seeing him in the kitchen is a scrumptious sight. He is dressed as usual in his signature tank top and trackie daks that sit low on his hips, showing the waistband of his Mitch Dowd boxers.

Tears from cutting the onions are running down his cheeks and standing up, walking around to the other side of the bench I stand up on my tiptoes, licking them from his cheeks.
"Babe, what are you doing?"
"Nothing, but you looked so hot in the kitchen and then you were crying," I laugh.
He laughs back in response, "Well onions babe, you know."

"I know," I laugh again, kissing his lips softly, "but I kind of wanted to kiss you."
"Oh really?"
I nod, licking my lips and tasting the salt of his tears on them.
"Well, babe, I can take you right here, right now, or cook your food, your choice?"
"Can't I have both?" I tease.
"Fine, one kiss and then I'll finish the food, but you're chopping the bacon."
I don't respond, instead push him against the bench crashing my lips to his. Taking control of the kiss, he moans against my mouth, instinctively wrapping his arms around my waist and pressing my body into his.

Lost in the moment, at first I don't hear the crash of the door slamming shut, announcing Jairus' arrival home from footy training.

"Bloody fucking hell, can you two get a god damn room?"
I jump back from Austin, a blush rising up my cheeks at again being caught in a compromising situation with my best friend.

Fighting my shyness, I spit at Jairus when he enters the kitchen to grab a beer from the fridge, "You're just jelly."
"Damn straight, sweetheart," he drawls at me, before taking a slow sip of his beer.

His eyes lock on mine, before proceeding to gaze down my body.

"Do you always dress in those ugly as shit scrubs?"
"No, just when I've got Prac."

"Nice, they hide ya hot arse though," he laughs, walking out of the kitchen.

Austin is silent, looking at me like his heart is shattering inside his chest.

"You ok Aust?" I ask, bumping his hip with mine.
"Yeah, but I don't like him talking to you like that," he says, nodding towards Jairus stretched out on the couch.

"He doesn't mean anything by it Aust, and you're the one who wanted a male roommate."
"I know, guess I'll just have to get used to it or knock him down a peg or two."
"Yeah," I reply, "so is there anything else I can do for tea?"
"Grab the eggs out, and go have a shower. It will be ready when you get out."

Handing him the eggs from the fridge, I kiss his cheek, "You're the best Aust, I love you."
Even as I round the hallway, the smile from my words has not left Austin's face and from the couch Jairus is staring at my arse while I walk away.
I really have no idea how I'm going to get through the days living with them both and the obvious tension that surrounds us.

Five | Crash Landing

After eating the delectable Carbonara Austin had made, I'm sitting in between his outstretched legs on the couch, my back against his chest.
He's playing with my hair, and it's surprisingly soothing.

Jairus is sitting on the other side of the couch, his eyes darting between the television screen and us.
The look on his face is amusing, as though he's trying to decide if watching 'House Rules' or Austin and I is better viewing.

Closing my eyes, I feel close to sleep when his voice shakes me awake, "Seriously what's the deal with you two?"
"No deal," I reply, folding my arms in front of my chest in the cross pose made famous by the television show, 'Deal or No deal'.

"You expect me to believe that drivel?"
"Yes," I snap, "we're best friends."
"Hmm, ok sweetheart, keep telling yourself that," he taunts, nodding at Austin when he stands up.
"And you man, own up to your feelings."

Austin pushes his hands into my back, forcing me to sit up as he gets to his feet and stands right in Jairus' face.

"What feelings man?"

Jairus scoffs, not responding with words, but shaking his head as he walks away.

"Aust? What feelings?" I ask, his back still to me.

"Nothing Anni, don't listen to him. He's obviously talking shit," he defends turning back around to face me.

"Hmm, yeah I guess," I muse, not entirely convinced myself.

He sits back down on the couch, with his head in his hands for a moment.

"Aust, are you sure you're okay?"

"Yeah, you know I love you Anni yeah?"

I smile, "Yes Aust, just as friends though yeah?"

"Hmm...yeah," he says a little too quickly, my heart skipping in my chest.

I was telling myself constantly on repeat that I wasn't still in love with Austin, but hearing him say 'I love you' no matter how he meant it kind of made me giddy.

Right in that moment I want to kiss him, and have him take me to bed, but I know that's a silly idea.

We both need space.

Without saying another word, I stand up to head to bed.

Turning back to look at him as I walk down the hallway, I see that he's laid back on the couch and has his hand in his daks.

Shutting my bedroom door behind me I giggle at the thought of what he was doing and only the still persistent pounding of my head was stopping me from running back out to help him.

~~

It feels as though I've barely been asleep for five minutes, when a furious bashing sound plagues my head, making me sit bolt upright in bed.

Clutching the sheets in my fists, I shake my head to focus and shake it away, but it persists.

I realise it's coming from the front door.

Jumping out of my bed, I run out into the hallway to find Austin standing in the doorway of their room, with Jairus right behind him, looking like he's about to yell a bunch of expletives at the top of his lungs.

"Austin, can you answer it?"

"Not a chance, Anni, it could be a fucking serial killer!"

"If it was a serial killer don't you think they'd have kicked the door in, rather than bashing on it,"

Jairus interjects, brushing past Austin, heading closer to the door.

"True, but I'm still not answering it," Austin replies, a genuine look of fear on his face.

"God, you two are such pansies!"

Now at the door he unlatches the deadbolt, taking the handle in his grasp and depressing it to open the door.

As soon as the latch clicks open, the door is pushed open from the outside, making Jairus take a step back and crash his back against the wall.

"Fuck, thank the lord," a girls voice curses, "I thought I was at the wrong fucking house."

She has stopped in the doorway, staring straight at me and my recollection is immediate. Running straight to her I wrap my arms around her in a tight hug,

"Bella!" I coo excitedly, "What are you doing here?"

"Other than freezing my tits off?"

"Well, dah!"

"Jace kicked me out," she replies sadly.

"Oh," I reply, not shocked by the words coming out of one of oldest friends' mouth.

She'd always been a bit of a floozy, getting with random guys all through high school and never really committing to anyone, until she met Jace.

They'd moved in together when Austin and I did, and seemed like the perfect, happy couple that everyone wanted to be.

We'd kept in contact, via the worlds of Facebook and Instagram, but it had been over a year since I'd seen her and it now made sense why'd she asked for my address a few weeks ago.

Clearly something had been going on with her and Jace that she'd kept close to her chest.

Looking back at Austin I ask, "Its cool if Bel crashes with us, yeah?"

"Fine by me Anni, but you should probably ask Mr Cranky pants," he laughs, pointing at Jairus who takes that moment to finally slide out from behind the open door.

"Yeah fuck you man, I'm not the one banging my best friend," he says, giving Austin the bird before he looks Bella up and down, licking his lips.

It seems he always thinks with his little friend in his too tight footy shorts, as it's clear he likes any woman that crosses his path.

"More than fine by me, sweetheart," he drawls, taking Bella's hand to shake it.

"I'm Jairus, by the way, not Mr Cranky Pants," he laughs, turning to Austin and giving him the biggest greasy.

Bella steps inside, grabbing the small backpack she'd dropped at her feet when opening the door.

Jairus shuts the door behind her, "So are you rooming with me or what?"

I shake my head at him, "Not a chance, Bel is bunking with me."

"Ooo...we'll just think about all the dirty things you'll be doing hey man?" he jeers punching Austin playfully on the bicep.
"OK man, whatever floats your boat, I'm going back to bed," he announces, walking away.
For a moment I think about following him, as he's definitely not acting like himself, especially when Jairus is around, but Bella takes my hand, "Show me where your crash pad is Anni."

Jairus shoots me a wink as I lead Bella down the hallway to my bedroom.
After I close the door the tears she was holding in cascade down her cheeks, she crashes against the bed.
Sitting down next to her, I stroke her hair comfortingly, "Tell me everything Bel."
"Tomorrow, Anni. I just want to sleep."

"Ok, but no spooning me," I laugh.
"I'll try not to," she laughs through her tears, scooting over to the other side of the bed and climbing under the sheets.
Laying in the dark, I listen to her sobs, wishing there is something I could do or say to make it better.

"Bel, I'm really glad you're here, even if it's not the best of circumstances."
"Yeah, why's that?"

"Living with those two hot as hell boys is testosterone overload."
"I bet, but we'll talk about it tomorrow Anni yeah?"
"Yeah, goodnight Bel," I say comfortingly.

Her reply doesn't come, as she's fallen asleep so quickly, I'm worried about why she's really left Jace. Thoughts wander through my mind as I drift to sleep, glad to finally have another female in the house.

Six | Morning Confessions

Rolling over in bed, I throw my arm over the body next to me.

"Eeek, Anni, get off me!" she screeches.

My eyes shoot open, and I shrink back from her, "Oh shit sorry Bel, I thought you were Austin."

She sits up, clutching the sheets to her knees. "Oh really? What's cracking with you two huh?"

"Nothing, we're just besties," I reply defensively, feeling my cheeks flush.

"Hmmm, so what Blondie said about you hitting the sheets is?"

"Ok, ok...we're besties with benefits....but..."

"But what? You still love him?"

"I don't know Bel...I mean I might...I just don't know."

"Yeah...I get you girl...but I'm sure getting it on with Austin regardless is pretty damn hot," she croons smiling.

"Oh yeah," I laugh.

"Are you sure they're both cool with me crashing?"

"Does it look like I care?"

"No, its just I've got nowhere else to go Anni."

"Bel, what happened? You and Jace were like the dream couple."

Biting down on her lips, she ponders what she's going to say for a moment, "I fucked up and if I tell you, you'll think I'm a..."

"Don't even go there Bel. I'll never think of you that way."

"Really? Even if I told you that I slept with Jaxon."

"What?" I spit at her, shocked that she would cheat on Jace and with his twin brother nonetheless.

"Um...yeah...Jace caught us in bed together and I..."

"What Bel? Tell me, ' I demand, touching her arm lightly.

"Well I was like wasted, and Jax had been crashing at ours a bit, and flirted with me like every damn second..."

"Yeah, not cool...but ok...so?"

"Jace and I had been arguing heaps...you know about money and shit...and I'd had enough so I went out to get blind again. When I got home Jax was home and well I don't remember anything until Jace came in later that night after work yelling at me."

"So, it wasn't a whoopsie?"

"Oh no it definitely was....In my drunken daze I thought he was Jace."

"Oh Bel! They're not even identical!" I laugh.

Thankfully she laughs back, "I know, beer goggles!"

"So, since it's Saturday, we now have the whole day to chill and get ready for tonight."

"What's happening tonight?"

"Drunken shenanigans and dancing until our feet hurt. Aust and I haven't been out in forever."

"Sounds like my kinda night. Is Blondie coming out?"

"He's not gay Bel!"

She laughs at my comment, "I didn't mean that! Is he going to come clubbing with us?"

"Stuffed if I know, but to be honest I haven't asked him and I'm not sure Austin would like him tagging along."

"Anni, you're going to get that damn fine arse of his to come with us or I won't!"

"Okay, and fyi he's all yours if you want him."

"Hmm, yeah as much as I think he's damn fine I think he's got the hots for someone else."

I slap her arm, "No he doesn't. He was totally checking you out last night."

"Need I remind you of the way he calls you 'sweetheart,' drawling out the word like he's kissing you senseless."

"That's just how he talks, it doesn't mean anything," I defend, my mind ticking over and thinking about how Jairus would kiss me, and whether it would be different to Austin's sweet kisses.

Blanking out for a minute, Bella waves her hands in my face, "Earth to Anni!"

"Sorry I was just um...thinking," I muse, touching my lips.

"Oh god Anni, you were thinking about kissing him huh?" she laughs.

Not responding I get out of bed, grabbing her hand to pull her up with me, before I leave her standing in my bedroom whilst I go to the kitchen to make coffee.

Just like he was the other day, Jairus is standing against the bench, again spooning Weetbix into his mouth.

Thankfully, he is wearing more clothes this time, even though it didn't make him look any less delicious.

"Morning sweetheart," he drawls at me, licking the milk that collected at the corner of his lips.

Scoffing I walk into the kitchen, standing in his personal space, "Do you mind moving? Or are we going to play that game again?"

"Depends sweetheart."

"On what?"

"If you want to play that game," he teases, grabbing me around the waist and pressing his body into mine. I can feel his growing arousal against my stomach.

"So, are you playing the game or not sweetheart?"

"Not," I gulp.

"Damn shame," he laughs, with a devious hot as fuck smirk.

"Why?"

"Wouldn't you like to know," he taunts me.

Freeing myself from his grasp, I huff at him, "You're so annoying."

He puts his hands against his heart, faking that I'm hurting him with my stupid insult.

"Oh harsh words sweetheart!"

"Not funny Jairus! And stop calling me sweetheart!"

"Not a chance, sweetheart," he drawls, teasing me again, like he knows Bella's words about kissing him are tumbling in my head.

"I don't like it," I spit at him, feeling like a ten-year-old telling someone they'd hurt my feelings.
"Yeah, well you wanna know something?"
"Not really but you're gonna tell me anyway, so go ahead."

He takes a step closer to me, leaning in to whisper in my ear, "Seeing how you react, sweetheart....", he pauses, taking a deep breath and exhaling in my ear, "turns me on so fucking much."
"Ehhh," I scoff, putting my palms against his chest to push him away.

He laughs, a deep bellied laugh, "You'll be begging me soon sweetheart, and until then I'll just jack off thinking about what you hide under your ugly as shit scrubs."

I feel the tears sting my eyes. I hate his crass words, but at the same time they make something odd stir inside my stomach.
Racing back to my room, abandoning my coffee yet again I let the silent tears fall down my cheeks as my mind races with thoughts of what being with someone else might actually be like.

Seven | Hot Damn

Standing in my walk-in robe, I stare at my clothes, trying to decide what's the best outfit for the night. The skimpy turquoise dress I'd brought on a stupid whim because I'd loved the colour was screaming at me, *'Wear me Anni, you'll look hot as sin'.*

Touching the jersey fabric, I pull it off the coat hanger and hold it up against my body, looking in the mirror on the wall, when Bella steps up behind me, towel drying her short chocolate locks.

"Damn Anni, are you wearing that?"
"I...um...I'm..."
She laughs, "Maybe I should've said Damn Anni, wear that!"
"You think?"
"Well, dah! You'll look as hot as fuck in that!"
"Okay, I hope you're right. I'm kind of nervous about showing so much skin."
"Don't be," she reassures, "have you got anything I can wear? Maybe not a dress?"
Smiling I reply, "Yeah, I know the exact thing!"
Pulling out the leggings I hold them up to her and she purrs excitedly, "Are they Black Milk wet looks?"
"Are there any others?" I laugh, handing them to her, "Have you got a top to wear?"

"Yeah, I have a black midriff tee in my backpack."
"Perfect, so um...give me a minute to put this on."

She pouts at me, "Anni, what are you wearing under it?"
"Undies, why?"
"VPL, bad," she laughs like a hyena.
"Oh, yeah, I didn't think of that."
"You wouldn't...do you have a G-string?"
"Yeah, I'm not that much of a prude Bel!" I snap at her, pulling open my underwear drawer and taking out the only G-string I do own, a lacy white one that has a small triangle at the front and elastic around the hips.

"Bonzer Anni, that will barely cover ya mappa tassie," she laughs again like a hyena at what she is implying.
"Maybe I should wear something else then?"
"No way you dill! You're wearing that dress, with that g, sans bra!"
"I can't do that Bel!"
"Oh, you can and you will," she winks at me, before stepping out of the wardrobe to get dressed herself. Undressing from my pyjamas I take a moment to look at my body in the mirror, tapping the tiny pooch of my belly with my fingers.
 Sometimes I dreamed of having a perfectly flat, washboard stomach but I wasn't exactly fat. My hips and boobs decided to come along a little later than they did for most people too.
Slipping my bra straps down my arms, I unhook the clasp trying not to think about how the low cut

draping neckline of the dress was going to expose me. I'm not big chested, but 'C' cup boobs generally need to be confined with a bra.

I shiver, now half naked, sliding my almost granny pants down my legs, before I step into the G-string. Carefully I bite the tag off the dress with my teeth, and drop the dress over my head. Stepping into some black patent black ballet flats, I take a moment to admire myself in the mirror, when I hear Austin calling out to me, "Anni, are you ready?"
"Yeah, I'm in the walk in," I call out, seconds later seeing him standing behind me in the mirror. Leaning against the wall he looks absolutely dapper, ripped black jeans clinging to his thighs, and a skin tight white V-neck t-shirt plastered to his abs, half untucked.

On his feet he has black and white Converse sneakers, his new signature shoes having had to replace his purple Nikes.
"Damn, Anni, you look hot babe," he comments, stepping up behind me in the mirror and wrapping his arms around my waist.
"You think?" I ask, with a smile at the corner of my lips.
"Oh yeah babe," he chuckles, kissing my neck.

Turning around in his arms, I press a kiss hard against his lips, "Mmm, Aust, you know I've only got a 'g' on underneath?"

"Damn babe, I'll be thinking about taking this dress off you all night," he grunts, "but we really gotta get going to make it before cover charge kicks in."

"Yeah," I reply taking his hand, and calling out to Bella, "Bel, are you ready?"

In the hallway, we stop to see Bella in the bathroom, putting the finishing touches to her makeup.

"You're so lucky Anni, you're flawless without a speck of makeup."

Austin smiles, kissing my cheek, "You don't need to wear it, babe," he coos.

"Well, I guess that's a good thing considering I hate how I look wearing makeup."

Bella follows us as we head to the front door. Jairus is sitting on the couch with a beer, and wolf whistles when he sees us girls.

"Damn sweetheart, I'm cracking a fat from over here," he taunts, biting down on his lip and looking down at his crotch, after he averts his gaze from my outfit.

Austin clutches my hand even tighter, as though he's trying to tell me I'm his.

"Blondie, are you coming out with us?" Bella asks Jairus, giving me a teasing smirk.

"Depends on where ya going?'

She looks at Austin and I for an answer, shrugging.

"Rivera," I inform him.

"Damn, that place is Ridgy-Didge," he replies, standing up, "I've actually got other plans with a mate, but maybe I'll catch you there later."

Bella's shoulders slump, leaving me wondering if she was hoping to get with Jairus for the night to forget about Jace.

"Ok, well we gotta go, don't wait up," I jeer at him, dragging Austin to the door to leave.

I'm ready to hit the turps and dance my arse off, feeling peppy at the thought of the songs that would be playing at Rivera on old school night.

Eight | Get Rotten

Stepping out our front door, I squeeze Austin's hand in mine, squealing in delight.

"You right there babe?" Austin asks, as we start walking down the laneway our apartment is on, towards the main drag of Richmond, the iconic 'Bridge Road.'
Considering how close we lived to the club strip of Richmond, we should have gone more often to hit the turps and get down.
I hated that since I'd gotten into the thick of my nursing degree, it being halfway through second year I didn't go off as much as I'd used to. My shyness still got the better of me ninety-nine percent of the time, but once I threw a few shots down my gob all my inhibitions went out the window.
 I'm hoping that will happen tonight, as I'm for one freezing my arse off in my barely there dress and I'm afraid that it will fall off for everyone in the club to see me in the nuddy.
"Anni, I asked if you're alright?"
"Yeah, yeah, I'm good, just freezing my fucking arse off!"
"I'd give you my jacket, but well..."
"You didn't bring one, I know...you're so chivalrous Aust," I laugh at him, leaning into his side so he can

wrap his arm around my waist to keep me warm as we continue walking.

Bella is slacking behind, texting madly on her phone.
"Bel, you good?" I ask.
"Yeah ripper, Anni," she replies, not sounding too happy.
"You sure?"
She looks up from her phone, shoving it into her small clutch, "Yeah, kind of pissed Blondie bailed out though."
"Why?"
"Why?" she asks back, blushing, "Because he's..."
"What Bel?"
"Hot as hell, and I want to..."
I laugh hard, clutching my stomach, "Oh Bel! You dirty bitch!"
Austin hasn't said a word, which is unlike him, and a little confusing.

There isn't time to ponder his iffy behaviour as we step up to the red carpet outside Rivera.
Thankfully as it isn't quite nine pm the line is only a few people deep and we don't have to wait long to enter. The cover charge didn't kick in until after ten, so that helped us get inside quicker as people didn't need to stop and pay.
Once inside, I drop Austin's hand from mine, taking Bella's instead, "Ready to go off Bel?"
"Damn straight, this song is my jam," she choruses, starting to belt out *The Way I are* at the top of her lungs, pulling me towards the dance-floor.

"Aust! Cowboy shots pretty please?" I call back to him, as he pushes through the small crowd to the bar. He nods, shooting me a wink and my heart skips, thinking about how well he knows me.

~~

As I'd thought, old school night at Rivera is definitely the grouse night I'd predicted, the songs playing the ones we'd listened to when we sang the words, having no idea what we were actually singing about. Bella looks so hot, swaying her hips to the beat, her arms above her head as she gets lost in the music. Following her lead though, I still look like a dag, partly because I've not had one drop of alcohol.
The song changes, *'Whistle' blaring* out, when Austin slides up beside me, leaning against my side.
In my ear he teasingly sings, *"Can you blow my whistle baby, whistle baby?"*
"Mmm," I moan even though over the music he'd not hear me.
Without warning, he grabs my waist, pressing his body against mine, grinding against me to the rhythm. Bella slides up behind him, dropping low to the floor, taunting him.
He shoots me dagger eyes, "Relax babe, let go."
"I can't Aust," I protest.
He smashes a kiss to my lips, reaching behind to swat Bella away from his back. His kiss is demanding and possessive; I know the song is still playing, but I can't focus on it.
The only thing on my mind is how arousing Austin's kiss is.

Breathless I pull back, laughing at the devious smirk on his face, "Fuck babe, you..."

"Don't go there Aust, let's just get rotten."

"Damn right," he replies, leading me over to the booth by the side of the dance-floor as the waitress saunters over with a tray of Cowboy shots and a stubby of beer.

Austin signals to her with a hand gesture and she places them on the table in front of us.

Bella rushes over, sinking into the booth opposite Austin and I.

We both grab a shot, clinking them together, chanting 'Ace!', before downing them as though it's water.

Austin lifts his beer to his lips, taking a long sip before he smirks at me, "You ready to get back out there or you want another round?"

Snatching his beer, I scull it, wiping a hand across my face as I slam it back on the table, "Damn babe, that was hot," he teases, kissing me fiercely and licking the foam from off my lips.

I hear Bella scoff, as she slides out of the booth to head back to the dance-floor to dance to my new jam, *'Turn the music up'*.

Beaming at Austin, after our second hot kiss, I drag him back out onto the dance-floor. The alcohol is starting to course through my body and I curse myself for being a Cadbury as my inhibitions fall away.

Nine | Drunken Knight

Jairus

Running a hand through my hair, as I board the tram, I try not to focus on the unease in my stomach of seeing Sara. I've been putting off seeing her for weeks, telling her that since signing on for the Tigers, I'd not had a moment to spare and was dead tired. But I'm dead set lying to her, texting her 'I love you babe' and 'Miss your face' when my mind is elsewhere, chock-a of thoughts of Annika doing the naughty with me.

She'd not left my mind for barely a minute, and the way she sassed me back in her responses to my teasing just riled me up in every way.

Stepping off the tram, I find Sara waiting at the stop. It irked me that I always had to be the one to make the effort to go see her and never the other way around.
Her smile is sickly sweet when she sees me, and stepping up to her I plaster a smile on my lips that I'm really not feeling. Pressing a soft kiss to her cheek, I greet her, "Hey baby."
"Jai, I hate when you call me baby."
"Why Sara? You're my girl."

"No Jai, I'm neither a girl or a baby. I'm a grown woman."

"Oh, come on Sara, it's a term of fucking endearment."

"So, Jai, I do have a name."

I scoff at her craziness, "I can't believe you've not seen me for weeks, and you're already trying to pick a fight."

Her response is a pout, "I'm not, I just miss you."

"You could have come to see my new digs, Sar...you know like made a fucking effort for once."

"I've been busy with work, it's report time Jai."

"Big fucking deal, Sar! You've always got an excuse."

"I'm sorry. Please Jai, can't we just go and have a nice dinner for our anniversary," she asks taking my hand and trying to lead me down the road towards the restaurant that I'd booked a month ago, knowing our two year anniversary was around the corner.

Snatching my hand back, I turn my back on her, about to cross the tram tracks when she runs up behind me, "Jai, wait? Where are you going?"

"To drink with the flies Sar, I need some space."

"Are we breaking up?"

I stop to look back at her, feeling a pang of guilt hit me right in the feels. There is no denying she's beautiful, but even as I press a sweet kiss against her plump pink lips I don't feel the same attraction to her I once did.

All because of a sweet, scorching hot blonde beauty that I want to have my wicked way with.

Focusing my attention back on Sara, I brush her cheek with my palm, "I really am dead tired Sar, but I'll swing by yours after the game tomorrow, ok?"
"Ok Jai, I love you."
When another tram slides to a grinding halt in front of us, I kiss her cheek again, "I love you too Sar," I repeat back, even though I'm not sure I even mean the words anymore.

She waves at me, as the tram leaves the stop and I watch her walk away, making sure she is heading in the opposite direction.

At the next stop, I jump off the tram and cross the tracks to flag down the one on the other side.
There is still time to get to Rivera and beat the cover charge.

~~

Walking into the club my eyes are immediately drawn towards the dance-floor where Annika and Bella are grinding against each other to the beat of some song I'd never heard.

Thankfully Austin appears to be missing in action, as seeing him grind against Annika would really irk me and make my perve session from the side of the dance-floor much less thrilling.

The song changes to 'Pony'; my jam and I start to walk slowly across the dance-floor, wanting to surprise Anni.

A burly guy steps up behind her, grabbing her arms and forcing them above her head, as he pushes his groin into her back. Her mouth opens as she shrieks, pushing her arse back to try and force him to move on.

But he makes no move to leave.

Rushing up to her, I step in front of her, grabbing her around the waist, sending dagger eyes to the stranger, a nonverbal 'She is mine' look.

He shrinks back from her and she falls into my arms, pressing her body close.

In her ear over the music I ask, "You good sweetheart?"

"Yes, thanks. When did you get here?"

"Just before that bastard thought he could have you."

"Mmm..." she moans, reaching down between our bodies and grabbing my growing fatty in her grasp, "and it seems you're happy to see me?"

"Damn right sweetheart, and this song is my jam."

"Of course it is," she laughs, taking her hand away but stretching up onto her tiptoes, her short ass dress hitching up over the tent in my slacks.

She grinds into me, singing, "My saddles waiting, come get on it?"

"Oh fuck, sweetheart," I drawl, "damn straight I want you to ride me."

Caz May

She doesn't respond even when I wrap my arms around her, grabbing her arse cheeks in my grasp, sliding my fingers underneath the hem of her dress to touch her skin.

I'm about to smash a kiss to her lips, but the song ends and she jumps back out of my arms, taking a step back straight into Austin.
"Oh no you fucking didn't man?"
"Aust, it's ok. We were just dancing."

"Didn't look like just dancing to me Anni," Austin says giving me an evil glare as he puts an arm around Annika's waist.
Scoffing I leave them both on the dance-floor, grabbing Bella's hand to drag her away, whispering in her ear, "What's with them?"
"If I knew I'd tell you. But forget about her, get with me."
"Sorry I can't....I..." she cuts my words off, crashing her lips to mine.
"Seriously Bella, where'd you get off kissing me?" I spit at her, pulling away from her unwanted kiss.
"Come on Blondie, it's just a kiss."
"Yeah...whatever, rack off! I'm going home, and don't get any ideas about following me."

Leaving her dumbfounded I walk out of the club, taking one last glance back towards Annika, to see her slow dancing with Austin whilst pashing him. My dick is aching for release and I have an uneasy feeling in my stomach.

73

I want her so fucking bad and thoughts plague me as I walk home.

You've got Buckley's chance of getting with her man, they aren't friends with
benefits, get over it, you've got a girlfriend remember

Reaching the apartment after unlocking the door I strip off my shirt.
Throwing it on the couch I go to grab a beer. In my bedroom, I flop onto the bed, drinking the beer to drown my sorrows. I curse myself for thinking with my wang again.

Ten | Chunder Queen

The gurgling in the pit of my stomach forces my eyes open. Glancing at the other person in the bed, I'm shocked to find Austin sprawled out next to me.
I can't remember getting home, nor the time we stumbled into bed.
The details of the night are fuzzy in my head.
For a moment thoughts of dry humping Jairus on the dance floor fill my mind, but I shake them away, trying to focus as he wasn't there.

It must have been a hot as dream, my body feeling the ache for release even though my stomach is in knots.
The gurgling increases; I can feel the chunder rise in my throat, I shoot out of bed racing to the bathroom.
Thankfully living with two males, means the toilet lid is up as I barely have a second to even bend over the bowl before I empty the contents of my stomach.
Clutching the porcelain, I try to think about the night's events, wondering if I'd even eaten anything or what I did in my drunken stupor.
Being one of those people whose inhibitions fell away when drunk I could have done anything; like dancing on a table top or humping hot as roommates on the dance floor.

The more I thought about it I knew it wasn't a dream.

Jairus had been there and I'd practically fucked him with clothes on.

But I'd woken up with Austin in my bed and my mind is too hazy to know if we'd slept together again for the umpteenth time.

Retching into the bowl again I curse myself for even suggesting a night out.

The next day always made me regret the choice of downing so much alcohol.

I'm not just cursing angry with myself about that though, it's also about Austin and his lack of commitment.

Even with my hazy mind, I remember kissing him, and his kisses were possessive, you're mine babe kisses that drew me in and made me forget that we weren't together.

I know that kissing him is wrong, as friends with benefits don't kiss just like I told him, but when Austin wants to kiss you, giving you that helpless puppy dog look with his chocolate eyes he's hard to resist.

But kissing him, was making me feel thoroughly confused, as though my heart was falling off Uluru.

~~

After what seems like hours, but is probably only minutes I jolt awake again, my head throbbing where I'd obviously hit my forehead on the toilet bowl.

Standing up, I flush the toilet, loving smashing the lid down in protest of living with guys.

About to strip from the pyjamas I'd somehow
managed to put on my body when I'd stumbled in
drunk, I flick the switch on the wall to turn the IXL
heat lamp on. I stand underneath it to revel in its
warmth. It makes me wonder about filling my heart
with warmth from love, and it isn't Austin who
flashes into my mind.

Quickly I grab some toothpaste, running it over my
teeth with a finger and spitting it in the sink before
taking a drink from the tap to get rid of the horrible
taste in my mouth.
All I want to do is wash the night away under the
warm water of a long shower.
Lifting my long-sleeved pyjama top over my head, I
look at my body in the mirror for a moment again
wondering what both Austin and Jairus see in me.
The door cracks open suddenly and he is behind me.
A hot as hell smirk crosses his face as I desperately
try to cover my nakedness from his gaze.

Eleven | Risque' Conduct

Jairus

Opening the bathroom door, the sight in the mirror straight ahead is glorious and damn hot. Annika is standing in front of the sink, wearing nothing but flannelette 'My Little Pony' pyjama pants.

Smirking I laugh, thinking back to her grinding against my cock on the dance floor to 'Pony' and now she is desperately trying to cover her nakedness whilst wearing daks with ponies on them.

"Jai! Don't laugh, get out!" she shrieks, her eyes locking on mine in the mirror.

The way she calls me 'Jai' sounds so sweet on her lips.

It makes the tent in my pants creep higher than it already is, damn morning wood from thinking about our hot as hell dry hump on the dance floor.

"Damn sweetheart," I drawl at her licking my lips, "I'm not laughing at how your body looks, but your daks."

Her hands are over her breasts, and she sweetly replies, "Why? They're my favourites."
"Sweetheart, they have ponies on them," I reply stepping up behind her, pressing my morning wood against her arse.
The recollection hits her at what I'm implying and she giggles.
"Last night?"
"Yeah sweetheart, you damn near fucked me on that dance floor."
"I'm sorry," she replies, biting her lip.
"Oh sweetheart, I'm not," I drawl again, putting my hands over hers that are still against her chest.
She lets out a little moan as I pull them away.
"Jai, don't...I..."
"Mmm, sweetheart, your body is exquisite," I moan against her ear.
"Don't tease me Jai," she protests.
"Why not sweetheart?"
"Because, there's no way you find me that attractive."
"Are you shitting me Annika?"
Her chest hitches, at my use of her name and her reply is a meek, "Yeah."
"Do you not feel my dick against your ripper arse?"
This time she moans, lifting her hands again to try and cover up but I grab them pushing them down on the counter in front of her.

Teasingly I run my hands slowly over her breasts and along the elastic of her pyjamas. Her skin heats at the sensation of my touch, furthermore as I slowly run them down her sides.

Brushing her luscious blonde hair from her neck, I kiss the sensitive skin beneath her ear, my lips just grazing her skin.

"Annika," I moan her name into her ear, at the same time hooking my fingers into the sides of her daks, plunging them to the floor.

The only item of clothing left on her body is the worlds skimpiest g-string, that has her bare erotic arse completely exposed.

She lets out a gasp, feeling my wood straining against her.

Gripping her around the waist, I lift her up, turning her body around to sit on the edge of the counter.

Stepping in between her legs, I gaze over her body, my mind racing with thoughts of kissing and licking every inch of her.

Running my finger over her lips, they part and her tongue darts out licking them.

"Fuck, sweetheart, I wanna kiss you so bad," I groan.

"Then kiss me," she says so sweetly I have to fight the urge to give in.

"I can't....I...I" I stammer, about to confess my relationship status when a loud pounding breaks the moment.

"Anni, are you in there?"

Stepping back from her, she jumps off the counter and I hand her top from the floor as she calls out, "Yeah Bel, just a sec."

"Are you naked?" Bella calls out.

I have to stifle a laugh at her friends' gall. Annika slips her pony daks back on and opens the door. I take my chance to slide out the door, as Bella steps into the bathroom giving me a smug look.

"Oh, hey Blondie," she teases, "thanks for the kiss last night."

I flip her the bird, "Up yours Bella."

"Mmm...sounds like a ripper idea, Blondie."

"Not a chance, Bella, keep dreaming sunshine," I spit at her, walking away to go deal with my morning wood, whilst thinking about my almost kiss with Annika.

Twelve | Innuendo Gossip

Bella enters the bathroom, slamming the door behind her.

Sitting on the toilet top she shakes her head at me.

Anger is bubbling inside my stomach, my mind spinning with words I want to hurl at her. I have no right to be angry at her for kissing Jairus, it's not like I actually have a claim on him.

It isn't just her that I'm angry at though, but Jairus too. Not even twelve hours had passed since we'd been at the club and he'd kissed Bella and tried to kiss me.

Bella looks up at me, "Anni, is there something going on with you and Blondie?"

"Um...I..."

"Anni, tell me please," she begs standing up to step closer to me.

Leaning into the counter I try to reply again, "We...um..."

"Anni, please...I'm sorry I kissed him, but..."

"Wait! What? You kissed him? He didn't kiss you?"

"Nah, yeah, after you guys stopped dry humping he was leaving and I smacked one on him."

"You saw that?" I gulp.

"The whole club saw, you dill!"

My cheeks flush, "Oh god, I can't believe I did that! I'm never drinking again!"

She laughs, "Oh Anni, you say that now, but you don't mean it."

"Bel, I dry humped him in the middle of the dance floor," I reply, not able to shake how mortified I feel.

"So this morning? Did I interrupt you really getting it on?"

My shoulders slump when I reply solemnly, "No...he...um...no."

"So you haven't even pashed him?"

"No, when you knocked, I'd just told him to kiss me and he said he couldn't."

"That bastard! I'm sorry Anni."

"Don't be...I'm obviously just not hot enough," I say, my head down, "he was happy enough to kiss you."

"Not exactly Anni, he rejected me last night and as you saw this morning to."

I laugh then, "He makes me as mad as a cut snake!"

"You like him, don't you?"

I feel myself blush again, "I...I don't know. He makes me feel so hot...like you know hot..."

"Oh, I know Anni, you only gotta look at that boy to feel that, but what about you and Austin?"

"That's another thing, he's been so possessive of me ever since Jairus moved in and I really hate it."

"I noticed hun, but I meant have you told him how you feel?"

"How I feel? What do you mean?"

"That you love him, you might have the hots for Blondie... but it's always been you and Austin."

"Bel, I don't know if I do love him anymore and he doesn't love me, that's for sure."

"Have you gone blind Anni?"

"No, what do you mean?"

"Austin is so clearly in love with you."

"No, he's not! We're just friends Bel."

"You honestly can't think that Anni, he just doesn't have the balls to tell you how he feels because friends with benefits is getting the best part of a relationship without the commitment."

"Yeah, I guess, but I don't know what I want either. Things with Aust feel familiar, but then with Jairus just the thought of being with him damn near makes me..."

"Ewww Anni, don't tell me," she laughs putting her fingers in her ears.

"Sorry, but you know what I mean."

"Yeah, I do, maybe just see what happens...and Anni?"

"Yeah Bel?"

"I'm sorry I kissed him, but can I tell you something?"
"Yeah anything?"
"If he kisses someone he doesn't like the way he kissed me, then if he kisses you you'll see fireworks."
"Really?"
"Yes, girl, that boy has got the hots for you, big time."
"Mmm, yeah," I muse.
"Don't deny it Anni, you've got the hots for him too."
"Ok...ok...I think he's damn gorgeous."
"Oh yeah," she laughs, winking at me.
"So Bel, who were you texting last night?"
"Jace."
"Oh, what's happening there?"

"He wants to meet up next week, he said we need to talk."
"Are you going to go?"
"Yeah, I still love him Anni...I might think Blondie is hot as hell, and yes, I stupidly kissed him, but I..."
"You don't have to explain Bel."
"Thanks...are you sure things are ok with us?"
"Yeah, I shouldn't have been jealous."

"Cool," she replies opening the door, "let's make some coffee and have a fry up, my stomach is screaming for some grease."

"Yeah, I'm starved," I reply, rubbing my stomach as I follow her out to the kitchen to find both the guys pussy footing around each other, giving each other dagger eyes.

Looking between them, I have to stifle a laugh, but can't help letting it out when Bel asks, "Something going on between you two or were you thinking about Anni and I getting it on in the bathroom?"

Jairus' gaze locks on Bella and he taunts her, "Wouldn't you like to know sunshine."

A deep chuckle comes from the pit of my stomach, laughing at the teasing banter between them, but when Jairus winks at me butterflies dance in my stomach instead.

I have to stop myself from rushing over to jump him and smash a kiss to his lips.

Austin looks straight at me then with a longing gaze that makes me wonder if Bella's words in the bathroom about him being in love with me are actually true.

Thirteen | Bloody Blue

Jairus

There is nothing better than running out onto the field with your teammates, hearing the club song blaring and the crowd chanting 'Go tigers'.
Playing Aussie rules had always been my dream and getting to actually live that dream playing full forward for such an iconic team as the 'Richmond Tigers' seemed a bit surreal.

Today is one of our biggest games of the year, against the 'Collingwood Magpies'. I was glad they'd not drafted me, as they'd have to be one of the teams in the league I actually disliked.

Out on the ground, we are kicking the footy around for warm ups and I practice a few goal kicks, cursing myself when I miss an easy shot.
Running back off the oval to continue warm ups before ball up, my teammate taps me on the shoulder, "Jai, mate? You alright? Not like you to miss an easy shot like that."
"Yeah Trav, I'm alright. Just something on my mind."
"Yeah, what's eating ya? Tell me now, so you don't take it onto the ground mate," he suggests.
"Just girlfriend issues, man."
"Oh yeah? Is she here?" He asks, hand-balling a footy to me.

"That's part of the issue, man. She doesn't support me at all."

"You don't need that Jai. How long has she been ya missus?"

"Two years and she's good for me man, but I don't know."

"Yeah, I get ya, but Jai?"

I look at him with an expectant look in my eyes, waiting for him to continue talking, "You're the best draft pick we've had in years. If this girl doesn't support you in the amazing career you've got ahead of you in footy, kick her to the curb!"

"Yeah I'll think about it. Thanks man. Let's get out there and crush the magpies!"

"Damn straight," he yells back, as we high-five and run back out the tunnel onto the ground.

Ripping through the banner and winning the toss we get the ball out of the centre with ease. A Collingwood team member starts the game off by kicking the ball straight into the inside fifty, to Trav who intercepts it before kicking it to me.

Reaching up, watching the ball coming straight for me I put my hands up, launching myself into the air from the bottom of my feet to mark the ball easily. The umpire whistles giving me clearance to kick from the fifty line. Lining it up, taking a deep breath in I run forward, my right foot making contact with the ball launching it towards the posts straight through the middle for a goal.

Caz May

Around me the crowd cheers, waving flags, whistling and screaming 'Jai the man, Jai the man!'

Trav high-fives me again, as we head back to the centre for a ball up.

~~

Back in the club rooms, after smashing the magpies by hundred points, in the circle, we chant out the club song,

'Oh we're from Tiger-land
A fighting fury
 We're from Tiger-land
In any weather
 You will see us with a grin
Risking head and shin
If we're behind then never mind
We'll fight and fight and win
 For we're from Tiger-land
We never weaken til the final siren's gone
Like the Tiger of old
 We're strong and we're bold
 For we're from Tiger
 Yellow and Black
We're from Tiger-land'

Trav comes up to me after as I'm packing my boots into my bag, "Ripper game Jai! Did you forget about ya missus to kick those ten goals?"

"Nah man, I imagined the ball was her head," I laugh.

"Good on ya mate, but go sort that shit out yeah?"

"I will Trav. Catch ya on Wednesday for training."

"No worries, mate," he replies, slapping my back as he walks away.

Slinging my bag over my shoulder I leave the club rooms to head to Sara's with a massive knot in my stomach at the conversation we are going to have.

~~

Twenty minutes later I'm pressing the intercom at Sara's apartment. Her voice is sweet when she answers the buzzer, "Hello, who is it?"

"Sar, it's me. Buzz me in baby."

The door clicks and I bound up the stairs to her second-floor apartment, knocking hard on the door. She opens it wearing a long-sleeved skater dress with a weird planet print on it.

"Damn, baby you look hot."

She ushers me inside, "Jai, please."

"What baby?"

"No baby talk ok?"

"Fine Sar. Can I have a kiss at least?"

"Mmm," she moans, closing the door and stretching up to kiss me sweetly as I drop my bag on the floor. Pulling back before I've even had a chance to kiss her properly, she asks, "Do you want a coffee?"

"No, Sar. Do you have anything stronger?"

"I've got Baileys," she replies meekly.

"Fine, give me a glass of that on the rocks."

"Ok, did you come straight from the game?"

"Yeah, do you think I'd be wearing footy shorts in the middle of winter otherwise Sar?" I ask following her across the small apartment and leaning against the bench.

"I guess not," she replies flicking the kettle on to boil.

Reaching up to get the Baileys down from the top shelf her dress hitches up showing her cheeky undies that barely cover her arse. At one point I'd have found that sight hot as hell but now even though I love her the attraction wasn't there like it used to be.

"Sar, what's the real reason you won't come to my games?"

Slamming the Baileys on the bench, she admits loudly, "I don't like football, Jai. It's a nonsense game."

"What? What's that supposed to mean?"

"Exactly what I said, a nonsense game! You get paid what a hundred thousand to prance around in those shorts for what? It's a fucking spectacle and a waste of your time."

For some reason I blush at her thinking I get paid a hundred grand.

Richmond had gone above and beyond to sign me, one being I was the top draft pick but also giving me a two-year contract offering me two hundred grand and a hefty rookie bonus as well as match bonuses.

What they offered me was practically unheard of and I was on track to be the first rookie in the AFL to earn close to three hundred grand in my first two years of playing in the league.

"Um, baby, you know I'm earning a lot more than a hundred grand."

"So, what difference does that make? Do you want me to quit teaching and just be your bitch?"

"What? Did you seriously just ask me that?"

"That's what you want isn't it? Someone to just have on your arm at all the stupid events you have to go to and who goes to the games to I don't know..."

"Yeah you don't know at all Sar, because you don't fucking give a shit about me!" I bellow at her, downing the Baileys she'd put on the bench in front of me.

"How can you say that Jai? I love you!"

"Really? You love me?"

"Yes Jai. I love you. How can I show you I still love you?"

"By supporting me, coming to my games...making an effort for once."

"Fine! I'll come to your game next weekend," she says unconvincingly.

"Um...that's probably not going to work Sar. We're playing in Perth next week against Freo."

"Oh...well what about the next week?"

"No can do either, unless you fancy a trip to Adelaide."

"Oh, for fucks sake Jai, this is what I mean."

"Sorry, it's part of the job Sar."

"It's not a fucking job Jairus! It's sport!"

"God Sara! I get paid nearly three hundred grand for
that sport, because I'm actually fucking good at it.
The least you could do is support me."

"I don't know how I can," she sniffs.

"Aww Sar, don't cry please."

"Don't worry about it ok?"

"I...I... want to support you Jai, but I can't give up my
job...I love teaching."

"I'm not asking you to quit Sar but I just want your
support yeah?"

"I know...but I don't know how to give you that...how
you want me to."

"Sar?" I ask, not sure what my next words are going
to be.

"Yeah Jai?" she questions me.

"Do you really still love me?"

"You know I do, Jai."

"Then please just make more of an effort, like maybe
checking out my new digs, meeting my roomies, you
know what I mean?"

"Yeah, I do...can I ask you something Jai?"

"Yeah of course Sar."

"Why are you rooming with others when you could
just get your own place?"

"Because I like the company and it's close to our
home ground."

"Fair enough, so what's the plan for tonight? I have
work tomorrow."

"Yeah, I know baby."

"Jai, I said don't call me that!" she yells at me, a hint
of cheekiness in her tone.

"Really? What will happen if I say it again?"

"Don't Jai, don't," she laughs taunting me.

Stepping closer to her I grab her around the waist, teasing her by whispering in her ear, "Baby, can I hold you tonight?"

She lets out a quiet gasp feeling my breath against her ear.

"Jai, please..."

"What baby?" I ask, brushing a stray hair from her cheek.

Her reply doesn't come as words instead she pushes my body against the bench, kissing me hard. It's been a long time since we'd shared such a passionate heated kiss and even though I'm not feeling the same attraction to her it turned me on.

Still kissing her I lift her arse up to carry her in my arms, loving the sweet little moan that escapes her lips when the callousness of my hands grazes across the small of her back.

"Where to baby?" I ask against her lips.

"The chaise," she replies, her lips still close to mine.

Carrying her over to the white chaise lounge I lay her down on it pulling my t-shirt over my head before leaning over her to kiss her again.

Pulling away to sit up and lift her dress over her head, she drawls, "I love you Jairus."

I don't respond, instead yank my shorts and jocks down throwing them on the floor and pulling the light grey blanket over my arse.

"Sar, please, I need to see all of you."

She shakes her head at me, "Jai, please, just..."

"I love you Sara," I whisper, my heart constricting as I feel like I'm lying to her.

Slowly she pushes her undies down pooling them at her ankles. I don't push her anymore to take off her bra, urgently just feeling the need for release.

Without thinking or any warning I plunge into her core thrusting hard and showing no mercy or care if I hurt her.

Slight whimpers escape her lips that seem pleasurable but may also be from how hard I'm driving my cock into her.

"Oh Sar, baby..." I scream out only moments later, my release way too quick for her to enjoy it.

As though she's angry she pushes her palms against my chest pushing me back on the chaise and racing towards the bathroom.

I think about following her, sitting up on the chaise a moment.

Something has definitely changed between us and I can't shake the feeling that I've fucked up this time.

Grabbing my clothes from the floor I quickly dress before walking to the door and grabbing my bag.

Walking out the door I wonder if it's the last time we'd be together and if that's what I want. I really feel like saying 'I love you' is one hell of a lie and I hate myself for the reason why I'm no longer in love with my girlfriend.

Fourteen | Hay Buddy

Sitting on the floor with my back to the fire, I sip my Milo, trying not to think about my almost kiss with Jairus a couple of weeks earlier. He was definitely about to tell me something important when Bella interrupted the moment.

Partly I was glad she had interrupted, as even though we weren't together kissing Jairus almost seemed like cheating on Austin.

Austin is busy playing some new game on his Switch and looks across at me out of the corner of his eye.

"Something up Anni?" he asks, still focusing on his game as he speaks.

"Yeah, Nah, just thinking."

He presses pause, turning his gaze and attention towards me, "About what?"

"Nothing," I mutter taking another sip of Milo.

"Are you sure? It looks like your thoughts are pretty intense, by the blush on your cheeks."

"Nah, nothing like that. I'm just feeling a bit warm from sitting by the fire."

"Ok, well I'm here if you need to chat."

"I know Aust, I might hit the hay actually."

"Ok, maybe I'll come in and snuggle later."

"Nah, Aust...I need some space yeah?"

He doesn't reply, even when I lean down to give him
a soft, sweet kiss goodnight.
"Goodnight Aust, love you.
"Love you too Anni, sleep well babe," he smiles,
blowing me a kiss as I dump my cup in the sink
before heading to my bedroom.
Plopping down on the bed, my thoughts continue to
wonder about whether I should have said 'love you'
to Austin.
All I really know is that I'm confused because I do
love Austin, with all my heart, as he was my first love.
But at the same time, I don't love him the same as I
did a year ago.
It is a feeling that I'll always love him but I'm not sure
that's enough anymore.
He is the only guy I've ever been with and I
sometimes wondered what being with someone else
would be like, how it would feel to kiss another guy
and sleep with another guy.
I can't help but drift to sleep thinking about if that
other guy was Jairus.

~~

Half asleep, I roll over to glance at the clock, seeing
one am in orange numbers.
The figure saunters into my room and I groan as he
slides into bed next to me.
Normally I'd take up the whole bed but tonight I'd
huddled closer to the wall side pulling all the
blankets against my body.
I know I've been dreaming something hot as my body
feels aroused and my undies are a little damp.

"Mmm," his voice groans against me as he puts an arm over my stomach, pressing his body close to mine.

"Aust, I said I needed space."

"Mmm," he moans again, sniffing my hair and inhaling the scent of my vanilla shampoo, "Mmm, sweetheart you smell like heaven."

His words, the name he calls me, flickers in my mind. In my half-asleep state, I don't register who is lying in my bed holding me close to his hot aroused body.

His hand grazes the edge of my pyjama pants, his fingers plunging into my undies and across my sensitive skin jolting me fully awake at the sensation.

"So wet sweetheart," he moans.

My brain realising with those words that it's Jairus in bed with me. Snatching his hand out, I slap it, "Don't Jairus, we can't do that."

I roll over to be face to face with him, only a breath away from his lips, "Why not sweetheart?"

"Because we can't...I can't," I say so close to his lips if I move even half an inch more my lips would be on his.

He moves back a little, as I exhale the breath I don't realise I'm holding in.

"Anni, I want to get so close to you, as close as possible."

"Um Jairus, are you drunk?" I ask, the faint smell of whiskey and beer on his breath.

"Maybe, I only had like one...no two drinks...oh I don't know how many," he stutters, confirming his drunken state.

"Hmm, well how about you head to bed."
"Uhuh....I'm sleeping here. I need to hold you close,"
he tells me, pulling me against his body again.

Running his hands up my torso he grazes my breasts
with his fingertips.
"Mmm, Jairus, that is amazing, but please stop."
"Only if I can hold you close, Anni?"
"Ok, but don't get any ideas."
"Never," he laughs as I roll over, feeling his arousal
pressing into my arse.
He feels bigger than Austin and again I fall asleep
wondering what it would be like if I hadn't just said
no to him.

~~

Thankfully, when I awake the next morning Jairus is
no longer in my bed. It makes me wonder if I'd
actually dreamt him being in my bed the night
before, but when I smell his cologne on my pillows, I
know it was no dream.

My memory of what happened and what was a
dream is a little fuzzy.
Quickly getting dressed I race out the door to head to
class, ignoring him when he calls out, 'Anni,
sweetheart can we talk?' from the kitchen where he
is eating his Weetbix again.
Grabbing my iced coffee at Gloria Jeans, I sip on it,
braving the cold morning air as I head to class,
hoping to block out thoughts of my two hot as hell

boys by immersing myself in the monotony of a Monday morning lecture.

Fifteen | Damn Tired

Austin

Stumbling into the house after Uni, I'm so damn tired I could've fallen in a heap as soon as I take one step inside the front door. Anni is in the kitchen, wearing a short as hell nightie that hitches up as she flits around to the music she has blaring from the stereo. The song is familiar and reminds me of when we were together, in our small hometown. Walking up behind her, I hug her from behind moaning at having her body close to mine. It feels like ages since we've even kissed, even though she'd given me a sweet goodnight kiss on Sunday.

It now being Wednesday though, Sunday seemed like months ago, especially as Tuesday and Wednesday are my biggest days at Uni.

Most of the classes of my Computer Programming degree fall on those days and considering it's a degree with a double major in gaming I constantly feel tired from the head trip of being immersed in coding; not to mention staring at a computer screen for eight hours straight.

Anni calls me a Bludger as on my Monday and Friday's off I sleep in until well past noon as I don't see the point of getting out of bed if I'm only going to play some type of Video game for the most part anyway.

Anni doesn't know how in depth my degree is, in a different way to hers, but I don't push it, instead ask her with my arms still wrapped around her waist, "How was your day babe?"

"Damn tiring, prac is kicking my butt Aust," she replies turning off the pasta sauce she's been cooking on the stove and turning around to face me.

"Yeah, I bet," I reply, about to lean in for a kiss when she presses her hands against my chest.

"No Aust, please I'm too tired."

"Come on Anni, it feels like months since we've been together."

"Don't be daft Aust! And what if I don't want to just fall into bed with you again?"

Taking a step back I try to hide the hurt I'm feeling but I know my eyes looking at her are glazed and the sheepish grin on my face is giving me away.

"But babe, you said friends with benefits is cool with you," I protest.

"Well, yeah, but I don't know Aust....I...want..." she starts to speak, and my heart leaps in my chest.

"Want what babe?"

"More Aust, I deserve more."

My heart pounds at her words, but I know I can't give her more.

Letting Annika in would only break my heart as I couldn't see our friendship surviving another breakup.

I need Anni as my friend more than I need her as a girlfriend.

It wasn't a secret to her that I'd been with other girls, but I always came back to her. Partly because being with her was familiar and partly because the sex was always off the charts.

What made Anni so sweet was her shyness, she was gorgeous but didn't honestly know how much and that drove me crazy.

I'd always hated the type of girls who knew they were attractive and flaunted it; although in high school before I got the guts to actually make a move on Annika, those were exactly the type of girls I got with.

Anni was the only girl that really got to me, she always had and losing her completely would damn near kill me. So as to guard my heart and keep Anni in my life when we broke up because of our constant fighting when we were together, I offered her the option of being friends with benefits. It didn't seem like the kind of thing Anni would do but she obviously didn't want to lose our friendship either, so she gave in.

"But Anni, we don't work that way."
"I didn't mean with you Aust," she laughs, her words hitting me hard.
"Oh, yeah, I'm just your fuck buddy," I feign a laugh to make it seem as though her words don't hurt like hell.

"Aust, I'm sorry...that was harsh of me," she says
apologetically.
"It's ok, but how are you going to make it up to me?"
I taunt, grabbing her around the waist again.

"Hmmm, well since Jairus and Bella aren't home,"
she teases, making me wait for what she wants to do.
"Oh really? How dare you tease me, babe!" I taunt
her again, smashing a kiss to her lips, melting against
her body in my arms.
Anni is mine, she always has been and the way she
makes me feel is addictive.
Pulling away from our kiss, I ask in her ear, "My
bedroom or yours?"
"Yours, but you better shut the door this time," she
laughs taking my hand and leading me down the
hallway.
My dick is aching, desperate for her mouth to be
around it, as tonight I'm too damn tired to fuck my
best friend and my heart is too tired of letting her in
too deep.

Sixteen | Ask Yourself

Sometime after giving Austin a little naughtiness,
I must have drifted to sleep as I wake up
wrapped in his arms in his king single bed.

He murmurs when I try to free myself from his
tight grip, "Aust I need to get up."
"Uhuh, babe...stay in bed with me."
"Aust, please I'm bursting and I'm hungry."
"Can I sneak in later?" he asks, letting his grip
around my torso loosen.
"Ok, but just to sleep, Aust."
"Of course, babe," he replies stretching up to
kiss me as I get out of his bed.

His kisses are becoming sweeter than usual, one
could say more loving and it has me a little
worried and confused about how I'm feeling.
In the kitchen, after a quick dunny stop, I spoon
some of the Bolognese sauce I'd made earlier
into a bowl to heat up when the pasta is ready.
Everything seems to be in slow mode, the kettle
is taking a hundred years to boil and the ticking
of the clock on the wall is making that

monotonous ticking sound that drives you crazy.

The only thing not in slow mode are the thoughts in my head. I've still not been able to stop thinking about my almost kiss with Jairus and his subsequent snuggle in my bed. It's crazy thinking about how much I do want to kiss him, the words Bella said to me about how hot kissing him would be.

It's not like kissing Austin isn't amazing but he's the only guy I've ever kissed.

The kettle flicking off breaks my thoughts and I pour the water into the pot with the Penne hoping it wouldn't take too long to cook. Penne was my go-to pasta, spaghetti couldn't be eaten with a spoon and for some reason there is always a shortage of forks in our house, as though we have a fork stealing bandit in our midst.

After setting the timer on the stove for ten minutes I sit on the stools by the bench, grabbing my phone off charge to go on Instagram.
I can't help myself, typing 'Jairus Brooks' into the search bar.

Caz May

His profile instantly comes up and it's not private.

Clicking on it I start scrolling through his pictures. Most of them are of football related stuff, pictures with his teammates. But about halfway down there are a few pictures of him on a post with a beautiful brunette. In one picture he is kissing her, another his arm around her smiling.

My heart pounds in my chest, clicking on the link to her profile, @sarbaby15, however, her profile is private.

Going back to Jairus' profile I continue scrolling back through his photos. He is undoubtedly gorgeous and I practically have to wipe the drool from the corner of my mouth looking at some of the shirtless pictures of him. I've seen him half-naked, right in front of me, but it doesn't make looking at photos of him any less appealing.

The front door cracks open then just as the buzzer sounds for my pasta.
 He greets me as I jump up from the stool, "Hey sweetheart, why you still up?"
"No reason," I reply, slamming my phone on the table.
Entering the kitchen, he glances at my phone, Instagram and his profile still lighting up the

screen.

Quickly I turn off the stove, knowing he is about to enter my personal space. He grabs my phone and I try to snatch it back, hoping the lock screen has taken effect.

"Were you looking me up on Insta?" he asks winking at me.
"No!" I defend, "It just came up in things I might like," I protest, hoping he buys my story even though it's so not plausible.

"Oh really?" he teases pressing back on the screen, "looks like you searched for me, sweetheart."
"OK, I did, but I..."
He pushes my body up against the bench leaning down to whisper in my ear, "Did you miss me, sweetheart?"
I want to defend myself, to say no, but that would be a big fat lie because I kind of did miss him. He'd not been around much the last few days, having a few late-night training sessions.

"Uhuh... Why would I miss you?"

"Because you want me," he teases, his lips again a whisper from mine, "as much as I want you."
I shake my head, "No, I can't Jairus."

Caz May

He sighs before freeing me from his arms and taking a step back, "Yeah and I shouldn't."
Not meaning to, I let out a 'huh', hoping he isn't about to tell me what I'd suspected when scrolling through his Instagram.
"I've...um...I've... "he stutters.
"What Jairus? You've got a girlfriend?"
He frowns when he replies, "Yeah...how'd you know?"
"Just guessing. But she's probably the beautiful brunette you're kissing in one of the pics on your Insta?"
"Yeah, her name is Sara."

"She's really pretty," I declare, my heart constricting because it hurts to say those words about someone he obviously cares about and it seems as though he has a thing for brunettes, not blondes like me.
"Yeah, pity she's a bitch."
"I'm sorry, what?" I spit at him, shocked he'd say something like that about his girlfriend.
"Yeah, we've been together two years and I don't know..."
"What Jairus? You can tell me," I suggest touching his arm, retracting it quickly when I feel an odd shiver run up my arm.

"We've been fighting heaps and I don't know if I love her anymore."

"That's no good, were you serious about her?
You know before you started fighting heaps?"

"Yeah, I was actually going to propose to her on
our two-year anniversary but she picked a
fight...and I um..."
"What Jai?"
"I met you, Annika."
"What have I got to do with how you feel about
your girlfriend?"
"Come on Anni, you can't deny there is
something between us."
"Maybe, but you obviously like brunettes and..."
"What? That's not an answer, sweetheart and
what a load of crap I only like brunettes."
"But your girlfriend is brunette and you kissed
Bella and she's brunette."
"God, sweetheart, do you hear yourself?"
"Yes...you don't want me Jairus. You just want
to..."

Pressing a finger to my lips to silence me, he
replies huskily, "Damn right sweetheart, I want
to kiss you and fuck you until you scream my
name but I'm not a cheater."
My heart is pounding. The way he'd just said
'fuck you' already had the desire pooling in my
underwear.

"I...I...but you kissed Bella?" I protest even though I know that Bella kissed him I want to hear the words from his mouth.

"No, sweetheart...Bella kissed me...and to be quite frank I'd rather have kissed a brick wall." I laugh at his response, "Hey, that's my friend you're talking about!"
"I know, I'm sorry Anni, Bella is a nice girl, but she's not you."
"And you want me? Why?"

"Good question...maybe because I can't have you and that drives me crazy...or maybe because you give my sass back to me."
"Hmm, yeah, so what are you going to do about your girlfriend situation Mr?" I taunt him.
"No idea," he confesses.
"Why have you been fighting anyway?"
"Because she's a bitch!"
"You said that," I laugh.
"Sorry...it's just that she doesn't support my choice to sign on for the Tigers and thinks I want her to give up everything for me."
"And do you?"
"No...I'd never ask her to give up anything that she loves. I love footy but she can't let me be happy."

"You'll work out what the best choice is. Do you want some Bolognese with me?"

"Sounds great," he replies peering into the pot, "you might want to cook some more pasta."

"Yeah, it looks like mush," I laugh, grabbing the kettle to refill it.

"Anni, will you come to watch me at training sometime? And maybe a game?"

I turn to look at him, seeing the pleading look in his eyes, "Yeah sure, sounds fun."

"That would be amazing," he beams kissing me on the cheek.

My heart leaps in my chest, my cheek feeling as though it's on fire and as he prepares the next batch of pasta my mind races thinking about what could be, as something has definitely changed between us.

I'm excited at the way just being around him makes me feel, but I'm also scared I'm falling for him and he can never be mine.

Seventeen | Overrated Words

Bella

No one was home as I prepared to get ready to go to see Jace. The trepidation is rising in my chest because he'd already changed the day on me once and I just want to get our meeting over with.
He never gave me the chance to say I was sorry, his words 'get the fuck out of my house Bella. Get the fuck out!' still torture my mind and hurt like knives in my heart.

Jace was my first love, my everything, he'd been there for me in my darkest days when my Dad passed and my whole world fell to pieces with Mum turning to the bottle.

So much fell on my shoulders, from taking care of my little sister Elyse to keeping things running at home when Mum couldn't.

Sometimes I feel as though I shouldn't have moved away but I needed the escape that Jace offered when he said we should move to the city.

Elyse was able to stand on her own two feet, being a little older and more independent but I still hated leaving her to care for Mum.

Taking a look at my outfit in the full-length mirror in Anni's walk-in, I sigh looking at my dishevelled appearance. I've not been sleeping the best since I'd started crashing at Anni's and working at Lush in the city Megamall was sucking the life out of me, like all my energy was being sloshed down the drain with the bath products I have to enthusiastically sell to earn a measly weekly wage.

Sometimes I regret my choice to not go to University but studying was never really my thing and I barely passed year twelve as it was, so it's not like I have much choice in terms of course options.

Pocketing my phone from beside the bed, I leave the bedroom.

Locking the front door behind me I hope that someone would be back to let me in later.

Quickly I cross the laneway running out to Bridge Road whilst flipping my hood on to not get soaked from the spitting rain that has started to fall.

Luckily when I get to the tram stop, a tram is just arriving.

It is thankfully empty and I easily get a seat after tapping my Taki ticket card on the reader.

The closer I get to the city the more nervous I feel and the more my heart pounds at the thought of seeing Jace again.
It has only been a couple of weeks, but it feels like months and I miss him so much it hurts.

~~

Walking into Click coffee I notice Jace sitting on a couch at the back with a coffee in his hands and one on the small round table in front of him.
It warms my heart that he's already ordered for me but at the same time a rush of panic overwhelms me that maybe he'd wanted to meet up because he wanted to introduce me to his new girlfriend.
Sitting down on the ottoman across from him I pick up the coffee in my hands to warm my frostbitten fingers.

"Hey Bel, I'm glad you turned up."
Taking a sip of my caramel latte I give him a half-hearted smile, "Why? Were you expecting someone else?"
"No, not at all, but I just thought you might have been too mad at me still."
"Why would I be mad at you Jace? I'm the stupid one who cheated on you," I declare shaking my head.
"That's not completely true Bel," he admits putting his head down so I can't see his eyes.
"What? Are you telling me that you were cheating on me?"

He looks up at me with a sheepish look on his face, "Yes Bel, but it was like a..I don't know.."

"With who Jace?"

"Just a random girl I met out one night....We hooked up a couple of times."

"I can't believe you, Jace! You're such a hypocrite!"

"I know Bella, and I'm so sorry...So incredibly sorry."

"Yeah well I'm sorry too... but it doesn't change what happened."

"That's true Bella, but I should have told you and I shouldn't have kicked you out."

"I did sleep with your brother though... that's worse than some random hook-up."

He doesn't reply instead focuses on someone walking up behind me, "Hey bro," the familiar voice says.

Turning around I find Jaxon standing behind me, "Hey Bella," he says choking on my name.

"Um hi Jax, what are you doing here?"

"Coming to set things straight with you, because my damn brother here is a wreck without you."

Looking back at Jace when Jaxon sits on the ottoman next to me a sweet blush flushes Jace's cheeks.

"What's there to tell other than the bombshell he just dropped on me?"

"Yeah other than that, look he told me about that....And..." he starts shaking his head.

"What Jax? Tell me!"

"Well, I kinda thought he'd told you...and that night between us I thought you guys had broken up."

"Are you shitting me?"

"No Bella, you know I think you're hot as fuck but I'd never have slept with you if I knew you were still my brother's girl."
"Oh, for fuck's sake!" I scream out slamming my coffee on the table before standing up and kicking the ottoman as I run out the door.

The footsteps are behind me almost immediately and I barely have a moment to think about which way to head before his arms are around me in a tight embrace.
"Bella, I'm sorry...but I love you," he says softly in my ear.

Pulling back a little from his hug I look straight into his eyes, "I don't know if I can forgive you, Jace."
"Please beautiful I'll do anything...I can't live without you, Bella."
"You...you..." I try to find the words, but I don't have any. He'd hurt me, but his brother had to and I feel so torn.
Undoubtedly, I'm still in love with him but I can't be angry at him for cheating on me when I did exactly the same thing.
"Bella? Come home beautiful please?"
"No, I don't want to but I..."
"Forgive me? Because Bella, I forgave you the moment I sent you out the door when I realised, I couldn't be angry at you for something I did as well."
"Then why didn't you come after me?"

"Because I thought it was best to give you some space...and send Jax packing."
I let out a light-hearted laugh, "I'm still not coming back to live with you J...but I forgive you."
"Oh Bella," he muses smashing a kiss to my lips that sends my heart pounding.
Kissing Jace feels like home and home is where the heart is.
Jace is my home.
"So does this mean we're back together?" He asks winking.
"I guess so," I reply, kissing him again.
"I love you, Bella," he whispers against my lips deepening the kiss a little.
A passerby wolf whistles causing us to break apart.
"So, Bella, where to now?"

"Your place to say I've missed you with more than just a kiss," I tease whispering into his ear.
He doesn't reply, instead grabs my hand to drag me towards the tram stop with a delicious smirk on his face.

Eighteen | Erotic Stories

Saturday night television is horrible, like they put on shows that are boring as hell, that make you want to scratch your eyes out and leave the house to spend money to better the economy instead of watching free television.

Sitting on the couch with Austin, he is in control of the remote as Bella is out with Jace and Jairus is in Perth for his game.

"Aust, put the footy back on," I demand.

"Why? You hate the footy," he rightly says back.

"Um, that's because I've never had a reason to watch it," I admit, my cheeks flushing with the guilt I'm feeling.

"And now you want to because of our roommate?"

"Well, yeah," I admit laughing sheepishly from being caught out.

"I can't believe you Anni. He doesn't want any more than a quick fuck," he reasons as though he's trying to convince himself and me.

"Isn't that exactly what you want Aust? I'm just your fuck buddy remember?"

"Yeah, Nah...but.." he stutters, a blush rising up his cheeks.

"But what Aust? We're just friends, yeah?"

"Yeah, bestie...but you..." He cuts his own words off turning his gaze back to the television when he flicks the channel to SBS.

It's getting late and an advertisement for the upcoming shows flash up on the screen. The next show to be aired, after the movie that is currently playing is 'Erotic Tales'.
I screech in excitement, "I used to watch that show on the TV in my room!"
"What? Anni, you dirty girl!"
"I know...but well, we hadn't gotten together yet...and you know..."
"Oh my god, babe..." he groans, "hearing you say that turns me on bad."
"Really?"

He doesn't reply instead pulls me down on top of him, both of us falling back down on the couch. Grabbing my cheeks in his palms he pulls my mouth to his for a desire filled 'I want you now' kiss.

He isn't joking about being turned on as I can feel his hard dick pressing against my belly.
As I'm about to deepen the kiss more he pulls back a little breathless, "God Anni, you...I..."
"What Aust? I what?" I giggle.
"Nothing, you're just perfect."

Sitting up I push my back into the armrest, "What's that supposed to mean, Aust? You're acting really weird lately."

"Am not," he defends sounding like a five-year-old who just got told he's lying.

"Don't deny it, Aust, something's up with us," I speculate hoping he might confess how he's feeling.

"Nothing has changed Anni. You're still my best friend. But I like being with you sexually, without all the bullshit of a relationship."

"Hmm, yeah I guess, but can you promise me something?"

"Yeah, sure I guess, depends on what it is?"

"Promise me the moment something changes about how you feel about me, you'll tell me?"

He sits up grabbing me around the waist, his forehead touching mine, "Yes Anni, I'll tell you if I fall in love with you."

He doesn't give me a second to process his words before his lips are on mine again, his kiss demanding but also having the same sweetness he'd been starting to do lately. With this kiss, he is breaking the promise already as it's clear he's in love with me.

I just don't know if I feel the same way anymore and I can't help but wonder if it's just because Jairus has come along.

Thoughts tumble in my head, thoughts of jealousy from Austin's side as he can see something is happening between Jairus and I. As I deepen the kiss licking Austin's lips to give me access to his mouth, I try to shake the thoughts from my head, just focusing on just being with Austin and not caring about the fact that he'd almost confessed he is in love with me.

Kissing for a few minutes I let myself feel, trying to give Austin the same fervour back that he is giving me. I wonder if I should say something, but when he pulls back breathless a few moments later his words confuse me more, "God, Anni, you're amazing...do you know what you do to me?"

"It's pretty obvious Aust," I laugh reaching down to graze my fingers over his crotch.
"Mmm, yeah and when you touch me Anni..." he moans.
I don't reply instead see out of the corner of my eyes that *'Erotic Tales'* is starting.
Crossing my legs, I sit back on the couch, my eyes fixed on the screen.
"Are we really going to watch it, babe?" he asks leaning back against the armrest on the other side of the couch and stretching out his legs, his feet in my lap.

"Yeah, this one is so funny. She seduces him to get in the tub with her after closing time to get a discount," I laugh seeing the title 'Wet' come on the screen.

"Fine. But after we are going to get wet, babe and I mean that in all senses of the word," he teases me smirking.

"Oh really, what happens if Bella comes home?"

He laughs, "Well I can't say we'll be quick, but if she hears you moaning, she won't knock."

"Aust, I don't moan during sex," I protest feeling my cheeks heat.

"Oh yeah, you do! And it's damn hot!" he jeers at me, rubbing his foot across my crotch.

"Well, so do you!" I spit back, laughing.

"Fuck, watching this show, babe. Come here, it's time to get wet," he teases as I shift to lay on top of him again.

"Are you sure we're just friends Aust?"

"Yes, Anni, you're my best friend and right now I'm going to kiss you until you beg me to fuck you."

Keeping his promise, he kisses me hard, more passionately than earlier and I can't deny the rush of desire it sends to my lower body.

It feels like months since we've been together so I pull away drawling out my words against his lips, "Fuck me now Aust please."

Moaning he grabs me by the waist lifting me up off the couch.

Instinctively I wrap my legs around his arse as he carries me down the hallway. We stumble past his room, stopping at the bathroom door where he puts me down.

"Um Aust, what are we doing?"

"I told you, we are getting wet," he laughs, the delicious smirk on his face again as he pushes me into the bathroom closing the door behind us and beginning to strip from his clothes.

Following his lead, I do the same, even though I know that having sex in the shower with my best friend, who is in love with me, is a very bad thing to do.

Nineteen | Shower Talk

Austin

Pushing my boxers to the floor I'm completely naked staring at Anni who is still taking off her clothes, torturously slow. "Need help, babe?" I teasingly ask.
"No, I'm just teasing you and I can see its working," she jeers at me nodding towards my obvious erection.
Stepping up behind her I enter the open shower. Turning the taps on I make sure the water isn't scolding before I turn back to find her standing behind me naked.

"God Anni, I love..." I start to say the words in my head; about to say 'you' but with the look of horror on her face I correct myself, "I love your body, babe."
"Really?" she teases.
"Really Anni, seeing you naked is a sight, babe."
She giggles sweetly before stepping closer to me, so close my dick presses against her belly. Her hands reach down grabbing my length in her fist.
"So, are you going to fuck me now?"
Shaking my head I drawl, "No babe, I'm going to tease you first, but only if you kiss me."
"Mmm...tease me how?"

Running a finger down her body stopping at her entrance, I speak against her lips, "By licking you, here," I tease brushing my finger over her clit.

She lets out a little gasp at the touch and I silence her by kissing her hard and demanding, slipping my finger in a little deeper to tease her. As she moans against my mouth, I break the kiss, still keeping my lips a whisper away from hers when I whisper with a teasing tone, "You're so wet, Anni."

Again, she gasps as I tease her a little more, "And now I'm going to taste you, Anni," I drawl focusing on saying her name like it's butter on my tongue.

Pushing her back against the shower wall I smash a quick kiss to her lips before licking and trailing kisses over her breasts, down over her belly button right to her entrance. Her gasp as I lick over her clit, teasing it with the tip of my tongue is almost vulgar and drives me wild.

I continue my delicious torture, feeling her body twitch as she fucks my face. Her moans are loud and I stretch an arm up to cover her mouth with my hand as she comes screaming out my name, "Oh Austin, fuck!"

Standing up I wink at her, smirking and she grabs me around the waist pulling me under the water and kissing me so forcefully she takes my breath away. Having her taste herself on my lips is so arousing.

I pull back taking in a deep breath, "Anni, oh my god that was so hot...so hot."

"Don't talk Aust, just fuck me now," she taunts, so unlike her usual shy self.

Not replying I brush her soaked hair away from her cheeks, kissing her furiously and grabbing her arse, lifting her up so she can slide onto my dick. Her legs wrap around my back as I thrust into her, our lips not parting for a moment.

This is by far the hottest, nastiest sex we've ever had and my heart is pounding in my chest, the words I want to say on the tip of my tongue.
I want to scream out, 'Annika, I love you' but instead as I thrust deeper into her hearing her moans increasing, I yell, "God Anni, I love being inside you. Oh Fuck!"
Her moans subside a little as I pound into her hard again. She grabs my wet hair in her hands pulling my face to hers, kissing me zealously.
Her climax rocking her body spurs my own release into her, as we speak with our tongues.
Pulling out of her body I grab her legs from around me helping her to stand up against the wall again. Caressing her cheek I whisper, "Anni, that was seriously incredible, are you sure your feelings haven't changed about me?"

She laughs, stabbing my heart a little that she thinks my question is funny.
"No Aust, you're still just my bestie."
"So you don't love me? Because sex like that babe...well..."
"I do love you Austin, but not like that. It doesn't mean that we can't have incredibly hot sex."
"Yeah, true...making you come is so damn fun."

She laughs reaching behind her to turn off the taps before she slides past me to grab a towel and wrap it around her body.

"Um, Anni?"

"Yeah, what?" she replies, her hand on the doorknob.

"We didn't use protection again, are we good?"

Kissing me on the cheek, she replies, "We're good Aust, shark week starts in a couple of days, don't stress."

"Ok, cool, I...wouldn t...want..."

"Me either Aust, trust me," she replies opening the door and walking out.

I hear her voice, "Oh hey Bel."

I know Anni would be blushing, being caught by her friend in just a towel. I don't hear Bella's reply, closing the door to wrap a towel around my waist. Looking in the mirror I shake the water out of my ears, trying not to think about how much Anni's words hurt.

I don't want to tell her how I feel if she doesn't feel the same way, as I know that would probably mean I wouldn't even get to be with her at all and that would be far worse.

Falling for your best friend is stupid but I've gone and done it. I can only hope that by being with her more she'd fall for me too.

Twenty | Nocturnal Gossip

Hearing Austin close the bathroom door I try to ignore the stare Bella is giving me, the tell me now stare.

"Oh, hey Bel," I greet her.

"Hey Anni," she greets me winking.

"Um, the bathroom isn't free right now."

"Oh really? And how would you know that?" she taunts me as I cross my arms over my chest to stop the towel from falling.

"Um...just guessing," I lie heading towards my bedroom.

She follows me, flopping down on my bed when I go into the walk-in to get dressed.

"Really Anni? Or were you getting it on with Blondie finally?" she calls out.

From the walk-in, putting on my underwear, I call back, "He's not home, he's in Perth remember?"

"Oh right, so you were in the bathroom on your own then?"

In my pyjamas, I sit on the edge of the bed feeling the blush rise up my cheeks.

"So Anni? Come on tell me, girl."

"Um...roommates don't kiss and tell Bella."

"Oh my God Anni, you and Austin really?"

"Um...yeah....but..."

"What? You weren't just pashing huh?" she teases sitting up on the bed and poking my arm in jest.

Feeling myself blush again I mumble, "We might have um..."

"Fucked in the shower, huh?"

I nod my reply, not sure of what words to say to my friend, feeling embarrassed.

"Anni, you dirty girl! Was it good?"

"Oh yeah...but I um...think he's in love with me."

"Anyone could have told you that Anni...so are you guys together?"

"No, we're just best friends, fuck buddies."

"Oh Anni, come on don't give me that shit."

"It's true Bel, I don't think I feel that way about him anymore."

"What about Blondie then?"

"I don't know...I'm just confused, Bel."

"Yeah, how?"

"I've only ever been with Austin and yeah things are pretty hot between us, but you know what I mean."

"Yeah, so get with Blondie then... it's obvious he's got the hots for you too."

"Yeah, can't go there. He's got a girlfriend."

"Seriously? Damn pity. If I wasn't back with Jace, I'd so try to get with him, not that I'd have a chance when he's got it so bad for you."

Laughing I reply, "Do you know what he told me?"

"No, what? Was it about me?"

"Yeah...he said he'd rather have kissed a brick wall."

She presses a hand to her heart, feigning hurt, "Oh Blondie, harsh words," she laughs breaking into a fit of giggles.

I can't help but laugh myself, "I know right...but Bel?"

"Yeah?"

"I don't know what to do," I say softly.

"Don't think about it, just be with Austin and see what happens. Maybe you'll fall back in love with him too."

"Yeah maybe, but I don't want Austin to be the only guy I'm ever with in my life."

"Totally, so get out there and get with someone else."

"I can't do that," I confess.

"Why? What have you got to lose?"

"I don't know...I can't do that to Austin and obviously, I can't get with Jairus."

"I meant someone else, Anni. And what's Austin got to do with it?"

"Because he's in love with me, if I get with someone else it will break his heart."

She laughs half-heartedly at my comment, "Leading him on is a hell of a lot worse than breaking his heart."

Her words hit me hard, as she is definitely right and I feel so incredibly guilty for my bathroom escapade. Austin is my best friend and I'm finally realising that friends with benefits maybe isn't the best idea, but it's so difficult to let go of someone when being with them is all you know.

Twenty-One | Filthy Twister

Jairus saunters into the house, home early from training to find Bella and I watching TV on the couch. He seems off when he greets us, "Hey chickas, what's cracking?"

I laugh at his crazy words, "Not your jokes obviously."

"I'm hilarious, don't you think sweetheart?" he taunts me coming into the lounge room and sitting on the chaise.

"So funny," I taunt back. Bella is trying not to laugh at the banter between us.

"So, have we got any plans for this Tuesday evening?" he asks with a sarcastic and suggestive tone.

"No, why are you asking?"

"No reason, except the gangs all here, we should do something."

"Austin won't be home until late though, he's got a late lecture or something on, I can't remember."

"More fun for me then," Jairus teases giving me a wink when he again suggestively says, "Do you have a Twister mat and spinner?"

"Yeah, who doesn't!" I beam.

"Then strip twister it is," he suggests, smirking deviously.

"No way Jairus, you'll cheat!"

"Oh you bet I will!" he taunts, "just to get you naked quicker of course."

Bella looks at me stifling a laugh, "I don't exactly want to see Anni naked, so how about down to undies and you can wear a hat instead of a bra." Jumping up from the couch I race to the cupboard to get the game out, spreading it out onto the lounge room floor.

"So, Jai, lay down the rules."

"Normal rules apply, however, if your spin lands on red you instead move an article of clothing, but have to then go back to the same position as before."

"Ok so what our clothing options then?" I ask looking at Bella.

"Well, as undies and bra don't come off its daks, tees, jumper...and hat instead of bra for you Jairus."

"Deal, so who's up first then? You and me, sweetheart?" he suggests winking at me.

"So, the loser is the first to underwear correct?"

"Yep, do you dare?" he taunts, winking and smirking like a damn devil.

It makes my insides flip-flop.

"Oh yeah," I laugh standing on one side on the mat near the word 'Twister' as Jairus stands opposite, licking his lips as he looks at me.

"Anni, pick a number between one and ten, keep it in your head, Jairus same and on the count of three say it out loud," Bella instructs laughing, "Ok one, two, three.... Number?"

At that moment I shout out five and Jairus shouts out eight. I'm already off to a shit start.

"Ok Jairus, first or second?"

"Second," he replies sending me another devilish wink.

"Sweet, ready Anni?" she asks flicking her finger against the spinner. It lands on right foot, green. Stepping on to the mat, I laugh hoping that Jairus lands on red.

Again, Bella flicks the spinner for Jairus' turn and it lands on right-hand yellow. He puts his hand down, leaning closer to me, "Just wait, you're going to strip first sweetheart," he teases with his devious smirk lighting up his face again.

"We'll see about that," I laugh when Bella calls out, "Anni, left foot red!"

"Oh shit, really?"

"Yep, take something off sweetheart," Jairus drawls at me. Lifting my foot off the green for a moment I yank my trackie daks off, throwing them on the couch before scissoring my legs open, one foot on green and one on red. Jairus licks his lips looking down at my crotch.

I know my whole body blushes with that look.

"Ok Jairus, left foot green," Bella instructs as Jairus follows the direction.

Again, she comes to my turn and I feel exposed as I again land on red, right hand.

Before putting my hand down, I remove my jumper, throwing that on the couch as well.

"Ooo...Jairus, right-hand red!" she beams winking at me as Jairus lifts his jumper and t-shirt off at once.

"It's only one piece of clothing, Jai," I inform him trying to concentrate on standing upright when I take in his half-nakedness in front of me again.

"I know, but I'm giving you an advantage, not that I plan on taking any more off."

"Oh right, well um Anni, left-hand red...sorry," Bella says.

Jairus licks his lips again, biting down when I lift my t-shirt over my head, falling against him as I try to move.

"You lose sweetheart, but it was so worth it," he whispers in my ear.

I scoff, "Bella are you ready?"

"Yes, girl, let's get Blondie naked!" she giggles giving me a high five as I spin the spinner.

As I instruct her, left foot blue, we hear a loud knock at the door, "Stay there, it's probably Austin having forgotten his keys again."

Wearing only a lacy bra and cheeky undies I run to the door, opening it expecting to find Austin at the door but instead find a brunette woman rugged up in about six layers of clothing.

"Oh, um hi," she blushes looking at my half-nakedness, "Is Jairus here?"

"Um yeah, and you are?"

"His girlfriend, Sara," she informs me, her tone when saying girlfriend vicious.

I didn't need to call out to Jairus as I feel him step up behind me and with his hand grazing against the small of my back, he leans against the door as he speaks to her in the same vicious tone, "Hi Sar, what are you doing here?"

"We need to talk and you haven't been answering your phone."

"I needed some space Sar and I'm kinda busy right now."

She looks me up and down before looking at Jairus who is still practically dressed.

"I can see that. I can just go if you want to get on with whatever this is," she says so meanly I think snakes are going to come out of her head.

"No, you said we need to talk and you're here, so talk."

"Can I come in then? Talk in private?"

"Fine," he spits at her pressing his hand harder against my back to lead me away from the door as Sara steps inside.

I watch as they walk towards his room and my heart sinks at what is going to happen between them behind the closed door of his bedroom. The fun night is ruined and I'm afraid I've already let myself in too deep.

Twenty-Two | Get Stuffed

Jairus

Once in my bedroom, shutting the door behind us
Sara winds her scarf off from around her neck and
shrugs out of her overcoat throwing them on Austin's
bed behind her.
I give her die bitch eyes.
"So talk then Sar?" I demand, taking a step back
closer to my bed.
"Well um....I..."
"What Sar? Don't play that game with me, you
wanted to talk so talk."
"Well... maybe you should start by telling me what's
going on with your roommates? You didn't tell me
they were girls."
"No, I didn't...because it doesn't fucking matter," I
object.
"It does so Jai, when one of them is prancing around
answering the door in her underwear!"
"We were just having a bit of fun Sar, plus she's not
into me."
"Bullshit Jai, she looked at you like she wanted to eat
you."
"What kind of look is that Sar? You wouldn't know
what that means...plus she's kind of got a thing going
on with our other roomie."
"Really? So nothing has happened between you?"

"No, God Sar, how could you think that I'd cheat on you?" I question her sitting down on my bed.

She moves closer, standing in front of me. Reaching out I grab her hips, about to pull her down to the bed with me when she wiggles away and sits down next to me.

"Please don't Jai, I'm not here to sleep with you."

"Sorry what? You actually do want to talk about what's up with us lately?"

"Yes," she says so quickly I wonder if she is about to say anything else but she is silent.

"Ok, well let me start by saying I'm sorry for not replying to your countless messages but being away for a game is pretty full on and..."

"It's just a text Jai, it's not that hard."

"Fine, you have a point, but sending a text isn't really making an effort Sar and your one to talk, showing up unannounced for the first time in forever."

"Well, yeah...because I..."

"What Sar? Spit it out!"

"I...I...k..."

"Fuck Sar, just fucking tell me!"

She looks across at me, pain in her eyes, her pupils dilated.

"I kissed someone else!" she blurts out, turning her face away.

"What? When? Who? Look at me Sar and tell me!" Her gaze turns back to mine, "After that night you used me on the couch."

"Oh, fuck Sar, come on... I didn't mean to hurt you, but fuck..."

"I'm sorry Jai, but it just happened after work one day...he could see I was upset and I told him that we'd had a fight."

"So, you were talking to some guy about our relationship?"

"Yes, but I was really upset...I had no one else to talk to."

"Don't give me that shit Sar," I spit at her standing up, "I can't believe I was going to ask you to marry me." She stands up, too close to me, making me feel like I'm suffocating.

"You were?"

"Yes, on our anniversary, before you decided to pick a fight like usual and then you go and kiss someone else Sar, I seriously can't believe it."

"I'm sorry Jai, it won't happen again..."

"No, Not with me it won't!"

"What? Are you breaking up with me?" she stammers.

"Yes Sar, I'm breaking up with you and do you want to know something?"

Tears sting the corner of her eyes when she mutters 'yes' under her breath.

"There is something between me and my roomie, I want her so bad it's killing me, but you know what Sar?"

"What?" she sobs.

"I didn't cheat, you bitch!"

"I'm sorry Jai, I'm really sorry!"

"It's too late Sara, I don't want you anymore. You can't support me and when things get tough you run to someone else telling him our private life and kissing him."

"Please Jai... it won't happen again... it was a mistake."

"Are you even listening to me Sara? I don't want you anymore."

"But I love you Jai, please?"

"Well, I don't love you, so stop fucking begging me to take you back and just get the fuck out of my house."

"Is that really what you want?"

"More than anything, seriously Sara, just get the fuck out of my life!"

Not saying another word I give her dagger eyes as she puts her coat back on, grabs her scarf and runs out the door in tears.

Sitting on the bed with my head in my hands I go over the last few months in my head, not believing her for a second that her indiscretion only happened once.

The door is still ajar and I don't hear Annika come in, not aware she is in the room until she sits on the bed next to me and says sweetly, "Jai, are you ok? That seemed brutal."

Looking up I meet her caring gaze, trying to focus on her eyes and not the fact she still hasn't put her clothes back on.

"Um... yeah... nah," I reply confused.

"Is everything ok with your girlfriend?"

"Not exactly."

"Really? What happened?"

"She cheated on me," I admit, feeling my heart constrict a little.

It isn't like it didn't hurt, I'd been with her for two years, loved her and was thankful for the time in my life I met her.

She'd dragged me out of a player lifestyle, got me to make a commitment to one person to the point I was going to marry her and now she throws it all away over one fight.

"Oh, I'm sorry Jai, that sucks."

"Yeah, but I..."

"What?" she asks touching my thigh with her hand reassuringly.

"I thought about cheating on her too..." I confess pushing her hand away, "with you."

"Really Jai?"

"You know I want you, sweetheart," I admit fighting with myself, wanting to just kiss her now but knowing I won't be able to stop myself from just kissing her.

"Um, yeah, but why?"

"Oh, come on Anni, you have to know how gorgeous you are."

Shaking her head she replies softly, "I'm not gorgeous, don't say that."

Her long blonde hair has fallen into her face and she shifts uncomfortably, turning away from my gaze.

Brushing it away from her cheeks I turn to face her, my knee up on the bed and my foot against her thigh.

"Sweetheart, you're damn gorgeous and I want you so bad."

Her sweet brown eyes look at me pleadingly as she bites down on her lip.

"I want you too, but I...."

"What Anni?"

"I can't...I..."

My heart is pounding now, normally before Sara, if I'd had a girl in my bedroom in her god damn underwear, she'd have been out of it in five seconds flat but I can't do that to Annika, no matter how much I want her.

Her sweet shyness is getting to me like no one else ever has.

"Anni, it's ok, come here," I suggest opening my arms for her to hug me.

Without saying another word, she falls against my chest and I wrap my arms around her.

Lost in the moment I don't hear him come in until he's right in front of us.

"What the fuck? How dare you, you arsehole!"

Annika jumps up reaching out to try and hold Austin back from launching himself at me.

"Aust, nothing happened, ok?"

He looks straight at her, the anger in his eyes calming down a little, "Doesn't look like nothing Anni, you're practically naked."

"Nothing happened Aust, we were just playing strip twister and then Jai's girlfriend showed up."

"Girlfriend?" he asks, looking at me with a questioning look.

"Yeah, my girlfriend who cheated on me and I just kicked to the curb."

"So, you just broke up with your girlfriend and put the moves straight onto Anni?"
Again, he tries to launch himself at me, his hands in fists and a stance of a boxer ready to pounce when I stand up.
Annika touches his arm, "Aust please it wasn't like that, I was just comforting him ok?"
"You expect me to believe that Anni, really?"
"Yes, I do Aust, I love you."
His eyes completely soften as he grabs her to pull her into a hug that stabs at my heart.
I have no chance of getting with her now and my heart hurts.

From the moment I'd caught them fucking I'd wanted her, slowly falling for her and now she'll never be mine.
Walking out of the bedroom I stop in the lounge grabbing my t-shirt to pull it over my head before rushing out the front door slamming it behind me and ignoring Bella calling out my name.
They could all get stuffed!
Or more rightly get fucked!

Twenty-Three | Blood Spill

Austin

It had been a week or so since Anni declared that she loved me, but my mind wondered if she'd even meant the words. She had been avoiding me, not coming in until late, well after her prac would have finished at Epworth hospital and barely said two words to anyone, not even Bella.

It is Monday and I've been wallowing in my own self-pity in bed, drinking too much coffee to sleep, but not able to drag my sorry arse out of bed. No one else is home, or so I'd thought until I hear a loud crash coming from the laundry at the back of our apartment.

Tentatively I jump out of bed, sneaking down the hallway to find Anni rummaging through the dirty clothes basket.

I step up behind her, "Anni, are you ok babe?"
Her head turns towards me as she clutches a hand to her chest, "Far out Aust, you scared the shit out of me."

144

"Sorry, you've just been like M-I-A lately."

"Yeah well, prac has been a bitch, as you can see I'm covered in blood and I can't find my other scrubs. If I don't wear clean scrubs tomorrow, I'm sure to get written up and I don't need that."

Tears had started to sting her eyes, jerking my heart hard.
I hated seeing her cry.

"Anni, babe, what's going on?"
"Nothing...I'm just doing really shit at this prac and I'm scared of failing."
"Come here," I suggest holding out my arms to her.
"I can't hug you in this Aust, can't you see I'm covered in blood?"

I laugh then, grabbing her by the waist pulling her towards me and lifting her up to sit on top of the washing machine.

"Then let's do something about that," I taunt, my fingers gripping the bottom of her scrub top.

She smiles at me as she lifts her arms above her head. I pull the top over her head and lick my lips seeing she has one of her sexiest looking lace bras on, that you can see the pink of her nipples through.

"Mmm, Anni this bra is hot," I tease, kissing her hard.

She returns the fervour in my kiss and moans against my lips, sending my dick rising. I pull back a little breathless, spreading her legs wide and stepping in between them.

"How about we get rid of these scrub daks too?" I suggest as I grab her arse and yank them down a little with her following my lead lifting her arse up a bit.
They pool at her ankles for a moment before they fall off her feet in a heap.
Not letting me think she kisses me again and grabs the front of my unbuttoned stripy black and white pyjama top to shrug it off my shoulders.

Her kiss is different to normal and I pull back feeling a strange rush of emotions.

"Babe, slow down yeah?"
"Why Aust? You're the one who always just wants to fuck."
"Yeah, well maybe I want more than that now," I confess hoping that she'd say the same back.
"Don't lie to me, Aust!"
"I'm not Anni! But it seems you are?"
"What's that supposed to mean?"
"You obviously didn't mean it when you said you love me last week."

The look in her eyes gives me her answer without words but still, she speaks, "I did mean it, Aust, I do love you, but not like that. You were about to lay into

Jairus when he'd done nothing wrong."

"So there's nothing going on between you then?"

"No Aust, what's it to you anyway?"

"Because I don't want you to be with him Anni."

"Why Aust? Are you telling me that you're in love with me?"

"No of course not," I spit at her, laughing to hide the truth, "I just don't think he's good enough for you babe."

"I think I'm more than capable of making that decision for myself Austin!"

"I didn't mean it, Anni, I'm sorry. I care about you that's all."

"I know Aust, so please just forget it and let up a little," she oddly says shifting as she jumps down off the washing machine.

Her body slides against mine and it makes my groin ache.

I smash a kiss to her lips, taking her mouth as though I'll never kiss her again.

She pulls away this time, "Aust please, I don't know if I can be with you like this anymore."

It's stupid, but I beg her, "Please Anni, I need you."

"Fine, but the promise stands about feelings and jealousy is a deal breaker."

"What the fuck do you mean? Jealousy?"

"If either one of us gets with someone else, not in a serious way the other can't be jealous."
"Fine, deal! And now you kiss me to seal the deal!" I demand, about to press my lips to hers again, when she turns her head so my kiss grazes her cheek.

She starts to walk out but turns back to look at me. "And Aust?"

"Yeah, babe?" I ask worried by her tone so much that her next words make my heart pound and my desire crash.

"Shark week is late."

She doesn't let me respond, instead, she rushes to her bedroom slamming the door behind her.

Only one thought crosses my mind as I pick up my pyjama top from the floor.

Oh Fuck!

Twenty-Four | Pink Lines

Lying in my underwear on the bed, the tears I'd held back from Austin break through.
Someone pounds hard on the bedroom door and I want to ignore whoever it is and just curse myself for being so stupid.

The knocking continues, so I bury my head under the pillow not responding even when Bella comes in and sits on the end of the bed at my feet.

"Anni, are you OK?"
Sobbing into the pillow still, I feel her hand on my back, "Anni, please tell me what's wrong?"

"I fucked up, bad!" I say sitting up and clutching the pillow against my chest in comfort.

"Austin said you needed to talk, so tell me what did you do?"

I look straight at her, the tears still stinging my eyes when I speak softly, "My...my...period is late."
Comfortingly she touches my arm, "How late?"
"Like about a week I think," I confess my heart pounding as thoughts fill my mind of the past month and the possibility hitting me hard again that I really

could be pregnant.

"Did you use protection last time?"

I shake my head, "No...I haven't used protection at all this month. I'm normally so sure of my cycles, so I didn't think it would matter."

"And if you are it would be Austin's yeah?"

I huff, "Of course Bella, you know I haven't been with anyone else."

"Sorry, I...um...so you haven't taken a test?"

"No, I don't have any. I'm scared to take one Bel."
"I know Anni, but wouldn't you rather know?"

"Of course, but what if I am? I can't be pregnant right now!"

"Let's not worry about that yet. We can cross that bridge if you are," she says so matter of factually I feel like she's been in the same situation herself.

"Bel, have you been in this position?"

"Of course, I have Anni."

"And were you pregnant?"

"No, just super stressed out; which you probably are so let's go get a test."

"Can you go get one for me? I have no idea what to buy and I'm embarrassed."

"OK, are you sure you're going to be OK?"

"No, not really, but..."

"Alright I'll be back soon; do you want to talk to Austin? He's kinda freaking out."
"OK, how long will you be?"
"Like half an hour."
I don't reply as she leaves the room. I can hear snippets of her conversation with Austin, and hear him grab his Ute keys off the hook by the door, throwing them at her with a cautionary 'don't you dare smash it.'

After Bella leaves, only moments after she's closed the front door Austin sits on the bed next to me, pulling me close for a hug that makes my heart ache.

"I'm sorry Austin," I say against his chest.

"What for?"

"Getting us into this situation."

Pulling back from the hug he looks straight into my eyes, "I'm just as much at fault if you're pregnant

Anni."

"But...I.."

"Don't OK, I'm here for you no matter what, I love you, babe."
"Aust, don't say that, please. You don't mean it."

"And what if I do mean it?"

"Then I'll feel even worse."

"Why? Can you honestly tell me you don't love me Anni?"

"Honestly Aust, I don't know really," I start, feeling my heart constrict a little, "but no I don't love you like that, I don't think."

"But Anni, I...after everything we've been through and now you could be having my baby...I just can't believe you feel nothing for me."

"You're my best friend Austin, and no matter what I'll have this baby and you'll be in our life, but I can't make myself love you that way."

He starts to reply but swallows his words, his Adam's apple bobbing up and down as he gulps.

"Aust, show me you love me."

Again, he doesn't reply, instead pushes my body down on the bed kissing me breathless. His kiss is consuming, wild and passionate, sending my heart pounding; my mind racing with thoughts that maybe I'm lying to myself about how I feel about him.

~~

As she promised Bella returns half an hour later with a bag from 'Chemists Warehouse'. Austin is lying next to me, an arm wrapped across my belly in a protective manner. It tugs at my heart a little, and for a moment I kind of want the test I'm about to take to be positive.

"Hey, how are you doing? You obviously talked things over?"

"Yeah, so um...did you get good tests?"

"Yes girl, here," she responds handing the bag to me with a three-pack box of 'First response' tests inside.

Pulling out the receipt I gape at the price, "Bel, these are a bit pricey."
"They might be, but they are the best ones Anni."
Sitting up I suggest, "Well at least let me pay you back."

"Don't worry about it girl, just go take one."

I look at Austin, biting my lip as I open the box, taking a test out and clutching the pink foil packet in my fist.

Taking one quick look at the instructions I head down the hallway towards the bathroom.

Not exactly looking where I'm going, I bump straight into Jairus as he comes out of the bathroom. Thinking quickly, I put my hand holding the pregnancy test behind my back.

"Woah sweetheart, what's the hurry? You OK?"

"Yep...yep I'm good, ' I stutter feeling exposed by his gaze locked on mine as I remember I'm still only in my bra and undies.

Still holding the test behind my back, I edge into the bathroom, about to shut the door when he asks, "Are you still coming to my training sesh on Wednesday?" "Um...yeah, of course. Just give me a couple of minutes, yeah?" I ask holding up my index finger of the other hand as I shut the door.

I wait a moment, to make sure he's walked away before I open the test packet as I sit down on the dunny.

My heart is pounding so hard I think it's going to explode out of my chest in anxiousness.

After peeing on the stick, I watch the first pink line cross the window before I put it on the counter beside me, too scared to see if another pink line comes up.

A knock comes loud on the door, "Anni, are you good? Did you take it?"

"Yeah, Bel, just give me one sec," I reply standing up and pulling up my undies, flushing the dunny before I open the door.

"So?" she asks.

"Can you look at it Bel? I'm too scared."

Peering at the test on the counter she smiles.
"What Bel? Why are you smiling like the Cheshire cat?"

"Do you want to know?"

"What do you think, bitch?" I half laugh, thankful for her lightening the moment.

"It's negative Anni, you're just late."

"Oh, thank fuck," I snap grabbing the test from her hand to look at it myself, never feeling more relieved to only see one pink line on a test.

When Austin appears in the doorway a moment later my heart crashes at his hopeful expression.

"So, are you?" he asks.

"No, I'm not pregnant Aust."

"Well, um...that's good yeah?"

"Yeah, but woah..."

"Yeah, maybe it's late because you're so stressed with prac," he suggests, his response a little too knowing for a guy.

"Yeah maybe, how'd you know that could be the case?"

"You forget I have sisters Anni."

"True," I reply giving him a quick kiss when Jairus appears back in the hallway.

"Who's preggo?" he jeers elbowing Bella.

"No one, nosy parker!" I snap at him, pushing everyone out of the bathroom.

Grabbing my hand Jairus pulls me back against the hallway wall, leaning against me and whispering in my ear, "You look hot in this bra sweetheart."
I let out a little moan at the contact of his breath against my ear.
"So, Wednesday?"

Putting my hands against his chest, feeling a rush of heat rush through my body, I reply, "Yes Jai, I'll be there."

He presses a kiss to my forehead and walks away,
leaving me feeling a little bit flustered.

Twenty-Five | Train Hard

Jairus

Slinging my gym bag over my shoulder I skid down the hallway to Annika's bedroom, stopping in the doorway calling out to her, "Anni, are you ready to go? I don't want to miss the tram."

"Yeah, I'm ready," her sweet voice announces as she stumbles out of her walk-in putting black ballet flats on her feet.
She is wearing black leggings that hug her delicious arse and a long-sleeved slouchy jumper that barely covers the small of her back. It's in that strange galaxy print that Sara was wearing the day I knew I wasn't in love with her anymore.

It looks super-hot on Annika though, in that way she doesn't know how gorgeous she is and how arousing her outfit choice is.
"Mmm, love the outfit sweetheart," I drawl, licking my lips.
She lets out a sweet giggle that makes my insides stir.
"It's comfy," she replies walking towards me.

Her hand brushes against mine, but before I can lace her fingers with mine she snatches it back as though she can feel the tingle I do.

Grabbing the house keys, she follows me out the
door to the tram stop.

"Anni, I really appreciate you doing this for me."
"I'm excited, I bet you're really good."
"Thanks, sweetheart," I reply blushing as we step
onto the tram that has just approached the stop.

Tapping our Taki's on the readers I have to grab Anni
to stop her from falling over as the tram jolts away.

Her body against mine is making my temperature
rise.
"Hold onto me sweetheart, OK?" I whisper in her ear
fighting the urge to wrap my arms around her and
pull her close, to kiss her.
I can feel enough eyes on us already and I want our
first kiss to be special, our own private moment.

Arriving at Punt road oval I don't hesitate to grab her
hand in mind, lacing my fingers with hers to drag her
off the tram. The warmth that rises up my arm
excites me and her sweet giggle filling the air excites
me as well.

Once we reach the training ground, I lead her to the
sidelines where friends and family are allowed to sit.

"I've got something for you sweetheart," I muse.
Sitting down she gives me a puzzled look.
"Oh?" she asks worriedly biting her lip as I unzip my

gym bag to grab out the Richmond snapback hat, I'd gotten for her.

Holding it up brushing her hair from her cheeks I put it on her head, kissing her cheek.
With a finger under her chin, I drawl "Look at me Anni."

Smiling she lifts her gaze to mine.
Cupping her cheek in my palm I whisper, "Do you know how gorgeous you look, Annika?"

A sweet blush rises up her cheeks, "Don't say that Jairus if you don't mean it."

"Sweetheart, I mean it," I reply not able to hide my smile, "I'll see you after, I've got another surprise for you."

Winking at her I delight in her sweet giggle and her words, "Train hard Jai."

Walking towards the goals I notice Travis has stopped kicking the ball. Throwing my bag by the goal post I sheepishly walk towards him, signalling for him to handball me.

"Uhuh mate, is that your girl?"
"No, man...but.."
"Don't hold out on me mate."

"Annika's not my girlfriend," I reply sure that I'm blushing.

"But you want her to be?"

"Fuck yeah...she's god...I can't even tell you how she makes me feel man," I confess, stretching, accentuating my lunges knowing Anni is watching

"You got it bad for her huh?"

"What makes you say that?"

"I could feel the tension between you from over here, mate. You've got the hots for that girl over there big time."

"Yeah, but she doesn't feel the same about me."

"Are you shitting me, man?"

"No, she's got some fucked up friends with benefits thing going on with our other roomie."

"Seriously man, make a move. She's got the hots for you too."

"You think so? I just don't know if I should, she's super shy too."

"Jai man, have you broken up with ya other girl?"

"Yeah but Trav I..."

"And you like miss shy over there, who can't take her eyes off you?"

"Yeah, I do man, a lot."

"Then make a move man. I didn't think you were such a pussy."

I elbow him hard, "I'm not a pussy mate, far from it but I don't want to mess things up with Anni."

"Trust me mate, kiss her once and it won't be the last time you kiss her."

I don't reply, instead grab the ball hurling it towards the goal posts to try to calm myself and stop myself from thinking about what I want to be doing with Annika instead of the routine of footy training.

The forty-minute training session seems to drag and Travis is right that Annika barely takes her eyes off me for a minute, except to lift her phone up and take a few selfies and pictures of around the ground.

I've never been gladder to hear coach Jenkins say 'That's a wrap boys', see you at the airport seven am sharp on Satdi'.

No sooner than those words left his mouth I race back to the stands to Annika.

Grabbing her around the waist I pick her up, lifting her over the barrier as she jumps into my embrace. She wraps her legs around my back falling against my chest.
Sweetly she looks up at me whispering so close to my lips, "Wow Jai, you were amazing out there."

"No Annika, you're amazing," I blush pressing my forehead to hers with the snapback grazing the top of my head.
Her breathing becomes raspy, her heartbeat rapid

like my own. Her hands are wrapped around my neck and my skin is hot just from the touch of her fingers. Just like on the tram having her close is driving me wild and this time I can't stop myself, smashing a kiss to her plump lip gloss stained lips.

Her fingers grab my hair as she pulls my mouth closer, letting out sweet moans that make the desire in my pants grow.
Her kiss is consuming, hotter than any kiss I'd ever had and I almost scream in pleasure when she bites my lip to part them and take my tongue as hers.

Pulling back completely breathless I groan as she slides down my body to the ground, "God Anni, fuck sweetheart that kiss... Fuck."

"Was it bad?" she asks innocently.
"Bad, are you fucking kidding me?"
"No... I've only ever..."
"Only ever what?"
"Kissed Austin...and I've never done the lip biting thing like that before."
"What? You've never kissed anyone else until now?"
"Yeah, so was it bad then?"
"Sweetheart, that was by far the hottest fucking kiss I've ever had."

"You're just saying that to make me feel better."

"Trust me, sweetheart, I wouldn't tell you that if it wasn't true."

"Mmm, yeah, ok."

Taking her hand, I lace her fingers with mine raising it up to kiss the back of it, "Are you ready for your surprise?"

"Kissing me wasn't the surprise?"

"No Anni, trust me I didn't plan on kissing you tonight."

"Oh," she snaps, as though my words hurt.

"Anni, sweetheart please don't be upset."

"I'm not upset, but why did you all of sudden want to kiss me?"

Dragging her over to pick up my bag I reply, "All of sudden?"

"Yes?"

"Anni, sweetheart I've wanted to kiss you since that first day in the kitchen," I drawl at her smirking.

"Really?"

"Really, I like you Annika, a lot."

She doesn't reply as I sling my bag over my shoulder, instead, she stretches up to press a soft sweet innocent kiss to my lips.

"So, what's this surprise?"

"If I told you, sweetheart, it wouldn't be a surprise."

"Fine, you're lucky I like surprises," she replies giggling again in her sweet way that makes my insides stir.

Travis is walking out as we leave the ground, and winks at me holding Anni's hand. I give him a nod back, squeezing Anni's hand in mine as I smile at her.

Her smile back makes my heart beat faster. It's the perfect night to share my favourite spot in the city with her.
I might have said 'I liked her' but the truth is I'm falling in love with her, hard and fast from just one kiss.

Twenty-Six | She's Mine

Austin

It was stupid to stay up waiting for Anni to come home from going to Jairus' training session with him but when it's getting close to midnight, I can't help but think something bad has happened to her, to them.

I try to focus on playing the latest Mario game on my Switch but all I can think about is whether Anni is ok. I'm also thinking other not so pleasant thoughts of him touching her, kissing her and who knows what.

You'd have to be blind to not see the tension between them and he'd made it pretty damn clear from his actions that he wanted her.

Anni is still behaving as though our arrangement to be friends with benefits is good with her but I hate admitting to myself that I want more from her now. Confessing I'm in love with her hasn't seemed to change how she'd feels about our arrangement at all. It's like I've told her too late and that any feelings she did have for me have vanished with the arrival of Jairus in our household.

Even though that thought hurts like a bitch I can't
hate the guy but I'm jealous of what he has with Anni
and I'm scared he's going to take my best friend away
from me.

Turning off my Switch after Mario has fallen to his
death for the tenth time in the same spot I'm about
to head to bed when the door swings open.

Jairus' arms are around Anni's waist as they stumble
in the door together laughing.

"Oh, hey Aust, why are you still up?"

"I was...um...just playing the Switch," I mutter, my
heart pounding.
"Cool, well um...we'll see you in the morning then,"
she suggests grabbing Jairus' hand.

"Um yeah, I guess...did you have fun?" I ask trying to
delay their obvious want to be alone together.

Bella is staying at Jace's for the night which normally
meant that I could sneak into Anni's bed but she is
giving me the impression that someone

else is going to be her bed buddy for the night and
it's making me super jealous.

She breaks my thoughts with her giggling, "It was
great Aust...I can see why they wanted Jai on the

team. He's amazing!" She coos elbowing him playfully making my heart sink further.

"That's good, so did you do something afterwards?" I ask feeling like I was her father interrogating her.

"Yeah Jai took me to the butterfly house in the botanical gardens, then we went to a rooftop bar and restaurant in the city. So amazing!"
"Um wow, sounds sweet," I reply, the jealousy rising in my chest.

It is plainly obvious something had happened between them.
Here I was thinking he just wanted a friend to go to training with him but he'd essentially taken Annika out on an amazing date.

I can't even remember the last date we'd gone on. Being friends with benefits for a year had wiped out most of the other memories of being together and I cursed myself for how wrong that was.

All I want now is to make new memories with the woman I'm in love with but looking at her with Jairus now I'm afraid she is falling for him.
I'm afraid I've told her how I feel too late and now I'm going to lose her.

Losing the friends with benefits part would suck but losing my best friend completely was the most worrying.

Annika is my world and I never should have been so
stupid to suggest friends with benefits. She'd told me
that one of us would fall in love; I just never thought
that one would be me.
"So Aust, we'll see you in the morning yeah?"

"Yeah, sure," I reply to her back as she pulls Jairus
down the hallway towards her bedroom.

~~

I've not even been asleep for an hour when I wake up
violently, in a cold sweat. Sitting bolt upright in bed I
gaze around the room shocked to find Jairus in his
bed across the room.

His eyes are open and he's lying on his side looking at
me.
Leaning on one arm he asks, "Are you, ok mate?"

"Yeah shit, I...um just had a fucked-up dream."
"Yeah, want to talk about it?"
"Um, fuck...sorry it was um...."

"It's cool man...you don't have to tell me."
"No, it's um...it was about...Anni died."

"Oh, shit man, that's horrible. But it was just a dream
yeah?"

"I know," I sigh.

"Man, can I be honest with you? I know we aren't mates or anything but?"

"Yeah, sure I guess, what's up?"

"I kissed Anni tonight."

Gulping I swallow the lump in my throat, "Oh just once?"

He blushes, "Um no, like three times."
"Oh, ok um," I reply sighing.
"I'm sorry, I know she's kind of your girl but I..."
He cuts his own words off but I know what he is going to say.

"Well, I don't blame you...I fucking love her so much but I think she likes you."

"Yeah, I don't know. I don't want to take her away from you man."

"Um yeah, but I just...forget it," I snap standing up clutching my sheets around my waist and stumbling out the door to Anni's room.

It is wrong but hearing Jairus tell me he'd kissed her makes me so insanely jealous I want to be with Anni, to make her see that she is my girl.

Twenty-Seven | Butterfly Kiss

I've never rushed out of the house quicker than I do the morning after my night out with Jairus.
 Austin is still asleep beside me and I feel a pang of guilt hit me in the chest recalling giving into him when he'd come stumbling into my room a few hours earlier.

He was super possessive, mumbling things like 'you're mine', but mostly 'I love you, babe'.
It's hard to hear him say those words to me after wanting to hear them for so long but now I'm not sure if he is who I want to be with.

Sleeping with him again was wrong, I knew that and this time he was slow in his actions, not fucking me but making love to me.
 I should have stopped him but I needed to feel last night, especially because Jairus had practically kissed me senseless and left me turned on, wanting a release that he didn't give me.

I'd been about to undress when he'd stopped kissing me, climbing out of bed and telling me 'No I can't sweetheart, not yet.'
I can't deny those words hadn't hurt like a bitch. I'd practically thrown myself at him, out on the football

oval jumping into his arms and his kiss then was so amazing I want more; so much more.

Jairus' kisses are so different to Austin's; more intense and arousing.
 I'm replaying the kisses in my mind that he'd given me on our night out in my head, especially the one in the butterfly house.

Jairus opened the door of the glasshouse, "After you sweetheart," he drawled smirking at me, making my insides flutter like the butterflies fluttering all around us.

Taking my hand, he led me down the boardwalk that ran through the middle of the glasshouse.

"Anni, I didn't plan on kissing you tonight...but I.."
"What Jairus?"

"Well, I wanted to bring you here, it's one of my favourite places in the city...I just wanted...god I don't know anymore."

"What do you mean? You're confusing me."

"I meant what I said about our kiss earlier."

"I'm sure it wasn't that good, you've probably kissed heaps of girls."

"True, but no one has made me feel like you do, sweetheart, ever."

"Really?"

"Really, you turn me on so bad Annika. Can I kiss you again to show you that the first kiss wasn't a one off?"

I muttered an 'mmm' in response as he pushed my body against the cold metal railing, lifting my butt up so I was sitting on the edge of it.

A butterfly landed on my head and he laughed, "Even they think you're beautiful."

Brushing the butterfly away he stepped in between my legs, wrapping his arms around my back, "Wouldn't want you to fall," he laughed his words laced with emotion.

"Yeah, we can't have that," I laughed back locking my eyes on his.

Not able to stop myself I grabbed his neck, fisting his hair to pull his lips down to mine.
The moment our lips touched he moaned, pressing his body against mine.

This kiss was even hotter than the first one as he ran his tongue along my lips, parting them and plunging his tongue inside to take my mouth as his.

As he kissed me back, he moaned more, as though he couldn't get enough.

Breathless he pulled back panting when he spoke, "Sweetheart, that kiss was even more arousing than the first time."

"Yeah?"

"Anni, seriously sweetheart, how do you not get how much I want you?"

"I told you, I've only ever been with Austin and it's never been like this with him."

"What? Never hot as hell? I want to take you right here, right now?" he taunted grazing his fingers along the seam of leggings, most definitely able to feel that my underwear was wet with the desire I feeling.

Letting out a little moan at his question he smirked at me, "Exactly like that, Jai."

"Well, sweetheart, as much as I'd love that I can't do that to you, and we need to get to dinner anyway."

"So, you're lying to me then?" I implied jumping off the railing and sliding down his body.
He wrapped his arms around me kissing my hair before he replied,
"No sweetheart, I'm not lying about the way you make me feel, but our first time together won't be somewhere with thousands of eyes looking on."

His words were serious but at the same time funny, as his pun about the butterflies flying around us watching on hit my mind.

"Yeah, these butterflies have had enough of a show," I laughed.

"They certainly didn't see a butterfly kiss," he teased bending down to give me a sweet tender kiss that made my heart pound.

Taking my hand, he asked, "Are you ready for dinner?"

"Yep, I'm starving," I replied winking at him.

"Me too, sweetheart, me too," he taunted as we walked out of the Butterfly house, our fingers laced together.

Stopping at Gloria Jeans I shock them by ordering a latte instead of my usual Iced Coffee. The warmth on my hands as I sip it on my walk to the tram is comforting.

My heart is still pounding thinking about my night with Jairus, my mind cursing myself for sleeping with Austin but thoughts keep cutting in about Jairus, that maybe I'm falling for him.

He may be crass at times but since he'd broken up with his girlfriend, he'd started to show me a sweet charming side of himself that makes me want to give into the way he makes me feel.

I'm just scared that I can't be the girl he needs me to be.

Twenty-Eight | Pillow Talk

Bella

Having had a little too much to drink, I stumble home from Jace's, straight into the bedroom, flopping down on the bed ignoring Anni's protest.

When I moan, she grabs a pillow from under her head, swatting me with it.
"Hey, bitch," I protest grabbing my own pillow, lifting it up ready to hit her back.
"Sorry, Bel."
"All good, I should have told you I was coming home late."
"Yeah, but I'm glad you're here."

"Yeah, why is that?" I ask playfully swatting her with the pillow next to me.

"I need to talk," she blurts out, blushing.
"Really?"
"Yeah…. I um…"
"Come on girl, out with it,"
"Jairus kissed me last night," she declares smiling.
"Seriously? You kissed Blondie, how was it?"

"Exactly like you said it would be," she replies blushing.

"So, nothing else happened? He just kissed you, once?"

Her blush increases, "Um..not once, but um well like..."

Again, swatting her with the pillow I have to draw it out of her, "Anni, tell me...did you sleep with him?"

It is her turn to swat me with the pillow, "No Bel I didn't but we..."

"Full on pashed?"

"Yeah, and I'm so confused."

"Why?"

"Because kissing him was so amazing, and he took me out for the night and it was so sweet."

Her expression is pained, "But what Anni?"

"When we got home, Austin was still up and he was super jealous."

"Do you blame him? He's in love with you, it's probably killing him to see you with Blondie."

"Yeah, I know, but I kinda did something bad."

"Bad, like what kinda bad?"

"Bad, as in naughty," she replies holding the pillow up to her face and muffling a shriek.

"But you said you didn't sleep with Blondie?"

Peering out from the edge of the pillow she meekly replies, "I didn't sleep with Jairus."

"What are you saying, Anni?"

Putting the pillow down she sighs, "Jairus came to bed with me and we pashed for a bit, but I was about to..."

"About to what? Tell me, Anni, please."

"About to get undressed when he stopped me, saying he couldn't and he went to his room."

"Seriously? I didn't think Blondie was a prude."

"Me either, but..."

"So, wait? What did you do that was naughty bad if you didn't sleep with Blondie?"

Again, she grabs the pillow, holding it up against her face, muffling her words, "I slept with Austin instead."

I snatch the pillow away, "You what?"

"You heard me, Bel, I slept with Austin again."

"Girl, how could you?"

"I know, but he came in and I was horny as hell and it just happened."

"Anni, I don't know what to say."

"I'm an idiot I know, but I'm so confused."

"You're not an idiot but you need to work out how you feel and sleeping with Austin isn't going to help you sort out your feelings."

"I know that Bel, I'm not that much of an idiot," she protests slapping me with her pillow.

"How are you feeling about Blondie, now you've kissed him?"

Her cheeks flush a deep crimson, telling me her answer before her voice does, "I'm not sure but I think I'm falling for him."
"Oh, shit Anni, really," I blurt out, cursing myself.
"Is that a bad thing?"

Slapping her with the pillow I'm clutching I reply, "Of course not dingbat!"
"But what if he's not feeling the same?"
"Are you seriously asking me that question?"
"Yeah, maybe he just wants to get into my undies."
"If that's all he wanted, he'd have gone there already, Anni."

"True, but do you really think someone as hot as him could fall for me?"
"Yes, you dill, that boy has the hots for you big time and I honestly think he's falling for you too."

She lets out an excited 'eeek' before she frowns, "But what about Austin? I don't want to break his heart."
"You have to follow your heart girl and by the sounds of it, your heart isn't Austin's anymore."
"Yeah, I don't know," she replies, "Thanks for the chat, Bel."
"Anytime Anni, what else are friends for?"
"Yeah," she laughs lifting her pillow up, "except early morning pillow fights."
She swats me hard, standing up on the bed giggling, "Oh no you didn't bitch," I jeer standing up and swatting her back.

Caz May

We continue swatting each other back, giggling until we hear someone speak in the doorway, "Well damn, that is definitely a hot as hell sight to see on this early Friday morning."
Annika jumps aside, "Morning Jai, we were just um..."
He laughs, "Don't stop because of me sweetheart, unless you want me to join in?"
"Not a chance, Blondie," I spit at him, throwing my pillow at him.

Picking it up, he looks at Anni, who I now just realise is only wearing cheeky undies and shelf bra singlet top, "Yeah, Nah, I could think of a lot of better things to be doing with Anni in that attire."
Anni giggles, "Stop Jairus, yeah?"

"Not a chance, sweetheart, but I gotta go. We have an early morning training session today so I'll see you later."

He winks at her, before throwing the pillow back and walking down the hallway.
We both erupt into a fit of giggles falling on the bed as we can't stop laughing.
He might have still spoken to her with the teasing tone, but the look he gave her in her underwear wasn't just lust.
He was falling for her, harder than a pillow to the head.

Twenty-Nine | Taste Test

Vairus

The boys had decided to go out for drinks after the game but having played a tough game, only winning by the goal I kicked after the siren, I'm dead tired.

Partly though I want to go home, because I know the chance of Anni being home alone is pretty high and since kissing her on Wednesday night, I'd thought of nothing else.

Her kisses drove me wild and it took a lot of restraint to not take all of her.

It's clear she wants more from me too but at the same time for the first time ever I want to take things slow in a relationship.

I'd rushed into things with Sara, sleeping with her after our second date and as much as I loved her for a lot of our relationship sex became the answer to all our problems.
If we had a fight, we'd just end up having sex to fix it and it never worked.

When I open the front door, dropping my bag down I can see Anni in the kitchen wearing the same slouchy jumper from the other night, sans leggings. It barely covers her arse and she is wearing cheeky knickers that sit halfway up her arse cheeks.

Her blonde hair is atop her head in a messy bun, like she has just pulled it off her face in a hurry.

She is stirring something on the stove that smells divine, whilst she looks delicious swaying her arse to the music playing from the lounge room.

As I walk towards the kitchen, she turns to look at me, smiling sweetly, "Oh hey Jai, hungry?"

Stepping up behind her I press my body against hers, "Mmm...you bet I am, what's cooking?"
"Garlic coriander chicken," she replies as I put my hand into the pan to grab a chicken strip.

Stepping aside, pressing my butt against the bench, I'm about to put it in my mouth when she snaps at me, "Jai, you heard me say coriander yes?"

"Yes, sweetheart I heard you." I laugh.
"So, you're not a coriander hater? Cause if you are, I'll never kiss you again."

I laugh at her sweetness, opening my mouth wide and biting down on the piece of chicken like a hungry crocodile.

"Well, luckily I'm a coriander lover then. I'd hate to not be able to kiss you again."

A sweet blush rises up her cheeks, "So you want to kiss me again?"

"Of course I do sweetheart, I've barely stopped thinking about kissing you all week."

"But the other night, you...you..." she stammers, a look in her eyes as though she's about to cry.

"Oh sweetheart, please don't cry, come here," I suggest grabbing her arm and pulling her gently towards me.

"I'm sorry Jai, it's just I put myself out there and you rejected me."

Touching her cheek with the back of my hand, I speak softly leaning closer to her, "Sweetheart I didn't reject you."

"Yeah you did," she spits at me, her words like snakes.

Not even thinking I cup her cheeks in my palms before crushing my lips to hers for a demanding kiss that sends a straight jolt to my dick.

"Still think I don't want you, sweetheart?"

She huffs, folding her arms across her chest, "You can't just kiss me like that Jai."
"Why not? Don't you want me to kiss you?"
"I...I... didn't say that.... but I..."
"Anni, you know I want you...but I want to take things slow. Is that ok?"
"I guess, but can I still..." she starts looking straight into my eyes, cutting her own words off by biting down on her lip.

She lets out a little murmur as she steps closer to me, grabbing my dick through the stifling fabric of my black jeans.

"Fuck slow!" I drawl grabbing her around the waist to pull her close to me.
Smashing my lips to hers again, I urge her to part her lips to deepen the kiss with my tongue as she teasingly keeps torturing my dick by running her hands over the front of my pants.

Still kissing her, I run my hands up her back, hissing when I realise, she isn't wearing a bra.
Breaking the kiss, I smirk at her, "Fuck sweetheart, you torture me."
She giggles, putting her arms up as an invitation to lift the slouchy jumper over her head.
Grabbing the hem of it, slowly I pull it off her, taking in the delectable sight of her practically naked in front of me again.

Her eyes lock on mine, her breath hitching in her chest as she tentatively puts a hand under the hem of my grey t-shirt.

A sweet hiss escapes her lips as she edges the t-shirt up, exposing more and more of my skin to her eyes.

When the t-shirt reaches my collarbone, I stretch my arms up and help her pull it over my head, throwing it on the floor beside us.
 A cheeky smirk crosses her face as she looks me up and down.

At the waistband of my daks, where the small patch of hair gathers under my belly button, she splays her fingers across my skin.
Giggling she then runs her index finger up my chest, over my Adam's apple, to my chin and runs it along my lips.
Darting my tongue out I lick it, not able to stop the moan that escapes my mouth.

"Anni, please sweetheart," I drawl, not even sure what I'm going to say.

She again giggles, bending down a little, pressing her tongue to the same spot her finger had touched before.
Licking across my stomach she fumbles to undo my jeans, pushing them over my hips to the floor.

After dakking me, her tongue delivers the same
sweet torture as her finger moments before until she
reaches my lips.
Her tongue runs along them, eliciting a moan from
me before I take her mouth in a hot as hell kiss.

When she pulls back breathless, her voice is raspy,
"You taste delicious Jai."

"Hmmm, really sweetheart, I bet you taste delicious
too."
"Why don't you find out?" she teases, her cheeky
smirk gracing her lips.
"Sweetheart, you know that sounds amazing, but we
really need to slow down."
"Why? she pouts at me, stepping away.
"Because I lll.... like you too much."
"If you like me that much, then why won't you sleep
with me Jairus?"

The way she says my full name is like a dagger to the
chest. I've gotten used to hearing her call me Jai in
the sweet teasing way, so hearing my full name roll
off her tongue is a shock.

"It's because I like you, Anni, that I'm not going to
sleep with you yet. I've made that mistake before and
wasted two years of my life."

Her eyes darken in confusion, "Sara?"

"Yes, Sara. I stupidly slept with her after our second date and rushing into sex set a precedent for our whole relationship."

"Oh ok, sounds complicated. But..."

Grabbing her hand, I press a kiss to it, "Anni sweetheart, please just trust me ok?"

"But I..."

"I want to be with you, more than anything, but taking it slow will be worth it. I promise."

"Ok, I guess," she pouts again, turning the burner back on to heat the chicken.

"How about we take a bowl to your bedroom to taste test it together?"

"Only if you stay in my bed tonight," she states.

"Only if I can hold you close, so close...." I drawl stepping up behind her and pressing my arousal into the curve of her arse.

"Mmm sounds delicious," she murmurs, leaning her head back into the crook of my neck inviting me to kiss her.

Spooning the chicken into a bowl a few minutes later, I grab a spoon from the drawer before following her down the hallway to her bedroom.

She is sitting cross-legged on the bed and looks so beautiful my heart pounds in my chest as I sit next to her.

Feeding her the chicken, she licks her lips and moans as she swallows it.
It makes my whole body ache with want, but I know I have to keep my promise to not take things too far.

Without a doubt I'm falling in love with her, no scratch that, I am in love with her and I'm not going to take the next step until I know she feels the same way as me.
That is proving to be the hardest thing I've ever had to do, as one taste of Annika has me craving more and it is going to be a test to my patience to not taste all of her.

Thirty | Tangled Sheets

Austin

Going out to get hammered, after boxing practice
isn't the best decision I've made recently but seeing
Anni with Jairus is like a stab in the heart and guts.

The way she giggles with him and responds to his
crass teasing stirs up resentment in my stomach.
It's like how it used to be between us, before I'd
decided that friends with benefits was better for us.

It doesn't seem as though they fight like Anni and I
did though but that is possibly only because
whatever is going on between them is new; the so-
called honeymoon stage.

The very thought of him kissing her and touching her
plagues my mind, making me want to tackle him to
the ground and pound him hard with my bare hands.

My head is pounding when I arrive home, partly from
the alcohol and partly from the knock to the head my
mate Kaden had thrown at me.

Stumbling to my bedroom I strip to my boxers,
glancing at Jairus' unmade but empty bed on the
opposite side of the room.

The house feels off, as though something is amiss
that I can't put my finger on.

In the kitchen that I'd wander into to get some
Nurofen and something sickly sweet to wash it down
with a pot sits on the stove with odd green looking
chicken in it, that smells like it would taste absolutely
rotten.

Even so, I grab a piece of chicken, so hungry the
rotten chicken looks edible. It's cold and has gone a
little rubbery.
Biting down on it I nearly spit it out across the
kitchen, when the soapy taste of coriander hits my
tongue.
Yanking the fridge open I grab the orange juice,
screwing off the lid hastily and pouring it down my
throat, swallowing hard to get rid of the rotten soapy
taste.

Before putting the juice back in the fridge, I down
two Nurofen tablets from the basket of random junk,
medicine and god knows what on the kitchen bench
before heading back down the hallway.
It's probably stupid, as Anni had started to make it
clear that our friends with benefits arrangement

wasn't what she wanted anymore but still, I head to her room instead of my own.

I want to be with her, take it slow and sweet until she comes apart underneath me.

It makes me feel like she's saying, *'I love you'* without words.
Her door is ajar and walking into the darkness when my eyes adjust, my mouth falls open at the sight before me.
In her bed, with his arm draped across her stomach holding her way to close, is Jairus.
He is clearly half naked, and very well could be completely naked, as no line of the elastic of his daks is visible under the sheet that is pulled tight across his hips and back.

Anni gasps, her eyes fluttering open when she realises I'm in the room.
Even though the room is dark, I can feel her, almost see her giving me dagger eyes.

She gently grabs Jairus' arm, lifting it off her stomach and placing it down on the bed as she gets out.

He murmurs, shifting in the bed but not waking up.
Anni is now standing right in front of me, a metre from her bed with her hands on her hips.

"Aust, what are you doing?" She asks anger lacing her voice in a tone that I don't like hearing coming from her mouth.

Without warning, I grab her arm dragging her out into the hallway.
My own anger is rising, as she is only wearing cheeky knickers and no bra.
"What were you doing in bed with him, half naked?" I stab at her accusingly.
"Nothing Austin, just sleeping!" she almost yells at me, using my full name for impact.

"Didn't look like nothing Annika!"
"Why do you care anyway?" she asks covering her nakedness with her arms as though I've not seen her naked before.

"Did you fuck him?"
"No, we just kissed Austin! But its none of your business anyway," she spits at me, stabbing me in the heart.
Her words hurt bad, as though I'm not even her best friend anymore.
Anni is slipping away from me, she used to tell me anytime she hooked up with someone when out and likewise, I told her whenever I hooked up as well.
Granted, my feelings towards her had changed but I kind of still wanted her to feel like she could share anything happening in her life with me.

"But you want to fuck him?" I question her, hoping she says no.

"I don't know Aust, ok?"

"How can you not know?"

"Because I don't Austin. You know what I mean," she replies blushing.

"Um Anni, I don't know what you're talking about. You've hooked up with other guys, you've told me that before."

She shuffles her feet on the floorboards, "I lied about those Aust. You're the only guy I've slept with and until Jairus, you were the only guy I'd kissed."

"What the hell Anni! Why would you lie to me about that?"

"Because it made it easier to deal with when you told me about your random hook-ups."

"Oh Anni, I'm sorry," I whisper, my heart breaking at her sweet innocence.

Not even thinking I grab her arms from her chest and wrap mine around her in a hug. She melts into me and for a moment as I hold her close in the middle of the hallway, I have my Anni back.

"I love you Anni," I whisper into her ear.

Abruptly she pulls back from my embrace, "Aust don't yeah? I'm just..."

"What babe? You can still talk to me."

"I'm just confused Austin, ok?"

Caz May

"Ok, how can I help?"

"Well, you can't really, but maybe not saying you love me."

"Sorry babe, but I can't change how I feel about you."

"Well, neither can I change how I feel about you Aust. Everything is just fucked up!" she says waving her arms in the air, "I'm going back to bed."

"You might want to send someone else to bed," I taunt, instantly regretting my words when she huffs at me as she walks off.

The fact that he is the one in her bed, holding her close makes my blood boil. Short of kicking him out of the house, to make it just us again, I have no idea how to make Anni see that she is meant to be with me.

195

Thirty-One | Test Fail

Getting home from the second worst day of my life thus far, I strip from my scrubs throwing them across the room as the wretched sobs cascade down my cheeks.

The first worst day of my life thus far was the day I found out Alex had died from a drug overdose and now this day is the second, failing my nursing practical.

Looking at the paper my supervisor handed me with my review and final grade on it, a big fat 'F' for fail on it tore my heart out.

I'd been killing myself for months, trying to complete my assignments as well as the shifts at the hospital.

To say I was stressed out was an understatement. Not only had my period been late a month or so earlier, but this month I'd completely skipped it.

I knew it was most likely from stress, but after the day I'd just had I grab the box of pregnancy tests out of my bedside drawer and head to the bathroom.

Austin sees me clutching the pink foil packet in my fist as I walk past his room in my underwear.

"Anni, babe, what are you doing?"

"I'm scared Aust," I stutter.

"Why? We used protection last time Anni."

"Yeah, I know but I haven't got my period at all this month."
"Oh shit, does that mean you might have tested too early or something?"
"I hope not," I start, reaching the bathroom with him following behind and leaning against the wall, "just give me a minute."
"Ok, let me know when you're done."

Closing the door behind me I quickly push my undies down, peeing on the stick the moment I sit down on the dunny.
My heart is pounding in my chest, hoping like hell only one line comes up again.

Putting it on the counter next to the dunny, I pull my undies up and call out to Austin as I flush the toilet and wash my hands, "Aust, you can come in."

He opens the door and pulls me into a hug.
"So?" he asks.
"I haven't looked at it. Can you?"
"Sure babe," he muses picking the test up and smiling.
My heart just about falls to the floor, as a smile from him looking at a pregnancy test probably means it's positive.
"Aust tell me please," I beg.
"It's negative Anni."
"Then why are you smiling?"

"I don't know."

"Well, that's the best thing to happen today, at least it hasn't made this fucked up day worse."

Putting the test in the bin next to the dunny, he looks at me confused, "What happened, babe?"

"I failed Aust."
He grabs my hand, pulling me out of the bathroom towards the lounge room.
"Failed what babe?"
"My prac Aust. I might as well tattoo 'F' for failure on my forehead."
"Don't say that Anni, you can make it up yeah?" he asks as we plonk our arse's on opposite ends of the couch.
"Yeah, but it means I won't graduate at the same time as the rest of my class and that I'll have to do an extra prac on top of the others."
"I'm sorry Anni, but you'll be a better nurse because of this, I'm sure of it."
"I guess," I start, unsure if I should even tell Austin how I'm feeling, "its shit Jairus isn't home. He'd make a joke out of it to make me feel better."

"Well I'm sorry Anni, I wish I could make you feel better, but I'm obviously not good enough anymore."

Leaning closer to him I reply meekly, "I'm sorry Aust, I didn't mean to upset you."

"Yeah well, you kinda did. You've been spending so much time with Jairus, I just kinda feel like I'm losing you, Anni."

Shuffling on the couch to move closer to him, I try to wrap my arm around him in a hug, but he shrugs me off.
"Don't Anni."
"Why Aust? I can't even hug you now? You're still my best friend Austin, I love you."
"No, you don't Annika. You stopped loving me the moment he walked in on us fucking."

"Oh, come on Austin, you're being an idiot. I've always loved you, as a friend, and right now you're not being a very supportive one."

He stands up, looking down at me with an odd glare.
"I'm sorry Anni, I am. I just don't know what else to say."
"There's nothing to say," I muse standing up and not letting him refuse my hug.
He melts into me, wrapping his arms around me.
"Anni, I know you like him."
"Yeah I kinda do Aust, but I'm really confused as well."
"Why? Don't you think he feels the same?" he asks sitting back down on the couch.
"Oh, I think he does, but it's so different being with him. It kinda scares me."

"Yeah I get you," he replies grabbing my waist to pull me down on top of him.

"Aust don't, I can't, we can't anymore," I protest feeling his heart beating fast against my chest.

"Please Anni, I miss you so much."

"I haven't gone anywhere Aust," I laugh, trying to free myself from his embrace but failing to wriggle free from his super tight grip.

"Not when I've got you pinned down," he laughs, using a boxing reference, "and I'm not letting you go until you kiss me."

"Aust, I can't," I protest again, feeling like I'm cheating on Jairus, even though we aren't actually together.

"Anni please, just one kiss...I swear or you..." he starts, licking his lips.

"Or I can what Aust?" I taunt him, running a finger across his lips.

"Hit me wearing one of my boxing gloves."

"Deal," I coo, leaning against his chest and pressing a kiss to his lips.

He moans against my lips and I deepen the kiss forcing him to open his mouth by running my tongue along his lips.

It may have only be one kiss but it's a hot kiss, one I'd never shared with Austin and my confusion level rises.

Breathless he pulls back, "Damn Anni, that was some kiss."

"Sorry, I um...."

"Don't be sorry...for another kiss like that I'd let you hit me with my glove more than once."

"Aust don't," I jeer poking him in the abs with my fingers.

"Sorry babe, but I've missed you and when you kiss me like that god I..."

The look in his eyes is lustful, not loving, which is odd and even though it's so wrong considering the past week or so I've spent with Jairus I slide further up on the couch.

My aching pelvis meets his aroused one and I bend down to kiss him again, grinding against him for release.

Mere moments later, I moan against his mouth, my lower body coming to a quick blissful release.

Austin pulls back, and has a wide smirk on his face, "Anni, did you just come from grinding on my dick?"

The blush rises up my cheeks, as I jump off his lap as though a fire has started.

Not saying a word or even looking back at him I race towards my bedroom, feeling the tears break free again.

Flopping down face first into the bed, I let the tears soak my pillow as thoughts fill my mind.

What in the hell just happened? And with Austin? I've officially fucked up, haven't I?

Thirty-Two | Pleasure Taker

Vairus

Arriving home in my brand new, red Kia Stinger, I revel in the rumble of the engine as I slip the gears down, parking straight out the front on the curb.

The feeling of driving such a sleek car gives me a giddy feeling, one I'd not felt since my tenth birthday when my parents had taken my friends and I to the waterpark for the day.

Walking up the massive spiral staircase to the top of the highest waterslide my heart pounded in my chest and an electric feeling rushed through me as I stepped up to the stream of water, pushing off and feeling completely free for the three minutes it took to descend the slide.

The giddy feeling that day was short-lived, my birthday forever tainted by the accident on the way home.
Mum's scream as the B-double truck jack knifed across the intersection into her door, and then across the front of the car crushing her and Dad whilst I sat in the back seat is a sound I will never forget.

Even now, stepping out of my car; my birthday
present to myself, tears sting my eyes thinking about
my parents and their passing fourteen years ago.

I'd refused to get in a car for most of those years,
much to my foster parents' annoyance.

They'd tried everything, but in the end, the only
thing that got me to go in a car again was when they
brought a brand new red Ford XR6 FG, close to my
eighteenth birthday.

I remembered Dad telling me that red cars go faster
and V6's go hard and that he'd buy me one for my
twenty-first.

My foster parents buying a car that was both finally
got me in a car again, as I thought in a car like that,
we'd be able to get out of an accident by speeding
off.

It was a silly thought for an eighteen-year-old to have
but knowing I had the power of that car behind me
when I got my license made me feel invincible.

Naturally, now still craving that invincibility, I've
chosen another car exactly like that for myself, this
one mine alone.

Walking inside I'm glad to find Anni home, sitting on
the couch watching some crappy afternoon drama on
TV.
Austin is in the kitchen, making some popcorn by the
buttery smell that is wafting through our apartment.
Anni looks up as I shut the door behind me,
shrugging off my jacket and hanging it on the coat
rack.

"Hey Jai, you look happy," she comments, taking in
my grin.
"Yeah, just bought myself something awesome."
"Yeah, like what?" She beams at me, ignoring Austin
who sits on the couch next to her.

 It's like I'm the only other person in the room and
that excites me, just as much as buying my car.
"Come over here and I'll tell you," I tease, my smirk
growing wider when she stands up and trips over the
coffee table on her way across the room. She rubs
her shin, mouthing an ouch as she steps closer to me.

It's slightly uncanny that she is wearing a short-
sleeved red dress that skims her knees with bare
stockings underneath.

After tripping over the coffee table, her feet betray
her and she slides across the floorboards straight into
my arms.
"I guess you want to know then?" I taunt.
"Yeah, of course," she laughs, grinning at me.

"Something red, "I taunt.
She looks down at her dress giggling, "You're such a tease Jairus!"

With her arms still wrapped around me, I back towards the door, holding up my keys in front of her face.
I can tell Austin is looking at us, but he doesn't utter a single word, just munches on his popcorn like we are a show to watch.

Sneakily, I nibble on Anni's ear, before whispering, "Wanna go for a ride?"

She turns to look back at Austin, who is now munching on his popcorn with his gaze fixed on the TV.

"Yeah, sounds fun," she replies, taking a step back from me as she picks up her ballet flats from by the door, putting them on her feet before grabbing her denim jacket from the coat rack.

Grabbing my own jacket back, I shrug it back on over my checked shirt.
"Ready?" I ask, winking at her as she opens the door, standing in the doorway with her back to me.

Stepping up behind her and wrapping my arms around her waist, I rest my chin on her head.
She gasps, "Is that your car? The red one?"

"Yeah, pretty sick, huh?"
"It's gorgeous, Jai," she beams stepping forward with
my arms still wrapped around her, "It must have cost
you a fortune."
"Yeah, about sixty grand, but so worth it."

Pulling away, as I shut the door behind me, she runs
towards the car, standing at the passenger side
looking at me with a hot as fuck smirk on her face.

When I reach the car, I grab her by the waist,
smashing a kiss to her lips.
"God sweetheart, you're so fucking gorgeous."
"Jai please, you have to stop saying things you don't
mean and kissing me like that…. I…I"

Brushing a hand across her cheek, I drawl at her,
"What makes you think I don't mean it?"

"I don't know, maybe because you're hot as and
could have any girl you want."
"And the girl I want is standing right in front of me
sweetheart. So still want to go for a ride?"
"Yeah, this car seems like a dream," she purrs turning
around and pushing her arse against my crotch as I
unlock the doors with the button on the key fob.

Grabbing the handle, she opens the door, a teasing
smirk on her face.
As I race around to the driver's side, she slides into
her seat.

"So where to sweetheart?"
"St Kilda beach, driver," she laughs.

Starting the engine, I glide the car off the curb,
changing the gears and loving how smooth they are.

"So, you think driving a stick impresses me?"
"I don't drive a stick for anyone but myself,
sweetheart."
"What's that supposed to mean?"
"I like the control it gives me over the car."
"Control?"
"Yes, control and no I don't want to talk about it."
"Ok, so how's the bass?"
"What kind of question is that Anni?"
"A car has to have good bass, music has to be felt Jai.
If the speakers aren't shaking, the music isn't loud
enough."
"Well, it would have to be good sweetheart; there
are fifteen speakers."

"Seriously? Fifteen?"
"Yeah and Car Play. Put Spotify on."

She lets out a little giggle, touching the screen display
and finding Spotify in the Car Play menu.
My playlist comes up and 'Seein Red' is at the top.
With a tap on the screen, it starts playing through the
speakers.
Anni turns the volume up until it's blaring out and
the speakers start rocking with the bass.

She squeals, "I love this song!" as she starts to sing the words.
There surprisingly isn't a lot of traffic for a Friday afternoon and I love how the engine purrs as we head towards the beach.

When the song ends, she turns the volume down and puts a hand on my thigh, looking at me puzzled.
"Is something wrong Jai?"
"Well, um, its..."
"Tell me please," she begs, pouting at me.
"I was just thinking about how you've changed me, Anni."
"What do you mean?"
"I don't know...I just feel like a better person when I'm around you."
"Aww Jai, that's sweet but I haven't done anything."

Turning down the esplanade, I swallow hard before speaking again, "No you've only made me fall in love with you sweetheart."

She blushes gasping, "You....you...don't mean that Jai."
"Yes, I do Annika, I'm in love with you."

I slide the car into an angle parking spot, right on the beach, cutting the engine immediately.
"Sweetheart, please say something. It's ok if..."
"I...I'm sorry Jai...I don't know what to say...I...I..mean I like you...a lot...but I..."

I cut her words off with a kiss, a soft tender kiss that
hopefully shows her my words are true.
It hurts a little that she isn't feeling the same way,
but I can only hope that soon she would, as I have
fallen head over my footy boots in love with her.

Thirty-Three | Fall Flat

Jairus

My day hasn't started out the best, rolling out of bed
later than I liked to on a game day, especially a night
game day as it stuffs me around the whole day
thinking about the game.

The whole week had been pretty shit, after I'd taken
Anni out for a drive, on my birthday.
She'd been avoiding me all week, since my
confession of being in love with her, and I was cursing
myself for opening my trap.

She'd left me a note on my pillow, telling me she
couldn't be at the game, as she had a late lecture.

My heart literally sinks, as I'm nervous about this
game, playing the second team on the ladder.
Having her, supporting me, at my games always made
me feel more confident.

Thankfully, she'd left her phone number on the note.
I laugh at the thought of why we'd not given each
other our numbers before.

As I grab my bag heading out the door, I send her a text.

Jai: Thanks for your number sweetheart. I'll miss you at my game

Her reply is almost instant, as though she is waiting for my text.

Anni: Hey Jai wish I was there...good luck smash them

Jai: Hopefully sweetheart. Can we talk later? xo

Anni: Um ok I guess...

Jai: Catch ya sweetheart xoxo

I want to type 'I love you' but her reaction to my confession a week earlier was almost a stab in the heart, so I think it best to not push it and just give her time to hopefully feel the same way.
Throwing my bag on the passenger seat, starting the engine I gun the car down the street, barely stopping at the intersection.
Coach had been in a bad mood earlier in the week and like us, he was stressing out about this game.
The last thing I want is to be late and piss him off more.

Once at the oval, I park in the designated spots, just as Travis is walking in.

Shaking my hand, he greets me, laughing, "Hey man, nice ride. You could pick a brother up you know?"

"Another time Trav, I had to gun it to make it on time today."

"Why? Something kept you up?"

"Nah, just slept in. Shit week to be honest."

"What's going on with your girl?"

"Seriously, I don't know man, she's hot and cold."

"Seriously, give up on her man... your cheer squad fan club would get with you in a second."

I scoff at him, "I don't want anyone else man.... I'm in love with her."

"Just get some action man is all I'm saying," he jeers at me, elbowing me in the side.

"Yeah, I guess but I kinda feel like I'd be cheating on her, you know?"

"Have you made it official?"

"No man, you know I haven't slept with her."

"Yeah, I know you haven't... I meant is she your girlfriend?"

"No, but I..."

He cuts my words off, "So, take the pick of your fan club then. I think Dana is pretty hot and she screams Jai the man pretty loudly," he jeers at me again, his tone teasing at his insinuation that she would scream my name during sex as well.

"Yeah, she's ok, I guess," I say half-heartedly, thinking that she is pretty but she isn't Anni.

"Seriously man, just take her in the change-rooms after the game," Travis suggests, lacing up his footy boots before he walks out winking at me.

~~

My concentration is lacking the whole game. I feel like a zombie on the field. Travis' words keep tumbling in my head, along with thoughts of what Anni would say if I sleep with someone else.

To say I played a horrible game would be highly accurate. I'm definitely not going to earn any Brownlow votes for my dismal performance.
We end up losing by twenty points, which just further cements my horrid mood.

Straight after the siren sounded, I waltz up to the cheer squad where Dana is sitting front and centre. A wide smile crosses her face when she sees me approaching.
Leaning over the barrier, I beckon her with a finger and when she steps up close, I whisper in her ear, "Do you wanna meet me for a quickie in the tunnel, in twenty?"
She nods a reply, blushing as she follows the cheer squad out from the stands.

My mind is still racing, twenty minutes later when I meet up with Dana. She is standing against the wall, wearing tight jeans and a Richmond guernsey with a black long sleeve top underneath.

She'd let her brown hair down and it fell over her
shoulders.

I can't deny she's hot.
Without saying anything I step up towards her, a
hand on either side of her, against the wall. I smash a
kiss to her lips and she moans, but I'm not feeling the
same fervour towards the kiss.
I can't stop thinking about kissing Anni, about how
Anni's kisses drive me wild and how kissing Dana is
so wrong and pales in comparison.

Dana reaches down grabbing my dick through the
front of my grey trackie daks, rubbing her hand up
and down. Still kissing me she yanks my trackies
down, finding that I'm commando underneath.

"So, Jai's not the man, huh?" she taunts looking
down at my crotch which has failed to come to the
party.

"I'm sorry Dana. It's not you," I apologise, feeling as
flat as my dick is.
"It must be Jai...you have a reputation."
"Really?" I enquire my heart constricting at the
thought of my past still following me.
"Yeah, every girl on the fan club wants to fuck you...
especially now you don't have a girlfriend."
"Yeah, I... um don't have a girlfriend but I'm sorry
Dana, I can't do this."
"Why? You asked for a quickie."

"Because I don't have a girlfriend... but there is a girl in my life, who's my everything and I want her to be my girlfriend."

"She's lucky then," she muses at me, her head down as she takes a step aside, not able to meet my eyes.

"I'm really sorry Dana."

"Don't be sorry. It sounds like you need to make her yours."

"Trust me, I'm working on it," I laugh softly.

"She really is lucky, Jairus, you're quite a catch, I'm sure."

"Thanks, I guess... so, no hard feelings?"

"Definitely not, but will I get to meet her soon?"

"Yeah, we're having a house party next Friday night. You should come along if you want?"

"Sounds great. What's your addy?" she enthusiastically replies.

"Twelve, Cope Place, Richmond," I inform her with a smile.

"Ok, I'll see you then, maybe around ten," she replies kissing my cheek before running off down the tunnel to leave.

Kissing her and my bodies non-compliance for a quick fuck, like I'd have done in the past means that I'm definitely in love with Annika.

She is now the only person my body craves attention from, the only person I'm attracted to and if I'm going to get her to fall in love with me, I need to face the past.

I need to tell her how much of a big deal my confession of being in love with her means and I can only hope that she feels the same.

Thirty-Four | Party Preparation

Standing in my walk in, I run my fingers along my clothes, unsure of what to wear for the night.
Part of me wants to wear a dress, after Jairus' reaction to my short red dress a week or so ago.
But I also know that a dress isn't exactly practical, considering I'm hosting and have to be sensible.

Bella interrupts my search, stopping to stand against the drawers.
"Anni, what's up? You don't seem too excited about tonight."

"I'm not... I don't know what to wear and I..."
"What?"
"I shouldn't have agreed with Austin to have a party."
"Why not? After everything with Uni, I thought you'd be up for any excuse to get tanked."
"I'm hosting Bel, I have to be responsible."
"Leave that to me Anni, but first some clothes and you can tell me what's really bothering you?"

She looks me up and down, standing there in my underwear.
Since she'd crashed into our house months earlier, we'd definitely become closer as friends and she was more like the sister I never had.

"Ok, I was thinking of wearing jeans and a t-shirt."
"Jeans yes, if it's those arse and thigh-hugging skinny 'Riders' I know you have hiding in here," she starts, thumbing her way through my daks until she finds them, holding them up.
"And a t-shirt?" I ask.
"No, you dingbat, you're not going to wear a t-shirt. I have just the thing," she replies bending down to rummage through her bag on the floor.
She pulls out a black corset type bodysuit, that has thick shoulder straps that dip down to a V.

She holds it up against me, "Perfect, no one will be able to take their eyes off you."
"I can't wear that Bel, its underwear."
She laughs, "Underwear made to be seen Anni, and you'll have Blondie drooling when he looks at you, even more than he already does."

I feel my cheeks flush at her mentioning Jairus.
"Um, yeah I guess but..."
"But what Anni? Has something else happened with Blondie?"
"Um..." I reply, biting down on my lip.
"Anni," she pokes me in the arm playfully, "Did you fuck him?"
I feel my core tighten at the thought of fucking him when I meekly reply, "No, but he told me he's in love with me."
"Damn Anni, when?"
"Like last week, when he took me for a drive in his new car."

"So, what did you say?"

"Not much, kinda that I like him a lot.... but things have been weird since then."

"How so?"

"He won't really talk to me about it, but he just seemed off."

"Hmm I don't know either, he has seemed less crass lately."

"Yeah, but he said something else that got to me too."

"What? Something other than being in love with you?"

"Yeah, he said he likes control."

Her eyes darken, as though she knows exactly what I'm thinking.

"He probably doesn't mean it in that way, Anni. You always think of the bad things."

"Yeah, I know. Can you help me with some makeup tonight Bel?"

"Yeah sure, if you want. Get dressed and meet me in the bathroom."

"Ok," I reply as she walks out.

Taking my underwear off I slip the bodysuit over my head, fastening it at my core that my fingers brush against.

I didn't mention it to Bella, but the thought of Jairus taking control over me in the bedroom, strangely excites me and I'm on edge just thinking about it.

After checking my appearance in the mirror, I shimmy into my jeans, fastening them at my waist.
Turning side on to the mirror, I admire the way the jeans hug the little curves I do have.

Walking out, after slipping my feet into some patent black ballet flats, I wonder what Jairus is going to think of my outfit and wickedly I think about the possibility of him taking it off me later.

~~

After Bella completes my makeup, highlighting my eyes with dusty pink eyeshadow, a wisp of eyeliner and a lick of mascara, I stand back to look at my face in the mirror.
"God, Anni, you're a knockout, girl," Bella coos from behind me.
"Yeah, you think?"
"Blondie isn't gonna know you."

I laugh, "Bella, why do you want me to be with Jairus so much now?"
Putting her hands on my shoulders, she turns me towards her, looking straight at me, "Anni, I've seen the way you look at him. Don't deny how you feel about him."

"But, Bel, what about Austin?"
"What about him Anni?"
"I... I don't know....I..."

"You need to sort out how you feel about both of them. Leading them on, Anni isn't fair to either of them. I'd be jumping Blondie if I found out he was in love with me."

I can't hide my shock, I know she thinks Jairus is hot, but she's also back with Jace and seems happy.
"What's happening with Jace?"
"Um, I don't wanna talk about that now," she replies frowning, turning to leave the bathroom.

Following her out to the kitchen I can tell I've struck a sore subject, "Sorry Bel, I didn't mean to pry."

"It's ok, but let's finish organising the food and stuff. We'll talk about it later, yeah?"
"Ok," I reply reassuringly touching her arm before I open the fridge to get out the dips to accompany the chips and crackers she was putting onto the plates on the bench.

Closing the fridge, I can feel his gaze on my arse and see Bella smiling out of the corner of my eye.
He steps up behind me pinning me against the cold stainless steel doors of the fridge, "Damn sweetheart, those jeans hug your arse."

I turn to look back at him, shifting so my back is against the fridge instead. His gaze shifts to my cleavage, that the corset has pushed up into a perfect valley.

His lips are just a breath away from mine when he whispers huskily, "And your tits, fuck sweetheart, hot as."

Against my thigh, I can feel the growing bulge in his white fitted chinos.

"Jai, don't," I protest, nodding towards Bella.

He leans in closer, his breath in my ear sending a rush through me, "Does it look like I care right now, sweetheart?

I let out a moan, the way his breath against my ear and his growing erection are doing things to me I have no control over.

He has the control.

Before I can even think, his gaze is fixed on mine, his eyes locking on my lips before he takes them in a heated kiss that makes me forget we aren't the only ones in the room.

Bella breaks the moment between us, "You seriously need to go get naked together. You make me sick."

Stepping back, clutching a hand against the front of his daks, Jairus drawls, "Don't tell me you haven't enjoyed watching Sunshine. I can see the lust in your eyes."

"You'll never know Blondie," she taunts, "But seriously take her now. She told me your little secret."

Bella winks at me, and Jairus' eyes dart between us both, stopping to lock his eyes on mine with a questioning look.

Shrugging I grab his other hand, dragging him down the hallway, as I shoot Bella an I'm sorry look. Reaching my bedrocm, I pull Jairus inside, slamming the door behind us, before smashing a kiss to his lips.

Thirty-Five | Preparatory Playtime

As soon as our lips touch, I feel his dick harden even more pressing against the waistband of my jeans.
He moans, deepening the kiss grabbing my hands and pinning them above my head, pushing me against the wall.
Just like I want him to, he takes control of the kiss, sending desire pooling at the crotch of my bodysuit.

Needing air, I break the kiss, "Jairus," is my only word, husky as I drawl it out between taking in a sharp breath.
"Yes, Annika?" he teases, saying my name so illicitly it makes my core throb with need.
I need more than a kiss from him now.
"Touch me Jairus," I beg, grabbing the front of his light blue shirt, fumbling with the buttons.
"Mmm," he moans, breathing against my ear again before placing kisses down my neck, towards my collarbone.
He stops when he reaches my plumped-up cleavage, just for a moment to let his shirt fall to the floor down his arms.
Just like I'd teased him a few weeks earlier, I press my tongue against the skin of his stomach, licking up over his belly button, up his rock-hard abs and his Adam's apple to his lips.

He lets out a carnal moan as our lips meet again, this time he parts mine with his tongue and bites my lip in between his teeth.

"God, Anni, I want to taste you so bad," he moans, sending the throb of my arousal higher.
"Then, taste me," I tease, smirking at him as I feel the blush rise up my cheeks.
"Are you sure, sweetheart?" he asks, his fingers brushing the waistband of my jeans about to flick open the button and slide the zip down.

"Yes, Jairus," I reply, feeling a rush of confidence when he groans.
Burying his face between my breasts he licks up my neck to kiss me again.

His fingers fumble with my jeans, but still kissing me he skilfully manages to undo them and push them off over my hips.
Breaking the kiss, his eyes lock on mine, as he yanks the press studs of the bodysuit open, and he runs his finger from my clit down to the pool of desire that only he can fuel.

"Fuck, sweetheart, you're so wet," he moans, inserting a finger inside my aroused core.
My hips jerk forward, as he finger fucks me. Teasingly he takes it out for a moment to brush my own arousal over my clit.

Inserting two fingers then he teases my clit with another, locking his eyes on mine.
"Sweetheart, I want to see you come," he drawls, smirking at me so wickedly.
Feeling brazen I tease, "I want you to taste me, Jairus."
"Sweetheart, I want to do so much more than taste you, but we have guests about to arrive and I need more than five minutes to enjoy tasting and fucking you."

The way he says 'fucking' always makes me feel turned on, more so than any other word rolling off his tongue.
"I want to come Jairus, please, please," I moan, as the pace of his fingers inside me increases.
My hips buck, driving his fingers further in, spurring my release hard and sudden.

Pulling his fingers out he brushes them over my lips, before putting them between his own lips and moaning as he licks them clean.

He kisses me again, zealously and wild.
I've never felt so turned on before.
His kisses always leave me breathless, and this time breaking the kiss, I drawl, "My turn now Jairus."
"You don't have to sweetheart, we've got guests waiting I'm sure."

I shake my head at him, undoing the buttons of his white chinos, pushing them and his tightey whitey jocks to the floor.

His hard as steel dick springs forward and I gasp at the length before licking my lips.

"Jairus, um... wow," I giggle, sliding my mouth over him.

He lets out a hiss, as I lick the tip and down the length of his arousal, taking all of him deep into my mouth.

Sucking hard, taking him in and out of my mouth, he groans, "God sweetheart, so good, fuck... so good."

I lick as I suck, desperate to milk his climax from him and feel it run down the back of my throat.

Being with Jairus took all my shyness and inhibitions away.

When I take his length out of my mouth for a moment, licking the tip and grabbing his balls in my fist he hisses his words, "Anni, if you put your mouth on me again, I'll come so hard sweetheart."

Moaning, I take his length back into my mouth, sucking hard and pushing him all the way to the back of my throat.

He grabs my hair in his fists, just as he teased I feel his dick pulse as he comes hard right down the back of my throat.

As I stand up, he pulls up his pants, as I do mine and he kisses me hard but sweetly.

Brushing a stray hair from across my cheek, his face is a whisper away from mine when he speaks, "God Anni, I love you.... that was the hottest fucking blowjob I've ever had, sweetheart."
"Sure Jairus," I laugh.
"I'm not kidding sweetheart."
"Yeah, well I've never come so hard either," I blurt out, surprising myself.
"I can't wait to make you come again," he taunts, "but now we have a party to host."

I pull him close for another kiss, not ready to share him with anyone, wanting to just stay in my room with him all night, "Do we have to?"
He laughs, "Yes Anni we do have to."
"But I want to stay here with you all night," I tease pouting.
"Soon sweetheart, I promise, but not until you know how you really feel about me."

His words stab at my heart, making it pound as I think about what he's implying.
Picking up his shirt, he shrugs it on when I hear my name being called, "Anni, are you ready babe?"

I call out to Austin, "Just a second Aust."
Kissing Jairus sweetly, I instruct him, "Wait a minute before you decide to make an appearance or you'll sport a black eye as part of your outfit."

"I don't doubt that for a second," he laughs, pulling me close for one more teasing kiss before he lets me leave the room.

Austin is clutching bags of various alcoholic beverages in his hands.

He puts them down on the dining table we'd purchased from gumtree, raking his gaze up and down my body when he speaks, "Wow Anni, you look hot as fuck babe, are you ok though? You look a little flustered."

"I'm f..fine," I stutter, tucking my hair behind my ears and pressing a sweet kiss to the edge of his lips.

"Ok, well let's get this party started then," he jeers, looking at Bella who has the biggest smirk on her face.

I laugh as I flip her off, mouthing, 'don't you say a word bitch'.

Her laugh fills the room, and when she brings some more food over to the table she asks softly, "So did you fuck him?"

"No, but....I...um..."

"Anni, you dirty girl," she beams.

Austin turns to look at us from the other side of the room where he's fiddling with the stereo.

As he presses play, he stands up beckoning me over with a finger, "Anni, babe, dance with me."

About to cross the room and fulfil his request, the party is about to be in full swing when the knocking on the door signals the arrival of guests.

I feel Jairus step up behind me, his hand brushing against the small of my back where the bodysuit meets my jeans. He whispers in my ear, "Let me get that sweetheart, you need to go play."

I take a deep breath in, exhaling it as I go to dance with Austin.
I haven't fucked Jairus, but going to third base with him has made me feel even more confused about my feelings for him.
I need to get drunk, to shake all thoughts from my mind for a while and forget how having two hot as hell boys in love with me makes me feel.

Thirty-Six | Port Escapades

Vairus

Opening the door, I'm faced with a couple of guests arriving, one is Travis and the other a guy I've not met before. He looks me up and down, before snubbing me and crossing the room towards Bella who is pouring herself a shot of vodka. She half-heartedly smiles when he steps closer to her.

Walking in, as I close the door behind him, Travis high-fives me, "Looks like I'm too early man. This party hasn't even started yet."

"It's only eight so yeah you're kinda early," I laugh.

The mystery guy has snaked an arm around Bella's side, pulling her close. He's giving Travis and I death stares.
Elbowing me in the side, as we go to grab a beer from the esky filled with ice by the table, Travis asks, "Who's the brunette?"
"Bella," I say giving him a questioning look.
"She's hot, man, fuck. Who's the shithead staking the claim on her?"

"Stuffed if I know man, I've never seen him before, but I'm guessing her man."
"Damn, I'd try to get in with that girl for sure."
"Come on Trav, you need to stop man."
"At least I get some action man," he laughs, flicking the top off his beer, throwing it on the table as he takes a swig.

I look down at the floor, taking a swig of my own beer, "Um, yeah I um...."
"You what?"
"Got some action, like just before you got here."
"What? With who?"
"Anni," I reply, not able to meet his eyes that are looking straight at me.
"But she's over there dancing with that other dick?"
"I told her to."
"Why? Wait! Is that the other roommate that she was fucking?"
"Yeah, her best friend."
"Fuck that sucks man, so did you finally do the dirty with her?"
"No, she sucked me off man and it was so damn hot."
"Nice, so um man, what happened with Dana the other night?"
"Nothing, I couldn't do it, man."
"I figured when she turned up on my doorstep later that night, desperate to fuck."
"I didn't know she was like that."
"I did, but I'm sick of that shit. I just wanna find a decent girl, not a fucking skank."
"Yeah, I know man. You will soon I'm sure."

"I hope so man, I really do," he muses, downing the rest of his beer, slamming it on the table as he sighs.
"Um, Trav?"
"Yeah man," he asks running a hand through his hair.
"I um kinda invited Dana tonight."

He laughs deeply, clutching his stomach, "Well at least if she turns up I'll have a willing and single brunette to take home for the night."
"Yeah true, help ya self to food man, I'm going to get some decent music cranking in here before some more people arrive."

Crossing to the other side of the room, I step up behind Anni, touching the small of her back. Her hips stop moving, and she presses her arse back towards me when I whisper in her ear, "Can we get some hotter music, sweetheart?"

Austin gives me a greasy, before shrugging and walking away to answer the door as more guests are arriving. Anni turns to face me, "What did you have in mind, Jai?"

"Something hot, you know what I mean sweetheart."
"Hmmm... yeah... pick something, I need a drink," she coos, stretching up to kiss my cheek, crushing my heart after our bedroom escapade.

She has no excuse now to not own up to her feelings.
I can't see her going back to Austin but still, she
seems confused.

At the door, Austin is ushering in another ten or so
guests, one of them is Dana who is arriving a lot
earlier than I'm expecting her to.

Pressing play on the stereo I turn the volume up and
find her standing behind me, "Hey Jai, I thought I'd
come a little earlier and help you get the party
started."

"Yeah, why do you think I just changed the song," I
laugh over the music.

"Yeah, this song is hot, so um who's the girl?"

"Black bodysuit, downing vodka shots like water at
the table."

"Oh, she's blonde?"

"Yeah I know, you're going to say not my usual type."

"Yeah, so are you going to introduce me?"

I laugh, grabbing her hand to lead her over to Anni.
Dropping Dana's hand, I wrap my arm around Anni,
whispering in her ear, "Sweetheart, you know that's
vodka, yeah?"

She looks at me like I'm stupid, "Yes Jairus, I know its
Vodka and I'm planning to get tanked."

"Well, before you're incoherent, this is my friend
Dana. Dana this is Annika or Anni."

Anni holds out a hand to shake Dana's, "We've met
when you've been at Jai's games."

"Yeah, you always cheer Jai the man, like super loud,"
Anni declares, a hint of her laughter in her tone.

Dana blushes, "Um yeah, so what's to drink Jai?"
"What do you want? We've got pretty much
anything."

Travis steps up behind her, grabbing her around the
waist, "Dan you'll have a beer yeah?" He laughs,
pressing a kiss to her cheek.
"Yeah you know me too well Trav," she replies,
freeing herself from his embrace as I go to grab her a
beer.
"Jai, get me one too, please," Anni calls out.
I hand both girls a beer, laughing at Anni who can't
get the top off hers.

Pouting she hands it to me, without saying a word.
Flipping the top, I hand it back and she sculls it.
"Sweetheart, I told you to slow down, remember last
time you drank too much."
"Nope," she laughs racing over to the lounge room,
pulling Dana with her, "Dance with me! Bella, come
dance!" she calls out, obviously heading to being way
more than tipsy.

We watch from the other side of the room, as they
wave their arms in the air, grinding against each
other as though they are deliberately taunting us,
knowing our eyes would be fixated on them.

The mystery guy from earlier comes over to stand
with us, "Damn women, they sure know how to get
to us."

"Yeah, so is Bella your girl?"

"Yeah, I'm Jace by the way," He says, holding his hand and shaking ours as we introduce ourselves.

"So Jace, you been with Bella long?"

"Yeah, about three years."

"Ripper, she seems like a nice girl," Trav replies, a slight smirk on his face.

"Yeah, anyway I gotta head out... have an early shift tomorrow," he says, once again giving us the death stares, like a non-verbal warning to leave his girl alone.

"Nice to meet you man, sorry you gotta head out," Trav again replies, worrying me with his tone.

The look he gives Jace as he walks up to Bella, saying something in her ear before pressing a chaste kiss to her lips, is one that has me a little worried about what he might do.

"Trav, what are you thinking?" I ask, grabbing another beer for us both after Jace has left.

"That I want to give her a kiss way hotter than that tool just did."

"Trav, man you can't."

"I know, I know, but damn she's hot."

"Yeah, just keep it in your pants with her is all I'm saying."

He laughs, sipping his beer before going up to dance with the girls, completely in his element.

A wicked smirk crosses his face when Bella starts to dance against him. I only hope he heeds my advice.

Thirty-Seven | Party Crash

My head is spinning, the music pumping and I know I'm beyond drunk, but I'm feeling so elated I couldn't care less. My new jam comes blaring out of the speakers and screaming, I yell out to Bella, "Bel, turn the music up! This is my song!"
"Anni, you're drunk girl!"
"No, no, turnnn it up!" I scream out letting my inhibitions fade as the music pumps out the speakers and into my veins, along with the Jager bomb I'd just downed.

Other people are dancing around me, talking above the music, but I'm in my own little world.

Looking around the spinning room, a crazy thought surfaces in my mind.

Eagerly, I jump up on the table, thrashing my hips and arms violently to the music, secretly loving that everyone's eyes turn to look at me.
I feel invincible.
A voice calls out to me, "Anni, sweetheart, get down. You're going to hurt yourself."

I ignore the voice, still dancing and jumping up and down on the table, beginning to unbutton my jeans. "Sweetheart, get down, please," the voice begs again, seeming closer than before.

That is the last thing I hear before the room fades into blackness.

~~

I've fainted before from drinking too much, without eating and I knew as soon as the room went black, feeling my body falling that it's happening again.

I feel weightless, free and can vaguely still hear the music pumping in the background, as well as screams of people calling out my name. One voice stands out, telling people to move away, to get out of our house now, the party's over.
His voice is comforting, a pleasant sound breaking through the throbbing in my head.
All the sounds seem to disappear suddenly and I feel safe and cocooned as though I'm being hugged and wrapped in a fluffy blanket.

Opening my eyes, I take in my surroundings, focusing on the figure lying beside me.

Evidently, I'm in my bed with Jairus outstretched beside me, his head on the pillow as he looks over at me.

"Hi sweetheart," he drawls at me, as I turn to face him, "How are you feeling?"

"Sore, confused," I mutter, touching a hand to my throbbing temple.

"I bet, that was quite the fall you took."

"Yeah?" I ask confusedly, not sure about what happened, "I just remember hearing 'Turn the music up' come on and now I'm here."

"Yeah, well you passed out when you decided to dance on the table, hitting your head on the lampshade before practically falling off the table."

"Oh, so did I actually fall off the table?"

"No, because I was there to catch you, sweetheart."

I smile at him, "Oh, so is anyone still here?"

"No, I sent everyone home."

"God, I'm sorry, I'm so embarrassed."

"It's ok, sweetheart. It was getting late anyway and I've got a big game tomorrow."

"Yeah, but Jai, can you stay with me tonight? I feel safe in your arms."

A huge smile crosses his face at my words, "Sure but only if you let me help you get into your pj's and don't mind me sleeping with just jocks on."

"Um, I'd be happy if you wore them or maybe nothing," I taunt, feeling my cheeks flush.

He laughs, teasing me, "Oh really? And what if I can't keep my hands off you sweetheart?"

"Um, I'd like that Jai, I..."

He moans, kissing me and fumbling to undo my jeans, pushing them over my hips. Without saying a word, Jairus sits up in the bed, taking off first his shirt and then his white chino pants.

He kisses me again, as I run my fingers up his chest teasing him, feeling his skin heat at my touch.

"Are you sure you're cool with me sleeping naked sweetheart?" he asks again, his tone seductive.

"Yes, can you help me get this off?" I ask, touching the straps of the bodysuit.

Jairus doesn't reply, instead reaches down to unbutton the bodysuit at my crotch as I slide the straps down my arms.

He yanks the bodysuit off, down over my hips, before pulling it and my jeans off at my ankles.

Grabbing all our clothes, we push them off the bed to the floor, diving under the covers together.

I can feel the heat radiating off his body as he pulls me closer.

"God sweetheart, you're beautiful. I love you."

I don't reply, instead kiss him hooking my leg over his to get as close as possible.

Breaking the kiss, I hiss, "Jairus, please...I want you."

"Really Anni? Tell me how you feel about me then."

"I....i..Ill..."

He silences me with a tender kiss, cupping my cheeks is his palms, taking my mouth as his and pressing his body against mine.

I want to tell him the words he needs to hear, but even though my body is aching for him to be mine completely I'm not ready to say those words.

Breathless he breaks the kiss, "Anni, sweetheart, I want all of you."

"I want all of you to Jairus. I like you a lot."

"I know, but until you feel the same way about me, as I do about you, I'm not taking that step."

It's childish, but I pout, "Why not?"

"You know why Arnika. I'm in love with you, and I'm not going to have sex with you until you're sure you love me too."

His words melt my heart a little, a part of me really does want to say, 'I love him' just so he'll take the next step with me, but logic wins out.

Instead, I kiss him, loving how his kiss makes me feel so aroused.

"Will you at least touch me again?"

"I'll do more than touch you sweetheart," he teases, lifting the sheet up and gazing over my nakedness.

"Mmm, like what?" I ask, lacing my tone with lust.

"Like licking your delicious honeypot until you cum all over my face," he moans before kissing me and touching me between my thighs.

Breaking the kiss on my lips, he kisses across my collarbone, before kissing and licking my breasts, making my nipples rise to attention.

His tongue and lips then lick down my torso, across the sensitive skin of my hips before he grabs my thighs spreading my legs wide.
His licking along the insides of my thighs sends a delightful shiver through my body.
"Jai, please, please..." I beg, grabbing his hair in my fists, trying to pull his mouth to my crotch.
Chuckling he obeys, biting my clit before licking down to my arousal, inserting his tongue, pushing it in and out.
It is absolutely delicious torture.
Lifting his head for a moment, he locks his eyes on mine, "Sweetheart, you taste delicious."
I laugh at his words, his taunt a direct hit back at the words I'd told him a few weeks earlier when we'd been alone in the kitchen.
Diving back under, he licks my clit, flicking his tongue against it, sending me so close to the edge.
I buck my pelvis up to his face and he moans as he licks lower again, his lips and tongue lapping up all my body is offering.

Mere moments later I can't help but scream out, "Jai, I'm coming! Oh, fuck!" My climax rips through me suddenly like a crashing wave.
Stretching up over my body, he kisses me, allowing me to taste myself on his lips.

"God sweetheart, I'll never get tired of making you cum. That was hot as."
"Mmm, I loved it Jai."

"I know you did, sweetheart," he laughs, lying beside me again and pulling my body close to his, "Now we need to get some sleep."
"Yeah, but can I have a kiss goodnight?" I ask sweetly, turning my head back to him.
"You don't need to ask me to kiss you, sweetheart, ever," he muses before crashing his lips to mine again in a soul-shattering kiss that makes my heart pound in my chest.

Thirty-Eight | Bedroom Secrets

Bella

Grabbing the half-empty bottle of Jack Daniels on the table, I head down the hallway bumping into the walls as I sway, feeling a little tipsy. Stopping at the bedroom door, I gasp hearing Anni's voice scream out 'Jai, I'm coming!'.
It seems like they are finally crossing the line, and I hate admitting to myself that I'm jealous.

Things with Jace had been pretty shit, he not been able to get it up and was acting like a complete tosser.
We'd not slept together since the day we'd gotten back together a couple months ago and I was as horny as hell. My vibrator just wasn't cutting it.
Standing against the wall, I take a swig of the Jack Daniels, loving the burn as I swallow hard.
 No other sound appears to be coming from mine and Anni's room, but I don't want to risk catching them with their daks down, even though seeing Blondie naked would have make using my vibrator a little more exciting.

Instead, I head to Blondie and Austin's room, partly hoping that maybe Austin was still up and partly hoping he isn't so I can just crawl into

Blondie's bed and dream he is fucking me instead of Anni.

It isn't like I'm in love with the guy, but I love his crassness.

It's a breath of fresh air, I also want to kiss him again to prove to him that kissing me isn't anything like kissing a brick wall.

I know I'd never get to be with him though, as it's clear he's fallen hard for Anni and she won't admit to herself, let alone someone else that she's in love with him.

Reaching his room, I find Austin sitting on the floor by his bed, looking like he's been crying. He also seems to have downed a significant amount of Vodka, as the bottle in his fists has maybe one mouthful left.

"Austin, have you been crying?"

He wipes an arm across his cheeks as I sit down next to him, taking another swig from my own bottle.

"No...just...um.."

"You can tell me Austin," I suggest, feeling a little sorry for him.

"I've lost her, haven't I?" he asks with a forlorn look on his face.

"Who? Anni?"

"Who else would I be talking about, Bella?"

"You don't know that Austin," I plead, even though I know he's right.

"She's with him now, not with me....and I just know."

"How do you know Aust?"

Caz May

"Because she looks at him the way I look at her," he muses, downing the last of his Vodka before putting the empty bottle down beside him.

"That doesn't mean she loves him, maybe it's just lust."

He laughs, "She loves him, Bella...I know she does. And he's...he's probably just lusting after her."

"Hmm yeah probably."

He doesn't respond, just sits there frozen staring at the wall, watching me out of the corner of his eye as I take a swig of Jack Daniels.

Out of the blue, he lets out a deep laugh, "Bella, does this remind you of something?"

"What? Does what remind me of what?" I ask confused and not making any sense.

"Me, you, a bottle of Jack in my bedroom."

He points at the bottle I'm holding, as the blush rises up my cheeks.

"Um...yeah....but there won't be any repeats of that night Austin."

"You loved it, Bella!"

"Did not!" I spit at him putting the near-empty Jack bottle on the floor beside me.

"Really? How about we do it again then? Maybe you'll love it this time."

He doesn't give me a moment to protest, a moment to think before his eyes lock with mine and he smashes a kiss to my lips, a kiss that is fierce and demanding.

247

A strange rush runs through me, and I moan as he kisses me deeper, parting my lips with his tongue. The taste of Vodka mixed with the taste of Jack Daniels is oddly arousing and I press my hands

into his chest fumbling with the hem of his t-shirt to run my hands over his chest. He moans, an appreciative hum escaping his mouth before he breaks the kiss.

"Fuck Austin, um...what just happened?"
"We kissed Bella, and you loved it," he laughs.
"And you didn't?" I taunt.
"I didn't say that," he protests, a smirk on his face that says it all.
"Aust, did you ever tell Anni, about that night?"
"It was before I got with her, so no and I didn't even realise you were friends at the time."
"So, she doesn't know that you almost lost your virginity to me?"
"No, and I intend to keep it that way."
"Ok...and maybe we shouldn't tell her about tonight's kiss either."
"Why? It's not like she's going to care," he snaps before the smirk crosses his face again.
"We aren't going to tell her Austin, because Roommates don't kiss and tell."
"Fair point....um Bella?"
"Yeah?" I ask winking at him, wondering what the hell has gotten into me.
"Can I kiss you again?"

This time I don't respond, instead, I grab his cheeks and pull his mouth down to mine. This kiss is setting my horny self on fire, and thoughts race in my mind that I'm kissing my friend's guy, but at the same time, I don't care.

When he pulls back breathless, his smirk crosses his face as he lifts his shirt over his head and grabs the hem of my camisole to lift it over my head.

"Bella, are you and Jace still together?"
"Define together?"
"You know what I mean Bella."
"Yes, but we might as well not be, and right now I don't care."
"Good, because if I kiss you again....well...." I silence him by pressing a finger to his lips, that his tongue darts out from between his lips to lick.
"I know Austin, roommates don't fuck and tell either."

He moans, pushing my body down onto the floor and kissing me hard. I can feel his hardness pressing against my belly.

Breaking the kiss, pulling down his daks I ask, "Austin are you sure about this?"
He laughs, "Wanna know a secret Bella?"
"Yeah, ok?"
"I might be in love with Anni, but I'm a guy and I always wanted to fuck you, so yes I'm sure."
"Ok, so have you got a franger?" I ask.

Bending up onto his knees, he reaches behind him opening the drawer and producing a box. He grabs out a franger, ripping it open with his teeth before sliding it onto his erection.

Undoing my own jeans, I push them and my G-string off, sliding them down my legs to my ankles.

"So, am I fucking you on the floor or the bed?" he asks teasingly.

"Bed," I reply, getting up and sitting on the edge of his unmade bed.

Smashing a kiss to my lips, he pushes my body down on the bed, plunging himself inside me and thrusting hard in and out.

I can't deny it feels good, better than good and when I began to feel my climax building, I again pull his lips to mine to silence the scream of pleasure that rocks through my body, to not let our roommates know that we're crossing that line.

After, he lays down next to me, pulling me close, "Bella promise you won't say anything to Anni yeah?"

"I won't Austin, roommates don't kiss or fuck and tell," I promise, "And Austin, this, us, won't happen again yeah?"

"Um...yeah I don't know, up to you, I guess. I can't deny that I loved fucking you, Bella."

"Yeah, I know what you mean," I muse, wiggling from his embrace and standing up, "I'm gonna sleep in Blondie's bed, just in case um..."

Picking up my G-string, I put it back on and slide into Blondie's bed, turning away from Austin's eyes on me.

What the fuck had I just done?
It felt damn good, but damn I've fucked up big time,
again...

Thirty-Nine | Man Down

Vairus

Like always, running out onto the field, knowing Anni is watching in the cheer squad makes me feel practically elated.
Travis is right that when Anni is at a game I play better; her support means the absolute world and today the love I feel for her is intensified after our party night a week ago.

I want nothing more than to take the next step with her, fully make her mine in hope that she'll confess she loves me too, but I know better from my past to keep it my pants until I'm sure the girl feels the same as me.

Sara confessed she loved me after we'd slept together, on our second date and I felt like she only said it because she loved the sex as that was usually the time she said I love you the most.

In the change room after warm-ups, Travis pats me on the back, "Did you make it official yet man?"
"No Travis, I didn't."

"Just sleep with her man, you'll know if you really love her then."

"I already know I love her man, having sex with her won't change how I feel about her, except for maybe making me fall more in love with her," I muse, lacing up my boots and pulling up my socks.

"How can you be so sure, man? What if she's a dud root?"

"Not a chance man," I laugh half-heartedly, feeling myself blush a little.

"Did something else happen, other than her giving you a gobby?"

"Yeah," I reply, blushing, too embarrassed to tell him, "we slept, actually slept naked together after I..."

"After you what man? Did you give her an Aussie kiss?"

Replying I swear my face is a deep shade of crimson, "I might have."

"Ripper man, you've got skills then to keep ya dick in ya pants after giving a girl an Aussie kiss."

"I won't deny I want to fuck her, but I'm not going to...yet."

"Suit yourself man, is she here today?"

"Yeah."

"Well, a good game is afoot then," he jeers, as we run out onto the field to prepare for ball up.

Running out onto the field, I throw the ball at my feet, running as I bounce it in front of me along the sidelines.

Anni is at the front of the barrier at the Punt road end, leaning against it with her arms folded.
She is wearing her blonde hair down, it loosely falls over her shoulders in waves and covers the front of the Richmond Guernsey she is wearing with my number on the back, the not so lucky number thirteen.

Cheers erupt around us, but all I can see is her, pressing a kiss to her lips, "I love you, sweetheart, cheer hard for me yeah."
"Of course, you're the man," she winks at me as I run out onto the field for ball up.
The game starts off with us scoring the first few goals unanswered by the Crows. It makes me feel like I'm floating on air, and vaguely in the distance, I can hear Anni screaming out, 'yes Jai the man,' and it makes my mind wonder momentarily as to what it would be like to hear her say that as she comes apart beneath me with my cock buried inside her.

Shaking the wicked thought from my head, I try to focus on the ball coming towards me and the Crows player trying to intercept it right out the front of our goals.
Without really thinking, I launch myself practically onto his shoulders, reaching out to grab the ball but fumbling and feeling the impact of the red leather hitting my forehead.
My vision goes blurry, the world disappearing as I fall backwards, crashing to the cold ground. Voices

tumble in my head, 'man down', 'unconscious,
suspected concussion'.

Feeling people lift my body up, I can't respond, my
eyes glued shut.
As I'm carried off the field, the only thing I can focus
on is hearing Anni scream out *'no!!!!! Jairus...no....I
love you!'*

At least in my knocked out mind I hear those words,
and I hope they are real and I'd get to see her
gorgeous face when she says them next.

Forty | White Walls

Watching Jairus crash to the ground, my hearts crashes to the ground with him. Screaming out 'No!' I'm about to jump over the barrier to run to his side, when arms wrap around me pulling me back and holding me despite my thrashing arms.

"Anni, calm down, he'll be ok," her words in my ear are soothing, but of little comfort.
"No, no....I...I...did you...did you see how he?" I stutter incoherently.
"Yes, Anni, I saw and it was horrible, but trust me he'll be fine."

Pulling myself away from her hold on me, I spit at her, "How do you know that Dana?"
She looks at me sheepishly, "Because it happens all the time, Trav got a bad hit, like a couple of weeks ago and he was fine."
"Yeah, well...we aren't talking about Travis here."
"Anni, can I ask you something?"
"If I say no, you're still going to ask so, ok."
"Are you in love with Jai?"
"No, why would you ask that?" I spit at her again, even though my heart is pounding just thinking about Jairus and the thought of losing him crushing my heart completely.

"Because no one else has a reaction to a player going down like this."

I don't have a reply for her, one that will throw her off, so instead I ask, "Why are you asking? Do you want him?"
"I've tried to get with him," she confesses blushing, "He said there was someone who meant everything to him and he was talking about you."
"Um....ok," I mutter, short of words.
"He's so in love with you, and I don't think you're going to lose him. Head down to the rooms and see if they've taken him to hospital."
"Seriously? Hospital?" I ask, worried about what she's implying.
"Yeah, don't worry Anni, it's usually just precautionary."
"I hope so...which hospital?"
"Epworth Anni," she instructs.
"Thanks, Dana and my name is Annika," I say to her politely, hating that she's calling me Anni.

She isn't my friend, and I don't like her thinking she has a claim on Jairus.

Being inside the Melbourne Cricket ground is all of a sudden making me feel claustrophobic, even though it's a huge, expansive and fairly open sort of building. I race out, running straight out the doors and sucking in the fresh outside air.
The Epworth is just around the corner, a short walk for me, but one that Jairus has most likely just taken

in the back of an ambulance. I hear sirens in the distance and my heart falls to the ground as I head to the hospital.

I'm worried about Jairus but also scared to walk back into the Epworth after failing my practical there a couple months ago.

The doctors weren't always the nicest, except for Doctor Thompson, so I cross my fingers that he's on duty as he'll at least tell me straight up if anything is wrong.

~~

After crashing through the hospital doors, I stop at the Nurses station finding that one of the nicer orderly's is on duty.

"Annika, dearest, you look frightful. What brings you in?"

"Hi Mary, has Jairus Brooks been brought in?"

"Oh yes dear, he's in room ten. Do you know him?" she asks winking at me and looking at my outfit.

"He's my roommate, and um maybe...."

"Oh, you lucky girl. He's quite the handsome young man."

"Thanks, Mary, is Doctor Thompson on today?"

"Yes, dear," she replies as I turn away to head to room ten.

Opening the door to the room, I find Jairus lying in the bed with his eyes closed.

Pulling up a chair next to him, I grab his hand in mine leaning over to press a kiss against his cheek.

His eyes flutter open, locking on me, "Oh hey sweetheart. What are you doing here?"
"You don't remember what happened?"
"Of course I remember...I took a ball to the head," he replies, touching a hand to his forehead where a large lump has made an appearance, "and it hurts like a bitch."
"Yeah, you've got a nasty looking egg on your forehead."

"Hmmm yeah, I can tell," he laughs.
"Are you sure you're ok?"
"Yes, sweetheart, I've been knocked out on the field before but I've never had...never mind."
"What Jairus?"

Again, he laughs before he reaches up to brush a stray hair from my cheek, "I've never had a girl by my side to kiss it better."
"Oh, is that so?"
"Yep, will you kiss me better sweetheart?"
I laugh at his little tease, bending over his chest and pressing a tender kiss to his lips. It doesn't matter if our kisses are sweet and soft or hard and passionate, I can't deny that I love kissing Jairus.
The thought of losing him makes my heart ache and I want to tell him how I feel, but my words are caught in my throat when the door cracks open and Doctor Thompson walks in.

"Well, fancy seeing you here Annika?"

"Hi Doctor Thompson," I meekly reply, squeezing Jai's hand I'm still clutching.

"How are you connected to my patient?" he asks looking down at our entwined hands.

"He's my roommate," I reply feeling a blush rise up my cheek and stifling a laugh at the smirk on Jairus' face.

"I see, well seeing as you've just woken up Mr Brooks, and took quite the bump to the forehead, we'd like to keep you in for a few more hours, just for observation."

"Ok, so what's the official diagnosis?" Jairus asks with a concerned tone.

"Mr Brooks, I'm not going to lie to you. You having another concussion is of concern considering you've had four previously, but most likely you'll be just fine with some rest and TLC from your nursing roommate here."

"Ok, thanks Doctor," he replies, firstly giving the doctor a curt nod, before he looks at me as if to say I'll tell you later.

"Annika, can I speak to you a moment outside?"

"Sure, Doctor Thompson," I reply, feeling my heartbeat begin to beat rapidly.

Stepping outside the room, he closes the door behind me and comfortingly runs a hand up and down my shoulder, "How are you doing? After your practical?"

"I'm ok thanks. I was...um...pretty devastated."

"I understand completely. If it was just my choice Annika, you wouldn't have failed."

"I'm sorry, I don't understand, you were my supervising doctor."

"Yes, that's correct, but I spoke with all the doctors you were on duty with you when you were here and a couple mentioned some incidents that you didn't handle well. They recommend we not give you a pass for this practical, so you gain some more experience."

"Incidents?" I ask, even though I know the exact ones he's talking about.

"Yes, there was the two drug overdose patients who came in and you refused to treat them, instead running out of the room screaming. I'm sure you know that is unacceptable."

"Yes, but my...my brother...."

"You don't have to tell me the details now Annika, but I will be in contact with the university to invite you back for another practical and I assure you I'll work closely with you to make sure you pass this time. You will be a wonderful nurse Annika and Jairus is lucky to have you as his girlfriend."

"Thanks, Doctor Thompson, I really appreciate the second chance and um Jairus....we aren't together."

"You could have fooled me," he laughs, "We'll chat later when we discharge him but don't worry, he'll be fine."

He walks away then, and I go back into the room, sitting back down in the chair.

"Everything ok sweetheart?"

"Yeah, that was my supervising doctor from when I did my practical here."

"Oh, did something bad happen? Did you kill someone?" he jokes seeing the tears stinging my eyes.

"No, I failed...but they are going to let me repeat it, so that's good."

"For sure, and did he say anything else?"

"Yeah, he said I needed to say goodbye to my boyfriend," I jeer at him, poking his chest and making him squirm.

"You have a boyfriend? Where is he?" he asks jokingly as he glances around the room.

"I don't know who he's talking about, you're the only one in this room," I laugh, smiling at him.

"Yeah, maybe the doctor got a concussion too," he laughs before frowning, and changing his tone, "Anni, I want you to be my girlfriend, you know that yeah?"

"Yeah, but I...." I cut my own words off, feeling like a fool for even thinking that I don't want to define what is happening between us with a label.

"Sweetheart, it's ok, I get it," he comforts me reaching up to caress my cheek with the back of his hand, "If I get to be with you, that's all that matters to me right now, ok?"

"Ok, are you sure?"

"Yes, I'm sure," he promises, "Just kiss me, sweetheart, please."

I don't reply, instead climb onto the bed to lie down next to him, before cupping his cheeks in my palms and kissing him harder than ever before.

He moans against my mouth, the words I want to say surface in my mind again, but I'm not ready to say them, so I kiss him deeper instead, hoping my kiss said what words can't.

Forty-One | How Sweet

After helping a tired Jairus with discharging himself from the hospital we have to take the tram home. He is in no condition to drive and I couldn't drive his car down a back road, let alone in Saturday afternoon inner city traffic.

At the tram stop, he looks as though he's going to fall flat on the ground again, so comfortingly putting an arm around his torso I tell him, "Lean on me, Jai."

"Aww sweetheart, I love you," he muses as we awkwardly get on the tram that has just pulled up.

From my bag, I tap my Taki, and the spare I always carry on the reader, helping Jairus sit down in a seat close to the door.

"Are you good, Jai?"

"Fine sweetheart, thanks," he muses again, putting his head on my shoulder when I sit down beside him. We've only gone a few stops when a kid bounds up to us from the other end of the tram, "Are you Jairus Brooks?" he asks eagerly.

"Yeah," Jairus replies softly, lifting his head to look at the scrawny boy in front of us.

"Can I get an autograph?"

"Yeah sure," Jairus smiles at the kid, signing a scrawly autograph on the piece of paper the kid fishes out of

his pocket, handing it over with the biggest grin on
his face.

"Can I have a photo with you?"

"You sure little mate? I've got quite the bump on my
head," Jairus enquires so sweetly it makes my heart
ache.

"I know, I just left the game and I'm like...so glad
you're alright. So please a photo," the kid begs
innocently.

"No worries," Jairus replies, as the kid steps closer
and he puts an arm around him.

He hands his phone to me and I quickly snap a photo
of them together, loving the sweet smile on Jairus'
face.

"Thanks, Jai, you're the man!" the kid beams.

"You're welcome, what's your name?"

"Terry Mattman," he replies, still smiling.

"I'll get you special tickets to the next game mate
alright, to sit in the cheer squad with Anni here
yeah?"

"That would be awesome! Is she your girlfriend?" he
enquires with childlike glee.

"No," Jairus laughs, "she's a nurse."

"Oh," Terry laughs, not understanding what his idol is
meaning.

"The tickets will be at gate thirteen for you, alright?"

"Thanks, Jai you the man," Terry jeers as we stand up
to get off the tram.

Walking from the tram stop Jairus is a little steadier
on his feet, not able to wipe the smile off his face.

"That was really sweet Jai."

"It's the least I could do, he seemed like a sweet kid."
"Yeah, and you were so nice to him."
"Part of the job, sweetheart," he laughs, stumbling a little, "hey can you text Trav on your phone to get him to bring my car home?"
"Yeah, sure what's his number?"
"0456 784 569," he recites, looking at me sheepishly.
I laugh at Travis' phone number ending with the number sixty-nine.
Jairus laughs as well, "I know I know...the phone number suits him."
Travis responds almost immediately.
Travis: yeah, no probs man, you all good?

Handing my phone over he types a response that makes me laugh when he gives my phone back

Jai: yep, got Nurse Anni to look after me

Once inside, we walk in to find Bella is in the kitchen attempting to cook something to eat.
She takes one look at Jairus before laughing,
"Blondie, did she beat you up or something?"
"Haha, sunshine! No, I took a ball to the head."
"Oh well at least nurse Anni can look after you," she teases winking at me.
"Yeah, um Bel, where's Austin?"
"I don't know, why would I know?" she replies with an odd tone like I'm accusing her of something.

"Sorry, I just haven't seen him much lately, that's all."
"Yeah, I...um think he went out with some friends. I don't know what time he'll be back though."

Blushing as I look at her, I ask, "So are you cool sleeping in Jai's room again?"

A blush rises up Bella's cheeks to which is a little weird, and makes me wonder if something happened between her and Austin.
I shrug it off when she responds, "Yeah, but Blondie you won't mind if I change the sheets? I hate smelling your dirty arse on the sheets," she laughs.
"Do whatever you need to sunshine," he laughs back.
"Sweet," Bella snaps, turning back to her cooking.

Taking Jairus to my room, I help him strip from his footy clothes, pulling back the covers so he can slide in.
Like a good little nurse, I tuck him into bed, "I'll be back in soon yeah? Get some rest."

"Ok nurse Anni," he laughs.
I laugh in response to him calling me nurse Anni. As I'm about to leave he pulls me down by the hand, to sit on the edge of the bed.
Not letting go of my hand he pulls me down more, my chest crashing against his as he brushes my cheek with his other hand and pulls my mouth to his for a lingering kiss that melts my heart.
"Mmm...do you have one of those hot nurse outfits sweetheart?"

"Get some rest and you might find out later," I tease, winking at him.

He licks his lips, thinking about my words before kissing me again. Every kiss is different with him, some sweet, some lingering, some quick and some so passionately soul shattering.

"God, I love you, Annika," he muses caressing my cheek.
"You're just delirious," I tease him standing up to leave the room.

Once out in the kitchen, I proceed to make a coffee, grabbing the milk out of the fridge. I look at Bella standing at the stove stirring something in the pot absentmindedly.
"Bel are you ok?" I ask, putting the milk on the bench and touching her arm lightly to turn her gaze to me.
She shakes her head but replies, "Yeah fine, why?"
"I don't know, you seem upset, in a daze."
"I'm fine, things are just a bit tough with Jace at the moment."
"Oh, wanna talk about it?"

"Nah all good...I told Austin the other night," she snaps quickly, swallowing hard like she is regretting her words.
"Oh, when?" I snap.
"The party night when I had to crash in Blondies bed."

I feel a blush rise up my cheeks remembering the night in my head, "Sorry about that."

"Don't be...so tell me how was it?" She enquires grinning.

"How was what?" I ask, kind of knowing what she means, but wanting to make sure of what she is actually thinking.

"Don't be so coy Anni," she laughs.

"I don't know what you're talking about," I lie, biting the inside of my mouth to hold my tongue.

"Was he a good root?"

"I didn't have sex with him, Bella."

"Oh...so you screaming out Jai I'm coming wasn't during sex?"

The blush creeps further up my cheeks when I sheepishly reply, "No."

"Oh, Anni! You lucky bitch!" she squeals excitedly, before slapping a hand to her mouth to stop a real scream from escaping.

"Mmm...yeah his Aussie kisses are pretty amazing...and pashing him Bella is something else," I muse feeling a little brazen after her reaction.

"Are you in love with him?"

"I don't know...maybe," I reply, her words ticking over in my head.

"Well, either way, enjoy it Anni...guys like Jairus don't come around every day."

"I know," I muse, nodding my head.

She's about to reply when someone knocks hard on the front door.

Running to answer it, I find Travis on the doorstep holding Jairus' car keys in his hand with his bag slung over his shoulder.

"Hey Travis, thanks for doing this," I reply, taking the keys and bag from him.

"Hi Anni, how's the patient?"

"Resting...but all good...his usual self," I laugh half-heartedly.

Travis' eyes look past me for a moment to Bella who's now leaning against the bench, staring at us like she's not sure if she should come over and interrupt our conversation.

He lifts a hand and waves at her, making Bella blush as she lifts a hand waving back.

Abruptly after the little moment, Travis replies,

"Good to know...tell him I'll text him if he needs to be at training on Wednesday."

"No worries Travis...thanks again."

"And if you need anything you have my number, ok?"

"I know...thanks...don't worry about him...I'm a nurse."

"Oh right...how sweet. I thought he was just joking about that...You should wear one of those sexy nurse outfits...that will make him feel better," he laughs winking at me.

"I'm sure it would. Goodnight Travis."

He takes a step back, turning to walk away and closing the door behind me I hear Bella's voice, "You need to tell me who that hottie is? He danced with me the other night but I didn't get his name before he left."

Sauntering back over to the kitchen to continue making my coffee I reply, "Travis Banes...he's number twenty and Jai's best friend."

"Mmm...maybe I should start coming to some games with you," she suggests.

"Anytime you want I'm down," I tease her.

"How sweet," she laughs, my mind tripping out that Travis said exactly the same phrase minutes ago.

"I'm going to go take Jai some food," I tell her, getting out some crackers and dip, "I'll talk to you later."

She smiles at me, grabbing a plate to spoon her food into as I leave the room, balancing the items and my coffee in my hands.

Once in my bedroom, I put the food down on the bedside table, hearing Jairus murmur in his sleep.

He rolls over to face the wall but doesn't wake, even as I go into the walk in to find my hot nurse outfit, hoping it still fits.

Forty-Two | Nurse Anni

After slipping on my hot nurse outfit, I sit on the edge of the bed sipping my tepid coffee watching Jairus in his sleep.

He murmurs, his face constricting as though he's in pain. It hurts to see him feeling like that, and I wonder if he's having a nightmare about something traumatic.

It dawns on me that I really don't know much about him, his past or what he really wants from the future other than his football career and me.

Downing the rest of my coffee, I brush a hand against his cheek when he rolls over to face me.

His eyes flutter open, looking me up and down.

"Mmm did I die and go to heaven, sweetheart?" he muses, a smirk crossing his lips as he takes in my outfit.

"No, you didn't die Jai." I laugh.

"Ripper, I'd hate to not remember seeing you in this outfit," he teases.

"Yeah, I brought you some food," I reply blushing, busying myself with opening the dip and fishing crackers out of the box as he sits up in bed against the wall.

Handing it to him, he licks his lips, muttering an appreciative 'mmm' as he puts the cracker in his mouth.

The sound and the way he again licks his lips to collect the dip at the corner of his mouth makes my stomach flip-flop.

"Mmm, nurse Anni, that tasted good, but I could think of something else I'd rather taste," he teases, signalling the flip-flop in my stomach again, sending the rush south.

Playfully elbowing him I jeer, "Jai stop, you've just had a concussion. You're not thinking straight."

"I'm thinking perfectly clear sweetheart," he says with the seductive panty dropping tone he knows has an effect on me.

"But Jai, I...everything that has happened between us in this last week...I...um..."

"What Anni? You can't deny you haven't loved every minute of the time we've spent together lately."

"I'm not Jai...but I'm scared...I don't want to label us and what I feel because that's only hurt me in the past."

"How? Haven't you only been with Austin before me?"

"Yes, but...ah...fuck I can't believe I'm telling you this."

"You can tell me anything sweetheart, I love you."

"Yeah, well maybe you shouldn't...."

"Anni stop ok! Nothing you say or do will change how I feel about you."

"Nothing? Nothing at all?"

"Nope, nothing sweetheart."

"Even if I can't tell you how I feel, because the last time I said those words they weren't reciprocated or can't label myself, us, because the last time I put a label on a relationship it ruined it."

"Even after that yes, and if you say those words to me, sweetheart, you already know I feel the same way about you."

"Mmm...so do you like my outfit?" I tease, trying to make the moment lighter, not ready to face how I'm feeling and glad he doesn't probe me for more.

"Why are you even asking me that question?" He laughs, nodding towards his crotch.

"I wore it for you," I try to tease him.

"Mmm, well you look hot as in it sweetheart, and I'd really love some special treatment from you," he taunts me as I edge closer to him on the bed, pulling back the sheets from the pool at his waist.

Just like his nod suggests, his dick is peeking out through the front of his tight boxer shorts, the tip poking out to say hello.

"So, patient, what kind of special treatment were you after?"

"Hmmm," he muses beckoning me closer with a finger to whisper in my ear, "I was thinking a kiss, and then maybe you riding my cock, nurse Anni."

I slap his arm, "Jai, no, we can't!"

"Sorry sweetheart, I want you so bad, you know that yeah?"
"Yes, but I can't," I apologise, feeling like an idiot,
"can we just pash and well you know?"
"I'm up for any special treatment from you sweetheart," he teases pulling me onto his lap, so I'm straddling him.

He lifts up the skirt of the nurse outfit, "What have you got on under here huh?"
"Just a G-string," I laugh, leaning over his chest and kissing him hard.

Moaning he deepens the kiss, parting my lips with his tongue to taste my mouth as he'd suggested earlier. As we madly pash, even though I know I shouldn't I rock my pelvis over the bulge in his boxers, feeling the ache intensify.
The fabric of my G-string barely covers anything and I'm so close to sliding my body straight onto his eagerness.
He breaks the kiss panting, "Sweetheart, as much as I love what you were just doing, you need to stop."
"Why?" I tease, feeling a little brazen, knowing he is just as affected as I am.
 "Because I won't be able to stop myself, and we can't go there yet."
"I really want to Jai, but..."

"I know sweetheart, trust me."
"Can I still kiss you?"

He laughs. "What did I tell you about asking to kiss me?"

"Not to ask," I laugh, stretching over his chest again.

"Exactly," is his reply, before he again smashes a kiss to my lips.

A kiss that both fuelled and tamed the desire in me.

Without a doubt, nurse Anni is falling for her patient.

Forty-Three | Lit Man

His voice hitting my ears the moment I walk in the
door is such a comforting sound, "Hey sweetheart,
how was Uni?"
"Shit, but when isn't it," I muse, crossing the room to
sit next to him on the couch.
He laughs. "Well, I wouldn't know, but I feel like a
fucking slob today. Missing training has made me feel
like shit. I need a workout."
"A workout huh?" I taunt, licking my lips.
"Oh really sweetheart, are you telling me you're up
for a tonsil hockey workout, right here on the
couch?" he teases, tapping the couch next to him.

I don't reply with words, instead, inch up onto my
knees and crawl across the couch towards him,
stopping when my face is just a whisper from his.
He moans, pulling me onto his lap, his lips on mine
before I can even think.
His tongue parts my lips, diving between them as he
laces our tongues together.
Cheekily I bite down on his lip, making him moan
again as he shifts to lie down on the couch, pulling
me down with him, our lips still locked.
 Kissing Jairus has become my new addiction, the
only thing that can make me feel better when I'm
down. Breaking the kiss, breathless I'm about to tell
him I'm ready to take things further when the sound

of the door slamming stops the words from rolling off my tongue.

Jairus laughs, not caring that someone is home as he kisses me again, knowing I can't resist kissing him back.

"What the fuck? How could you? Can't you keep things in the bedroom, where I can't see?" Austin yells at us, standing next to the coffee table with his hands on his hips.

Jumping back from Jairus' lap I apologise, "Sorry Aust."

"Are you together now?" He snaps, looking first at me and then to Jairus who replies, "No mate, we're not."

"So, you think you can just kiss her, use her and take her away from me, like I'm gonna be ok with that?" Austin taunts, his hands clenching into fists.

"You know I didn't mean to mate, but I can't help that I fell in love with her."

"Yeah well..." Austin starts, cutting off his own words as Jairus stands up, entering Austin's personal space. I want to look away, scared that Austin is about to do something he's going to regret.

Time seems to be a ticking time bomb as Austin raises his clenched fist to hit Jairus.

Instead, his hands fall at his side for a moment, unclenching before he pushes his hands into Jairus' chest, taunting him angrily, "You are going to lay off her! She's mine!"

"And if I don't?" Jairus jeers back with a questioning tone.

Austin is seething, his chest visibly moving in and out beneath his shirt as he tries to curb his anger.
"You'll meet my fists!" He yells.
Jairus is surprisingly calm when he replies, "What the fuck for mate? I haven't done anything wrong."
Austin's anger rises as he pushes Jairus again, this time to the floor.
His fists ball again, as he's about to punch him hard.
A breath hitches in my chest, knowing the power of Austin's punches.
I step over Jairus, blocking the path of Austin's impending hit.
"Don't Aust, please he didn't do anything wrong," I beg to my best friend, who at that moment is breaking my heart, his actions, so out of character, I feel like I'm looking at a different person.
"Get out of the way Anni! I don't hit girls outside the ring," he bellows at me, his words as he looks at me hitting me hard in the chest like he's actually hit me.

He pushes me aside, harshly clutching my calves.
Looking down at Jai I beg, "Get up Jai please...I'm not worth fighting over!"
"Yes, you fucking are sweetheart," he replies sitting up and clambering to his feet knocking Austin back a few steps as he stands up.
I cover my eyes, peeking out through my fingers as they start laying into each other, fists beating against each other.

Finding my voice, I scream at them to stop as Austin hits Jairus in the eye and Jairus curses, clutching a palm over his eye to suppress the pain.

"Fuck, I'm sorry man," Austin apologises, regretting his actions.

I give him dagger eyes, when I spit at him harshly, "Really Aust? You're sorry now? You could have hurt him! He had a concussion last week for fuck's sake!"

"I'm sorry Anni...I...I."

"Just leave yeah," I snap at him, shaking my head, "I don't want to look at you right now!"

Austin sheepishly walks away, his head down as he heads towards his bedroom, not daring to look back to meet my furious gaze.

Carefully I pry Jairus' hands away from his eye touching it lightly to see where it hurts, hating when he lets out a little whimper of pain.

"Well, it's definitely going to be a shiner. Are you ok?"

"Yeah sweetheart, I'll be fine, but I'm not sorry," he replies, locking his eyes on mine.

"I know, you don't have to be. I'll talk to him when we've both calmed down."

"You're not still in love with him though, Anni, are you?"

"No, I'm not. You're the only guy I want to be with now Jairus. I'm falling for you."

"Mmm, Anni sweetheart, that's music to my ears, and worth fighting Austin to hear," he replies, his tone seductive.

He kisses me, as though that will take the pain away, before he replies huskily, a little breathless, "I know I'm about to sport a black eye, but how about we go out for dinner? You know to give him some space?"

"Sounds good, can we go to Terrace?"

"Anywhere for you sweetheart, go get changed," He taunts tapping my arse cheekily as I walk off to get changed.

Forty-Four | Open Wounds

Jairus

Leaving Terrace, the look Anni is giving me is making my dick ache. I want her so bad, but I need to keep my promise to her that I won't take that step until I'm sure she loves me just as much as I love her.

Even so, it takes a hell of a lot of restraint to not pull the Stinger over and take her hard on the back seat. The only thing that stops me is the pounding of my heart, my mind kicking in, telling me 'you love her Jai, make the first time special'.

Once home though I can't help myself, pushing her against the door the moment we step inside, taking her mouth to mine in a zealous kiss. She moans, driving my desire for her higher.
I can feel the hem of her dress tenting over my aching dick like she'd done the night I'd danced with her at the club.
Again, she is grinding on me, kissing me so hard my head is spinning and pulling back my voice

comes out as barely a whisper, "Sweetheart, god please, I want you, all of you."

"I can't Jairus. I'm not ready."

"Anni, how can you say that? We've had months of foreplay."

"I'm sorry, I just can't yet."

"Ok, sweetheart, can you just hold me then?" I ask, looking at the strange look on her face.

"You don't want to be with me now, because I won't have sex with you?"

"God Anni, do you hear yourself. If sex was all I wanted from you, don't you think I'd have already fucked you?"

"I guess," she muses looking at the floor, not able to meet my eyes that are searching for an answer more than the meek reply in her eyes.

"Sweetheart, we need to talk."

Her eyes darken and she bites down on her lip, looking at me worriedly.

"Why? Don't you want me anymore?" She asks, her bottom lip quivering.

"Oh sweetheart, of course, I still want you, but we need to talk about my past because you might not want me when you know the truth."

"I doubt that Jai," she smiles, taking my hand and leading me to the bedroom.

Reaching her room, I want to stop her, but fail when she sits on the edge of the bed pulling me down with her.

"I know I said I'm not ready to sleep with you, but can we lie naked together under the covers again while we talk?"

"Mmm...sounds distracting, but undressing each other sounds like fun."

She lets out a delightful giggle, grabbing my hard dick in her hand.

"Is this for me?" she taunts, grazing her finger along the waistband of my jeans.

"You know it, sweetheart," I drawl, grabbing the hem of her short dress, smirking at her as I lift it over her head.

Dumping it on the bed next to her I grab her around the waist, pulling her close for a kiss. Moaning against my mouth she reaches down, fumbling with the button-down fly before she yanks them down my hips.

Only when they reach my knees does she break the kiss, looking at my aching crotch in my tight maroon boxers.

"Mmm," she muses licking her lips, letting out a whimper of longing as I lift my t-shirt off, throwing it on the floor behind me.

"God Anni, you're so fucking beautiful and you're mine."

"Yes, I'm yours Jairus, no matter what you tell me," she replies wrapping her arms around my neck to pull me down further onto to the bed and to her lips for a kiss so intense my heart is sent racing.

She has no idea what she does to me; the more I think about it I can't help but think I'd fallen for her the first day she sassed me back in the kitchen.

Breaking the kiss now, she is about to take her bra off, but I shake my head, "Sweetheart, we need to talk yeah, and I'm already distracted enough without you removing any more clothes."

"Ok, so let's talk then, I'm ready to listen."

"Well," I start softly, rolling off her to lie down next to her, propping myself up on an elbow and taking her hand with my other.

Lacing our fingers together, I smile, telling my mind that it's time.

"My parents um..." I whisper my chest hitching at actually saying the words I've not told anyone before, not even Sara.

Anni squeezes my hand, "What Jai? I'm here, you can tell me."

"They died in a car crash when I was ten, on my birthday."

"Oh Jai, that's horrible, I don't know what else to say," she comments brushing a hand over my cheek, wiping away the tears that drip down them.

"And that day I took you out when I got my car?"

"Yeah?"

"That was my birthday. I wanted to tell you then, but it was too perfect a day to ruin it."

"Oh Jai, you should've told me," she mused at me giving me a soft kiss.

"I know, but being with you made it the best birthday I've had in fourteen years Anni, I'm not kidding."

"Well, I'm glad Jai, but that can't be all you had to tell me?"

"No, it's not," I agree before I swallow hard, "I kind of went off the rails big time after that."

"Well, I can understand why...what happened?"

"I um...got put with a really great foster family, who gave me everything but they couldn't keep me and I lost it."

"What did you do?"

"Tried to burn down their house and trashed my school...got myself expelled."

"Oh Jai, really? Why would you do that?"

"I don't know...they were trying to be my parents; kept telling me that they loved me and I don't know it just made me angry."

"So, did you end up in another foster family?"

"Yeah, and things didn't really get better there. I stayed with them until I turned twenty-one, but I didn't get in a car again until I was eighteen and it really pissed them off."

"I can understand that, so did you do anything else horrible?"

"Got expelled again," I laugh.

"For what?"

"For hooking up with a couple of girls in the locker rooms, multiple times after footy practice."

"Jairus, you didn't," she jeers laughing as she lightly punches my abs.

"Yeah, I was a douche. I wasn't lying when I said you've changed me, Anni. I don't even want to count all the girls I've been with."

A look of pain flares in her eyes, and I mentally kick myself in the nuts for my stupid confession.

"So, why do you want to just be with me now? You could just fuck me and move on with your life?"

"Not a chance sweetheart, I'm better with you and I like having company in my life."

"But what about Sara? Weren't things better
once you got with her?"

"I thought so...fuck I thought I loved her too, but
what I felt for her doesn't even compare to what
I feel for you, Annika."

She doesn't reply, instead rolls over to push me
down and straddle me again.

"What will happen if I tell you how I feel about
you?"

"You'll have all of me sweetheart, my body, heart
and soul. I'm absolutely in love with you Annika."

"Mmm, I...um...I" she stutters.

Grabbing her hips, I pull her down to me, just a
breath away from my lips, "Don't force the
words, Annika. The fact you're still here tells me
everything I need to know."

"I...I...II.." she stutters again but stops when I
press a finger to her lips.

"What did I just say, sweetheart?"

"Don't force it," she laughs smiling cheekily.

"Exactly, can I ask you something?"

"Um...I guess so," she replies biting her bottom
lip like she always seems to do when she's
nervous.

"What's your middle name?"

"Elizabeth, what's yours Jairus Brooks?" she
taunts.

"Kingsly," I proudly reply, "It was my Dad's name."
"Oh that's awesome," she beams, pressing a kiss to my lips quickly, before her words nearly make my heart skip a beat, "I ll...like like you, Jairus Kingsly Brooks."

"Yeah I kinda gathered that, Annika Elizabeth Mathers, but I don't like like you," I tease smirking at her.
"No? Then I guess we can't kiss anymore," she teases, laughing as I start to tickle her.

"Oh, we'll be kissing, because you know that I don't just like you, I love you more than you know Annika Elizabeth Mathers."

She laughs, brushing her hair back over her shoulders, squirming as I continue to tickle her and sneakily reach around her back to unclasp her bra, loving watching as it falls down her arms to the bed.

"Whoops, how did that happen?" I laugh pinning her down on the bed to kiss her whilst I knead her bare breast in my hand.
She whimpers in pleasure, breaking the kiss and bucking her pelvis against mine.
"Say the words Annika, say the words and I'm all yours."

"I...I can't...but..."

"But what?"

"Kiss me Jairus," she moans looking down towards her lacy underwear.

"Mmm, are you asking for a kiss here?" I taunt, sliding my finger over her wet slit, her underwear so wet I lick my lips just thinking about tasting her again.

"Yes, Jairus, please give me an Aussie kiss," she begs her tone husky.

I groan, hooking my fingers in the elastic of her lacy underwear, ripping them off her.

"Sorry if you liked those, sweetheart," I laugh running my finger over her clit.

"Mmm, Jai, please..." she begs again.

I tease her more, putting the finger in my mouth to lick it clean before I kiss her mouth hard, teasing her arousal by grinding my hard dick against her.

"Are you sure you haven't got three words to say to me?"

"Um...kiss me now," she replies smirking.

"Oh, you fucking minx, sweetheart," I taunt, licking down her body slowly until I reach her arousal.

I bite her clit, licking it and I love her hot as moans.

She's so turned on I barely lick her, barely get a chance to taste her folds, before her hips buck against my face and her climax rips through her.

Lying back down next to her I tease, "I love making you cum, sweetheart, and you wanna know something?"
"I guess," she replies, her tone a little husky.

"When I make love to you, you're going to cum so hard you won't be able to stand."
"I look forward to it," she teases kissing me so hard and passionately I again have to fight the urge to give in and have her now.

Without a doubt, having sex with Annika Elizabeth Mathers will be the most amazing sex of my life.
I damn near blow my load just thinking about it.

Forty-Five | Why Him

Austin

After a tough boxing session, I think about heading out for a drink, but headaches have been plaguing me for the past week and I feel like I was coming down with some nasty flu. Opening the front door, I drop my bag by the door, hooking my keys on the key rack as I look towards the lounge room to find Anni sitting on the couch munching on salt and vinegar red rock deli chips.

"Hey Aust, you OK?" she greets me, as I sit down beside her sighing.

"Hey babe, yeah I'm OK, I guess, killer headache though."
"Are you getting sick?"
"Don't know, I've felt like I'm coming down with something for the past week."
"Aww Aust, really?"
"Yeah, can you check my head?" I ask with a childlike tone.

Leaning closer to me, the front of her singlet top falls forward, exposing her cleavage and I let out a little whimper.

When she presses her hand against my head, I hiss at how cold it is.

"Aust, you're burning up."
"Yeah, I'm freezing."

"Go to bed Aust," she demands, as she sits back down, crossing her legs.
"I um...wanted to talk to you about the other day."
"What about the other day? I'm sorry I should have thought about how you'd react seeing us together."

I reach out to touch her arm, "I'm the one who should be sorry babe...I shouldn't have reacted that way. It just hurts."
"What hurts Aust?"
"Seeing you with someone else, when I want you so bad Anni."
"Aust, I'm sorry, I don't know what to say but I don't feel that way about you now."
"Did you ever?"

"You know I did Aust," she replies meekly, her head down.
"But now, you're in love with him?"

"No...I don't know actually."

"Well he loves you, and I can't blame him for that. Any guy that gets to be with you Anni, would fall for you."

"Aust don't, OK," she protests, playfully punching my arm.

"Don't what babe?"

"Say stuff like that," she replies, her sweet insecurities about how beautiful she is surfacing again.

"Anni, you know you're gorgeous."

"Aust, stop please," she begs.

"Sorry babe, I just.. I love you and I want you to know how beautiful you are."

"Thanks, Aust, can I ask you something?"

"I guess."

"Why now? Are you only in love with me now because of Jairus?"

"I don't know babe, maybe. I think I've always loved you, but I was afraid to tell you because even though we were together, I thought it would change us. That we wouldn't be best friends anymore, you know?"

"Yeah, I get you, but you know I've always loved you, Aust, and a part of me always will, but I...."

"What babe?"

"I don't know...I'm really confused. I really love being with Jairus, but I don't know."

"You're not in love with him?"

"No...I really like him..a lot...but love, I don't know, the thought just scares me, like how could someone as gorgeous as him be in love with me."
"Come on Anni, don't be crazy!"
"I'm not Aust! I just think, why me?"
"Yeah, well I think why him, Anni? Why do you want to be with him, when I'm here and I've always loved you?"
"I don't know Aust, OK!" she snaps in reply, before turning her eyes away from me, "but being with him makes me feel like I never have before."
"Fuck Anni, that hurts. Have you fucked him?"
"No Aust, I haven't OK...he doesn't want to fuck me...and that's part of the reason I'm so confused."

"Well, he's a fucking fool, Anni, cause being in love with you only makes sex with you a hundred times hotter."
"Aust, stop," she protests again, playfully slapping my arm.

Without thinking I push her down on the couch, about to kiss her when she turns her cheek to meet my lips instead. She pushes me away, "I may not be sure of my feelings for Jairus, but I don't want to be with anyone but him Austin. We are just friends!'

Standing up, I spit at her, "Fine Annika, just friends. But I don't want to know anything that happens with you and him."
She doesn't reply as I head to my bedroom, to sleep off the headache that has only intensified from our conversation. Not only does my head hurt but my heart does too. She might not be able to admit she's in love with him, but she clearly is and I've lost her for sure. Downing a couple of ibuprofen tablets, I crawl under the covers, pulling them up over my head, feeling hot tears sting the corner of my eyes.

I feel like I'm being a pansy, crying over a girl, but Annika isn't just some random girl. She is the love of my life, and I've lost her to someone else because I was too scared to say three little words to her, until it was too late.

The only thoughts in my mind, as the tablets kicked in and I drift to sleep are, 'You're a fucking idiot Austin, you let the perfect girl go because you couldn't admit ya feelings for her'

Forty- Six | Ruby Carpet

Jairus

I've never been more nervous to attend an event in my life. It's only the second time in my life I've donned a suit, the first time being my parent's funeral and I feel a pang of sadness hit me as I fix my bowtie in the mirror.

The nerves are bubbling in my stomach too, and they intensify when I walk into Annika's room finding her in the walk-in wearing only a strapless nude coloured bra and cheeky seamless knickers.

"Is that all your wearing sweetheart?" I ask stepping up behind her and wrapping my arms around her waist, "I won't complain if it is, but well?"

Running my hands across her hips, she whimpers in pleasure, "Jai, don't touch me there, it tickles."
"Ooo sweetheart, have I found your sweet spots?" I tease, brushing my hands across the same spot again eliciting the same hot as whimper from her, as she turns in my arms.
Grabbing around my neck she pulls me down for a kiss, moaning into my mouth as I take her tongue with mine.

My dick aches, pressing against the front of my slacks against her stomach.

Just kissing her makes me ache with longing for her, and when she again grinds against me, intensifying the kiss I want to strip from my suit and take her up against the mirror behind her.

"Fuck Anni, sweetheart, I just got into this suit, you kissing me like that makes me want to strip it off and fuck you against the mirror," I taunt stepping into her personal space and slamming a fist against the mirror.
"Sorry, Jai, but I told you not to touch me there," she teases.
"I'm not sorry, I'll be touching you there again if I get a kiss like that again."
"Yeah, and I also couldn't resist you," she confesses smirking.
"You like this suit? Is it better than my birthday suit?"
Biting down on her lips, she looks me up and down before replying, "Well no...it's not better than seeing you naked but you do look pretty ripper Jai."
"I'll show you my birthday suit later then," I tease, kissing her forehead, "and sweetheart, as much as I love this outfit you need to put your dress on."
"Can you help me? It's kind of hard to zip up."

I lick my lips, as she takes the thin strapped red sequinned dress off the hanger.
As she steps into it, I watch her with a smirk on my face.

It hugs her arse and hips, dipping into a V-neck over her delectable cleavage, that her strapless bra has pushed up into two perfect mounds, that I want to bury my face in.

Brushing her long blonde hair over one shoulder, she turns to look back at me, "Zip me up please, Jai."
"Mmm, only if I can unzip this hot as dress later, sweetheart," I tease, making her giggle.
"Jai, don't tempt me."

I laugh, bending down to kiss the small of her back where the zipper starts, slowly edging it up and kissing her skin as I go, all the way up to her neck. Pressing a kiss against the soft skin under her ear, she murmurs.
"You look so fucking beautiful, sweetheart. This dress is exquisite and it matches my car and the red carpet."
"I didn't think of that, should I wear a different one?"

"No fucking way sweetheart," I reply, taking her hand and bringing it to my lips to kiss.

She only has the bare minimum of makeup on, a simple touch of blush on her cheeks, a lick of mascara on her lashes. Grabbing a clutch in her other hand she drops mine for a moment to take out lip gloss and swipe it across her lips. It smells delicious, like chocolate mint ice-cream.

"Why are you putting that on? I'm just going to kiss it off again sweetheart."

"Later yeah?"

"Definitely, so are you ready?"

"Kind of, I'm super nervous about being photographed."

"I know sweetheart but it's ok, you'll be the most beautiful girl there."

"I doubt that Jai, but... '

"To me Annika you are," I reply kissing her forehead, before opening the car door for her to slide in.

Once we arrive at Crown Casino, I park the car in the designated parking area before making our way to the red carpet.

Photographers and reporters are everywhere, and Anni takes my hand squeezing it hard in nervousness. I don't mind having her glued to my side when we walk up to a reporter who bails me up for a chat.

"Jairus, Jairus, over here!" A voice calls out, shoving a microphone in my face.

"Is this your girlfriend? She looks stunning tonight."

"No, but hopefully she will be soon," I reply to the reporter, winking at Anni who's pressed against my side.

"So, no red carpet kiss then?" the reporter asks, smirking at me and looking Anni up and down.

"I didn't say that," I laugh, turning to kiss Anni sweetly.

"So, you saw it here first," the reporter starts looking at the camera, "Jai the man is officially off the market again, right?"
"You'll have to ask this beautiful girl," I drawl, picking up her hand and kissing it.

Anni blushes but doesn't say anything and the reporter turns his attention back to me.

"So Jairus, you're a hot contender for the Brownlow medal...how are you feeling?"
"Super nervous," I respond, squeezing Anni's hand, "but I've just tried to play my best game."
"Yeah, well good luck you've definitely had quite the year."
"Thanks," I reply, smiling as I led Anni inside.
As we weave through the array of tables I whisper in her ear, "Sorry about the kiss sweetheart."
"It's ok, I was just a bit shocked that's all."
"I know I'm sorry, I should have warned you something like that might happen."
"Do you think you've got a chance of winning?" she asks sweetly.
"I don't know...maybe."
"You deserve it, Jai."

Finding our seats, Travis is already seated, sipping on a beer. He hasn't brought a date and I'm a little shocked. I thought he'd have at least invited Dana to come along as they seemed to get along in the bedroom and they looked good together.

Sitting down next to him, after sliding Anni's chair out for her to sit down I ask, "Why'd you not bring a date?"

"No one to bring my man, but your girl looks beautiful."

"Yeah," I reply kissing her forehead, "she's the most stunning girl here."

Anni blushes and rubs a hand up and down my thigh, under the table.

"How's her friend?"

"Single I think, but to be honest she's probably still with her guy. Why you still lusting after her?"

"Yeah, you've seen her? You get what I'm talking about," he laughs taking another gulp of his beer.

"Yeah, I should have asked Anni to bring her along for you."

"All good man, another time," he muses, downing the last of his beer.

We sit through dinner, having a few drinks to wash the food down, food that should be illegal to eat because it's so fancy.

"You ok sweetheart? You've been quiet."

"Yeah, I'm fine. I just feel so out of place here."

"I know, but it means so much that you're here with me."

"I know, Jai."

The announcer is going through each round, and I know he's said my name a number of times, but from the alcohol, my head is spinning a little and I can't add up how many votes I've received.

Anni takes my hand. "Jai, baby, they are about to announce the winner."
"Sorry, what? Really?" I reply looking at her and brushing a stray hair from her cheek.
"Yeah," she laughs.
"Did you just call me baby?"
"Yeah, I did," she blushes, turning away from me shyly.

I turn my focus back to the stage hearing the final votes were being announced, before the words "I declare the winner of the 2017 Brownlow medal, Jairus Brooks of the Richmond Football Club."

Standing up, I make my way to the stage, accepting the congratulations and handshakes before I step up onto the stage to receive the medal around my neck. Looking out at the crowd, I smile wide as all the official speeches are made before they ask me to say a few words.

"Thanks for all the votes, this year has been a whirlwind and an amazing start to my career. I'd like to thank the beautiful girl I brought here with me tonight, Annika, without her support this year, I'd not have been able to play my best game and Travis my man, you've been like the brother I've never had and I've loved every minute of playing this great game with you. I love you both! Thanks again all, this is such an honour!"

As I step off the stage, applause erupts as the highlights of my year play on the big screen above the stage. Running back to the table, I wrap my arms around Anni as she stands up to congratulate me.

"I love you, Annika, I couldn't have gotten through this year without you.'
"I..." she stutters, but I don't let her say the words, instead I capture her mouth in a passionate kiss.

There isn't much more that would make my year complete, the grand final is looming and we have a good chance of winning.
I have some thoughts in my mind about other ways to make the year complete and the most important one is to do with the most beautiful woman who is kissing me back, right here in a crowded room like there is no one else here.
I never want to let her go.

Caz May

Forty- Seven | Final Play

Jairus

Glancing up at the scoreboard, my heart is pounding hard in my chest. There are only fifteen minutes left in the last quarter of the grand final.

Part of me is elated to be playing in a Grand final as a rookie, I'm riding the coattails of my Brownlow win as well, but the other part is panicking at how close the score is.

There is a goal between the Crows and us, six points down and I want to win more than anything.

To end my first year in the Australian Football League with a bang!

Snatching the ball from the centre bounce, I run before kicking it to Trav who sets it up for me to perfectly mark the ball just outside our goals.

It's an easy kick, but still, as I kick it I see the ball veer to the left and hit the post for a point.

Cursing I shake myself back to reality, looking back towards Travis who is intercepting the ball from the Crows outside their fifty.

The time is dwindling and my panic is increasing.

I want this so bad, so I run outside the fifty into a
swarm of Richmond players, one being Travis who I
signal to pass to me.
Nodding at me, he hand-balls the ball towards me
and I grab it easily in my grasp.

Bouncing it front of me, I run inside the fifty, telling
myself to breathe, to focus on the goals and nothing
else.
I don't dare look at the scoreboard, as I kick the ball,
hurling it towards the goal posts.

Closing my eyes, time stops the moment it leaves my
foot.
I hear the applause, cheers erupting around me, I
feel my teammates slapping me on the back in
encouragement. I know I've kicked a goal then, and
my stomach flip-flops as the siren sounds.

Opening my eyes, I see Travis step up to hug me,
"Fuck Jai, you did it man!"
"I what?" I stammer, shocked at his words, even
though I know exactly what he means.

"You kicked the game-winning goal man!"
"Oh yeah," I laugh, as Anni runs straight up to me,
jumping over the barrier and into my arms.

Kissing me, she nearly squeaks, "I...L...wow Jai that
was amazing! Congratulations!"

Putting her down, I kiss her forehead, "Thanks sweetheart, I can't believe it. I gotta go down to the rooms with the team before the trophy's presented. I'll see you after."

I watch her as she goes back to Bella and Austin who came out for the grand final, to sit with her and cheer us on.
I'm still absolutely overwhelmed as we head towards the rooms.

After singing the club song, dousing ourselves in celebratory champagne, Trav pulls me aside before we head back out, "Have you slept with her yet man?"
"To be honest, no, " I reply.
"Why man? You should totally tap that! I'm surprised you didn't after the Brownlow win."
"Trav man please. I'm in love with her man and I don't know, she won't let me take that step with her."
"She's a virgin then man," he suggests puffing his chest out.
"Oh, no man, I know for a fact that's not the case," I reply shaking my head.
"How so man?"
"The night I met her...I caught her fucking our roommate."

"Oh, shit man...is that still going on then?"
"I don't think so...well I hope it's not. It'd break my fucking heart."

"Hmm...well I don't know man... a guys got needs...love aside if she doesn't put out completely."
"Trav man I can't believe you. It's not all about sex."
"Sorry man...I shouldn't have said that...if it's even possible since she's been here supporting you, you've played better and I don't think we would have won the fucking grand final without you."
"Yeah, I still can't believe it! We are the 2017 AFL premiers!"

We high five, following our teammates back out onto the ground with the club song blaring through the speakers as we cross the ground onto

the stage to be presented with our premiership medals and the trophy.
It all passes by in a blur, and as I get my medal around my neck, I kiss it, holding it up as I blow a kiss to Anni who's excitedly jumping up and down in the crowd like she's floating on the same air I am.

God, I love her so fucking much, I should make things official in every way

Caz May

Forty-Eight | Inky Hearts

Jairus

Since our premiership win, things quietened down a bit.
The team trip to Hong Kong is around the corner and I'm both excited and scared out of my wits to head overseas.
I've only ever lived in Melbourne and didn't have the type of upbringing after my parent's death to see much of Australia, so leaving the country is a big deal.

It's the first really nice warm day we've had in months and I decided it's the day to get a permanent reminder of the success I've achieved.

"Anni, sweetheart are you ready to go?" I ask, knocking on her closed bedroom door.
She opens it to me immediately, smiling wide when she replies, "Yep, but you haven't told me where we are going?"
"Somewhere special."
"That doesn't tell me anything baby," she taunts at me, her high ponytail shaking from side to side.
She's wearing her tight as skinny jeans again, with a tight V-neck t-shirt that outlines the delectable

curves that she always likes to tell me she doesn't have.
My mind wanders back to the last time she wore those jeans, and I want to delay our leaving by dakking her to give her the same dirty pleasure again.

"I love those jeans, sweetheart," I drawl at her, grabbing her butt and squeezing it.
"Jai, stop," she begs in a teasing tone that tells me she doesn't want me to stop in the slightest.
Leaning closer I press my forehead against hers, "You know I love teasing you, sweetheart."
She tries to kiss me, but I pull back and take her hand, leading her out to the car.
"You can kiss me later,' I jeer, "if we don't go now, we'll be late."

In the car, driving down Bridge road she cranks the stereo volume up to fifteen when *I like me better* by Lauv comes on the radio.
She's singing at the top of her lungs, her infectious smile pulling me under with a rush of love for her.
When I met her five months ago, she was so sweet and shy around me, but now her inhibitions
have fallen away and it's uncanny how the song sums up how I feel about her.

Sliding into the carpark out the front of our destination, turning the stereo down as I announce, "We're here."
"And where is here exactly?" she asks glancing up and down the street through the front windscreen.

Pointing straight ahead at the Tattoo parlour, I declare, "There."

"Huh? We are going to the tattoo parlour?"

"Yes, I'm getting a premiership tattoo and I want you to help me choose what to get and where to put it."

She takes a deep breath, blurting out innocently "Where to put it? Um."

I laugh at her comment, "Sweetheart, I'm not going to get a tiger on my arse unless you think I should?"

She slaps my arm playfully laughing. "Jai, don't."

"What? Do you mean don't get a tiger tattoo on my arse?"

"Don't tease me," she snaps, getting out of the car. Taking her hand to walk inside I whisper in her ear, "Sorry sweetheart, but I'm sold. I'm getting a growling tiger tat on my arse."

Inside the parlour, we are greeted by a punk looking girl covered almost head to toe in tattoos herself, with multiple piercings.

"Hey, so which one of you is getting a tattoo today? Anni points at me, blushing when I reply, "Me, on my arse and lower back."

"Nice, man," the punk girl replies, eyeing me up and down, before blurting out, "You're Jairus Brooks yeah?"

"Yeah Jai the man," I laugh, "and you're?"

"Aisha...so I'm guessing your um, here for a premiership tattoo then?"

"Yep and this beauty convinced me to get it on my arse," I jeer slapping my own arse and lower back with my palm.

"Right, so what were you thinking of?" she gulps, glancing over my body again, knowing that I'll have to be practically, almost completely naked to get the tattoo where I want it.

"I was hoping for a growling tiger, his claws leaving scratch marks on my arse cheek and then above his head on my lower back the words 'Richmond Tigers Premiers 2017'."

"Oh fuck, that sounds um..." she bites her lip, "super hot. You'll um have to strip down to your underwear though."

"All good," I wink at Anni who has decided to clutch my hand in hers like she's declaring a claim on me.

"So, um, just give me a minute to draw something up for you and we can get started."

"No worries," I reply, turning to Anni as Aisha walks away.

"You good sweetheart?"

"She's...she's...going to...see...you naked Jai," she stammers, not able to look at me.

"Sweetheart, it's part of her job. She'd see a lot of naked bodies."

"But Jai," she protests, "are you forgetting who you are? She recognised you."

"Yes, that's true, but most of the players on the team who have tatts have been here Anni, and they are highly professional."

"Fine, but I don't like the way she looked at you either," she spits at me, a sweet blush on her cheeks.
"And how was that sweetheart?"
"Like she wanted you."
"Is someone jealous sweetheart?" I taunt, smirking at her.

"No!" she protests folding her arms across her chest defiantly.
"Sweetheart, you don't need to be jealous. You know I love you."

She huffs at me, locking her eyes on mine as Aisha comes back into the room.
"Show her then baby," she taunts, her arms dropping down to her sides, her tongue darting out of her mouth and across her lips.

Growling I kiss my Anni hard, forgetting for a moment that we have an audience.
"Um sorry to interrupt your pash, but what do you think?" Aisha asks holding up a drawing that is beyond what I pictured in my mind.
"It's perfect," I beam.

"Great, so I'll get the colours and needles sorted if you want to slip behind the curtain there to strip down to your underwear."

I follow her instructions, waiting until she's left the room to pull Anni behind the curtain with me.

"So, sweetheart, tell me again where you want me to get this tat?"

She stretches up to whisper in my ear, "On your hot arse, baby."

"Fuck Annika," I growl, kissing her hard again, biting her lip and moaning as she gives me entrance to her delectable mouth.

Her hands grab my arse, still kissing me as she daks me, pushing my Nike trackies to the floor.

Our lips part and I scramble to lift my t-shirt over my head.

Trailing kisses down her neck, she moans pushing her body against mine.

Pulling back, I groan, 'Sweetheart, fuck, we need to stop or I'm getting a tatt with a fucking hard on."

"Sorry baby," she replies, blushing.

"Don't be sweetheart, you just turn me on so bad. You know I can crack a fat from just looking at you."

"Jai," she protests in her sweet innocent way.

"So, sweetheart before I go out there, can you kiss where I'm getting the tatt? Just so I'm sure of exactly where you want it," I tease, smirking at her as I turn around.

Grabbing the elastic cf my boxers, she edges them down my right arse cheek.

Bending down, she presses her soft lips against my skin, licking a small circle before she stands up.

"Mmm," I moan.

"I want the claws where I licked your skin, baby," she teases.

"Anything for you sweetheart," I reply as Aisha calls out that she's ready to start.

~~

I'm straddling a chair, with my back facing Aisha. My boxers are halfway down my right arse cheek and I hiss every time a needle pierces my skin.

Anni is watching, intrigued, her eyes locked on mine as I bite down on my lip to not yelp in pain when Aisha starts doing the words across the bony part of my lower back.

Feeling the coolness of the cream on my skin as Aisha spreads a coat over my finished tattoo covering it up with paper towel, I let out a deep exasperated sigh.

Anni's smiling at me, so I ask, "Do you want a matching one sweetheart?"

Her reply is meek, as she bites down on her lip, "No, but I kinda want one."

Aisha gets me to stand up, using the chair to steady myself, "Then do it...get something that means a lot to you," I suggest.

"You think I should, does it hurt?"

"Yeah, sweetheart it does."

She bites her lip again and looks at Aisha.

"I can do a simple one for you right now, with the leftover colours. What would you like?"

"Um, maybe my brother's name in a heart underneath my breast. Will it hurt there?"

"Yeah, but I can numb it a bit first. Would you like to go ahead?"

I take her hand, "Do it, sweetheart, you won't regret it."

"Ok, so his name is Alex and I want his name to be the outside of the heart with the A in red and the rest in black. Is that ok?"

"No worries, just give me a minute. Just take off your t-shirt and take a seat."

Helping her lift her t-shirt off, I kiss her cheek, down her neck and over her breast before pressing a final kiss where she's about to have her ink virginity taken.

Aisha comes back and quickly gets to work.
It's a simple design but it looks amazing, and Anni's a trooper, grinning through the pain and squeezing my hand only a few times when she winces at a particularly tender spot.

After a final wipe over Aisha covers it with cream and puts a cover over it. Quickly I sneak back behind the curtain to get dressed before taking her hand and leading her out, Aisha hands me an instruction of care leaflet before I pay for both.

Walking outside holding hands, I look at Anni,
"Sweetheart that looks really great...does it hurt?"

"Like a bitch," she laughs.

"Yeah but so worth it, yeah?"

"Definitely! Jai, can I ask you something?"

"Yeah anything," I reply as we step up to the car.

"What's the meaning behind your to the blue sky and back tattoo?"

"It's something my mum said to me...."
"Yeah?"
"She used to say I love you to the blue sky and back,"
I muse, my breath catching in my chest hearing my
mum's voice in my head.

"Aww Jai, baby...that's beautiful."
"Yeah...and so are you sweetheart," I drawl, her legs
crashing against the car.
"Jai...please," she protests, her tone like she's telling
me off but begging me for a kiss at the same time.
"You are beautiful, Annika," I moan, not letting her
reply, as I push her back against the hood of the car
kissing her passionately, not caring that people are
walking past until I hear a familiar voice behind me.

Forty-Nine I Come Back

Jairus

"Jairus is that you?" the voice asks, her words making my thoughts fuzzy as I tear my lips from Anni's.

Fuck!

"Yeah," I reply, standing up and turning to face her when I continue with malice in my tone, "Sara, what are you doing here?"
"Um...just going shopping and was hoping I'd run into you actually," Sara coos, fluttering her eyelashes at me.

I grab Anni's hand, squeezing it, as she leans into my side a little glaring at Sara like she's going to pounce on her.

"Why is that?" I ask, dreading her answer.
"Well, I was actually going to come by yours....we um need to talk."
"Really, I thought we talked about everything months ago Sara ...you know when we broke up."
"Well...um...not really," she stammers, scuffling her feet on the footpath.

"What then Sara? What else do you have to say to me?"

"I'm...I'm.." she stammers, angering me a little.

"Come on Sara, out with it for fuck's sake."

"I'm...I'm pregnant Jairus...and it's yours."

Hearing the words from Sara's mouth Anni snatches her hand away from mine, sliding down the side of the car and yanking the door open.

Getting in she crosses her arms over her chest and stares at us through the window with an angry look in her eyes.

"Mine! Seriously Sara...you don't even look pregnant, at all, let alone what, five or so months pregnant."

"Well, I'm carrying well," she interjects like that is all the explanation I need.

"Yeah ok, whatever," I snap, about to leave.

"Are you with her now?" she points at Annika as she speaks.

"Her name is Annika and yes I am."

"Oh...do you love her?"

"Yes, Sara, I do love her."

"Oh cause I...um...kind of wanted to get back together."

"What seriously?" I snap, running a hand through my hair, "You think you can just turn up after nearly six months telling me you're pregnant and I'll just take you back no questions asked."

"Um..." she mutters, her head down.

"You're crazy Sara! Seriously just fuck off out of my life! I don't believe you for a second that you're having my baby!" I yell at her.

"I am Jairus...please believe me," she begs stepping closer to me.

"Sorry, Sara I can't. You'll have to do a paternity test before you get a cent out of me," I inform her as the thought crosses my mind that she's playing me for money.

"That's really cruel Jairus," she accuses, waving her hands frantically.

"Might be Sara, but you broke my heart and proved that I can't trust a word that comes out of your mouth so you leave me with no choice."

"Um...ok..." she replies, meekly kissing me on the cheek.

Pushing her away I snap, "Don't Sara! I don't want Anni getting the wrong idea."

"Ok well...bye Jairus. It was good to see you. Congrats on the Brownlow and premiership," she bleats out feigning sincerity.

I scoff, before going around to get in the driver's side and gunning the car away.

I can't deny the thought of mounting the curb and running Sara down doesn't cross my mind, but jail isn't somewhere I want to go and even though I dislike her I don't want her dead, especially from a car accident I caused.

Putting a hand on Anni's knee, I try to comfort her but she pushes it away.

"Don't Jairus," she snaps at me angrily.

"I'm sorry sweetheart, but she's lying."

"Really? Why would she lie about that? She can't be more than three months along Jairus. She's not showing at all."

"Exactly Annika," I snap back, hating that my words sound so callous.

"What's that mean Jairus? Did you sleep with her whilst you were making moves on me?"

"No, I didn't! How the fuck could you even think that?"

"Once a player, always a player!"

"Oh, for fuck's sake Annika. I love you! I'm not nor have I been with anyone but you for months."

"Yeah seems like three months..." she implies.

"Yeah, it might seem like that but the last time I slept with Sara was about five months ago before anything happened between us."

"Whatever Jairus! Don't fucking talk to me!"

Arriving home, we don't say another word to each other, going inside and straight to our bedrooms slamming the doors behind us.

Flopping down on my stomach on my bed Sara's words tumble in my head.

I know they aren't true and a wretched feeling is bubbling in my stomach having had my first fight with Anni.

It makes my heart ache and I'm afraid that it's the beginning of the end before I really got to be with

her and show her with my whole body and heart
how much I love her.

Fifty | Flying Out

Jairus

Walking through Tullamarine airport with my suitcase at my heels I'm feeling a mix of emotions. Nervous, anxious but mainly heartbroken.
I've barely even seen Anni, let alone spoken to her since our fight after Sara's announcement.

Nearly every word that had come out of Anni's mouth since then had stabbed at my wounded heart, words that weren't like her sweet shy self.
I'd tried to make amends, sneaking into her bedroom one night but in her half-asleep daze she snapped 'fuck off Jairus' and it literally was like a knife in my heart.
The way she'd started to call me 'baby' made my heart pound, just as it did when she called me Jai.
So, her using my full name was a deliberate dig at me and it hurt like hell.

Travis is following behind, slapping me on the back as I hand my passport over to the woman behind the check-in counter.
"You alright man?" he asks, concern in his tone.
"Not really, but nothing I can do about it now," I reply, taking my passport and boarding pass and hoisting my suitcase up to be weighed.

"Tell me, man, I've never seen you so fucked up," he informs me, as the check-in counter woman gives him a scornful look for his language.

After we've both completed the check-in process, along with the rest of our teammates we head towards customs.

"Jai, tell me what's going on man?"

"Well, the day I went to get the premiership tatt done with Anni, we um...ran into Sara after."

"Sara, your ex, yeah?"

"Yeah, and she told me she is pregnant with my kid."

"What? She's preggo?"

"Apparently, but I don't know and if she is, I don't think it's mine."

"Why's that? You were rooting her yeah?"

"Yeah, but she wasn't even close to showing and I last slept with her like five months ago, nearly six before I got with Anni, so it just doesn't add up."

Travis is shaking his head, his mouth upturned in the corner like he's thinking about what to say.

We have to zip our mouths for a bit as we pass through the passport gates to head towards customs and the scanners.

Panic rushes through me, as I put all my belongings on the tray and walk through the detector.

Travis follows and once through he sighs in relief.

"I hate going through that shit," he laughs, "So you think Sara is lying?"

"Yeah, she did cheat on me before we broke up, so I have a feeling it might have been going on for a while and maybe he dumped her arse too."

"You could do a paternity test, if and when the kid is born?"

"Yeah, I told her that," I confirm, sitting down at a table in the terminal food court.

"So Jai, this doesn't tell me why you're so down, man?"

"Well, Anni and I weren't exactly together, but we had a fight about it and she's not... "

I sigh, pushing my elbows into the table in front of me, covering my face with my hands.

"What Jai?"

"She has barely spoken a word to me since, and I fucking miss her so bad."

"Fuck man, that's shit. Did you tell her that you thought it wasn't yours?"

"What do you think Trav? She's training to be a nurse, so she didn't exactly believe me given the fact that Sara doesn't even look pregnant."

"Oh, right yeah, I forgot that. Well, I don't know man, you need to just suck it up and enjoy the trip."

"Yeah, I guess," I muse, as a couple of other teammates sit with us.

"You're technically a free man Jai. Forget about Anni, and find some hot ex-pat to root."

"Seriously Trav, I love you man, but you've got to stop thinking with ya knob."

He laughs, a deep belly laugh as the announcement for our flight reverberates through the terminal. Standing up I sling my bag over my shoulder, heading towards the gate with even more emotions running through my body.

I'm about to board a plane to fly nine hours away, overseas and my best friend is being a completely unsupportive dickhead, shrugging off my feelings like Anni is just some random hook up.

Reaching the gate, we board the plane and we're shown to our seats in business class by a pretty young flight attendant.
As Travis sits next to me, after we put our bags in the overhead storage he elbows me, "She's a looker, you should join the mile high club."
"No thanks Trav, I'm just going to try and get some sleep."
"God Jai, you're so whipped, man. When we get home, I'm going to make sure you get ya girl back, because you're a fucking sad sack of shit without her."

"Yeah, you got that right," I confirm, settling into my seat and closing my eyes.

Two weeks away from Anni is going to be torturous. Slipping my hand in my pocket to grab my phone to text her I have a momentary panic, jumping up in my seat.
"Jai, sit the fuck down man, we're about to take off."

Caz May

"I don't have my phone, I...I can't text her."
"That might be a good thing, man."
Stifling a scream of frustration, I sit back down,
buckling my seatbelt as the plane starts moving away
from the gate to take me to two weeks of hell in
Hong Kong.

Fifty-One | Break Me

It has been a few weeks since my fight with Jairus, on the way back from the tattoo parlour. My tattoo has healed up nicely, and I can't help but admire it every time I look at myself naked in the mirror.

I feel a little guilty that Jairus has opened up about this past to me, letting me in and I've not even mentioned Alex to him at all. He didn't question why I got his name as a heart for a tattoo, and I didn't even get the chance to tell him before his crazy ex decided to show up with the worst news ever.

Even though we've barely spoken and I was a complete bitch to him, I have to admit I'm missing him whilst he's away. He's not even sent me a text the whole time.

I know he's due back sometime in the next day or so, but I have no idea what I'm going to do or say when he's back. It was stupid to have pushed him away, without letting him explain.

I just not sure if I believe him that he hasn't been with her. But the real reason I feel wretched from pushing him away is that I miss being with him, miss how his kisses and touch make me feel.

For the past week, I've been moping around the house, in my Peter Alexander 'My Little Pony' pyjama pants, because they were the ones I was wearing when Jairus first tried to kiss me.

I want to remember the giddy feeling I felt that day.

I'm trying to focus on my revisions for the upcoming exams, but I might as well be staring at a brick wall as nothing is going in.
Sitting on the couch I'm surrounded by textbooks, open to pages that I know have stuff on them that is important, but it all looks jumbled and blurry.

Tears have started to fall down my cheeks, and I inhale a deep breath breaking down into sobs, when I hear the crash of Austin closing the door behind him as he arrives home.
He looks at me on the couch, asking, "What's wrong babe?"
"Everything Aust," I declare, huffing.

"It can't be that bad babe," he muses, sitting on the end of the chaise.
"It is...I pushed him away and I'm gonna fail my exams and he's going to get back with his ex," I blurt out, not even taking a breath.
"What? What are you talking about Anni?"
"Jairus, his ex-girlfriend is pregnant with his kid...and he's probably going to get back with her," I inform Austin, wiping my bare arm across my teary eyes.
"Anni, slow down...breathe," he suggests calmly.

"Didn't you hear me Austin? He's going to get back with her...he lied to me...used me."

"Annika that's not true," he speculates like he isn't sure of his own words.

"How do you know that Austin?"

"Because it's obvious that he's so totally fucking in love with you!"

"Whatever, it was all lies Austin! You're the only one who's ever loved me."

"Well, yeah, I do love you Anni but I know you don't love me back. Believe me I'm trying to move on."

"Really?"

"Yes, really Anni, you're in love with Jairus, just admit it to yourself and him when he gets home," he suggests, a smile at the corner of his mouth.

"I can't Austin...he broke me, he broke us before we even got a chance to be together."

"Is his ex really pregnant or was she just trying to get back with him to ride his coattails?"

"I don't fucking know Austin!" I spit at him, glaring at him like I'm asking 'are you stupid?'

"Maybe you should find out and just face your feelings, Anni. I hate seeing you like this."

He leans forward brushing a stray hair from my cheek, murmuring, "God Anni, I really wish you loved me back."

"I...I do love you Aust but I..."

"Love Jairus more?" He states, more like a question.

"No differently," I respond sniffing the tears back.

"Yeah so um...how's the studying going?"
"Shit, I'm gonna fail Aust. I know I am."
"I'll help you tomorrow but I think you need to head to bed."

I let out an audible grunt at the thought of moving from the couch, "Can't be fucked, too much effort."

He doesn't reply, instead grabs me around the waist, throwing me over his shoulder as he heads down the hallway towards my bedroom.
"Aust put me down!" I screech, beating my fists against his hard chest.
"Nope, I'm putting you to bed!"

After he carries me to bed, he gently throws me on top of the unmade sheets before tucking me in. Snuggling into the sheets, just as he's about to leave I mumble, "Aust, can you sleep in here with me tonight?"
"Babe, I don't think that's a good idea."

"Please Aust," I beg, grabbing his hand and pulling him down so he's sitting on the edge of the bed at my feet.

He looks down at me, smiling before he lies down against my back. Snuggling up close to me he murmurs as he closes his eyes.

Closing my own tired eyes my mind wanders to thoughts of Jairus and I can't help but wonder if he's thinking about me too.

Fifty-Two | Malice Undone

The sun has been up for hours, it nearing lunch time when I finally wake up bleary-eyed from crying in my sleep.
I'd gone to sleep thinking about Jairus; thinking not only about being with him but also about the guilt of not telling him about my past and Alex's death.

My dreams or nightmares more so were plagued by that day, the day my world was shattered by an odd text message from Alex and then the subsequent news from the police in Melbourne about his death.

Even now dreaming or thinking about it brings tears to my eyes. Stumbling out of bed to the kitchen I decide to make pancakes for brunch. They were always Alex's favourite breakfast food and starting to make them my mind drifts.

Hoisting myself up I sat on the island bench in the kitchen, laughing at my older brother who was mixing the gooey mixture in the bowl he was clutching against his chest with the biggest wooden spoon I'd ever seen.

"Al, you're gonna spill it, Mum will crack it."
"I'm not going to spill it An," he told me lifting the spoon up and letting the pancake mixture drip off it.

"Al! Stop! You'll get it everywhere!"

"The only place it's going is in my belly," he laughed, putting the bowl down next to me and rubbing his stomach.

He stepped closer to me, "An, can you get out the strawberries and the Nutella?"
"Really, I can help you?"
"Yeah, little sis, and then we can surprise Mum and Dad with breakfast in bed."

Excitedly I jumped off the bench, grabbing the ingredients Alex asked for.
Holding them up to him proudly, he ruffled my hair when he replied, "Put them on the bench, and you can help me plate up when the pancakes are ready, OK?"
"OK Al," I beamed, loving how he made me feel included.

"I love you An, you're the best little sister ever!"
"Love you more, Al."

Wiping the tears from my cheeks, I hear Austin behind me, his feet shuffling on the floorboards as he enters the kitchen.
"Babe, are you crying?"
"No, I'm not, I'm f..fine," I sniff, pouring the batter into the pan.
"Anni, are you making pancakes?"
"Yeah, do you want some?"

"Of course, but were you thinking about Alex? You only ever make pancakes when you've been dreaming about Alex's death."

Sniffing I reply, "Yeah, all night Aust."
"Awww babe, I'm sorry," he muses, crossing the room to hug me, holding me close in his embrace.

We stand there for what seems like ages when a loud vibrating and trill sound fills the room, causing us to jump apart in shock.
"Is that your phone Aust?"
"No, is it yours?"
"No mine is charging in the bedroom."

Plugged in the power point next to the kettle is a phone. Glancing at the screen as it vibrates, the name and picture on the screen makes my heart lurch in my chest.

Picking it up and realising it's Jairus' phone, I wonder why I haven't noticed it on the bench for the past two weeks. Sara is calling non-stop, as the screen is full of missed calls from her.

Picking it up as it rings again, I hold it up to Austin, showing him who is calling.

"Answer it, tell her where to go," he laughs.
"No way Aust! I'm not doing that, maybe she'll text."

Putting it down I proceed to finish the pancakes,
pouring another round of batter into the frying pan
and watching it bubble up.

Austin gets out the strawberries and Nutella as I'm
cooking. Smiling at him, as I flip the last pancake on
the plate, I tell him, "Aust you know me too well."
"You're still my best friend Anni," he reminds me.
I don't reply, instead pull up a stool at the breakfast
bar. I've only gulped down one mouthful when I hear
Jairus' phone ping from across the kitchen.
Austin gives me a knowing smirk as I jump off the
stool to grab it.

There is a text from Sara lighting up the screen.
Sara: Jairus are you there?
Austin laughs when I hold it up to him, "Text back,
pretending to be him," he suggests.
"What if he has a passcode?"
"Just try Anni."

Swiping my finger across the screen, a passcode
screen hinders me.
Thinking for a moment, I try to work out what it
would be.
Hesitantly, hoping I'm right, I type 6, 10, 13.

The message from Sara pops up in the message app,
making me squeal.
"What?" Austin asks, laughing.

"I guessed his passcode," I confirm, holding the phone up to him again.

"You've got it bad, babe," he laughs, "you know him better than you think you do."
"Yeah," I muse, reading the message again before I reply.

Jairus: Yes Sara I'm here. What do you want now?

I hold the phone up to Austin, "Is that good? Should I send it?"
He gives me a thumbs up, his mouth full of pancakes.

Pressing send I wait for her reply, which is almost instant.
My heart is galloping in my chest. I feel so guilty but I can't help myself.

Sara: to say I'm sorry
Jairus: for what? Ruining my life?
Sara: no...well..um
Jairus: what kinda answer it that?
Sara: I lied to you
Jairus: wtf
Sara: yes I lied
Jairus: So are you pregnant or not Sara?
Sara: yes I am, but I only just found out like a week ago and I'm only six weeks along
Jairus: so the kid isn't mine?
Sara: no

Jairus: who's is it then?
Sara: the guy I told you about at school
Jairus: were you cheating on me with him Sara?
Sara: yes and I'm sorry Jairus...I never meant to hurt you
Jairus: yeah well you did
Sara: I'm sorry...I meant it that I want you back
Jairus: why?
Sara: he broke it off when he found out I was pregnant
Jairus: oh...well you broke my relationship too...so you can fuck off

Austin snatches the phone to see what I'm frantically typing, and laughs at me, "Anni, you can't write that!"
"I just did," I laugh pressing send.

Sara doesn't reply again.
"Are you going to tell Jairus when he gets home?"
"Yeah, I feel no malice now."
"Yeah, I can't believe his ex is such a bitch."
Laughing I reply, "She's one of those stuck up, to pretty for my own good types."
"What does that mean Anni?"

"I don't know," I laugh realising my words sound stupid.
"Show me a pic of her."
"Why Aust?"
"I don't know, I just wanna see what she looks like."

"Fine," I snap, opening up Instagram on Jairus' phone and scrolling through his posts until I find the ones of them together.

Austin looks at the pictures, and the corner of his mouth turns up in a scowl.
"Well, um...I guess she's kinda pretty..but not as pretty as you babe."

Playfully I slap his arm, "Aust, don't say that!"
"You know it's true babe," he muses, leaning closer to me.

He presses his forehead to mine, whispering, "I'll always love you, Annika."

His breath is warm on my face, and I know he's about to kiss me.
My heart is pounding, and my mind is racing.
 I don't want Austin to kiss me, I want Jairus to kiss me and as I'm about to pull back from Austin the front door squeaks as it opens.
Austin's kiss meets my cheek, as I stumble getting off the stool.
"Austin, don't!" I screech at him, pushing my hands into his chest.
His stool wobbles and he grabs hold of the bench to steady himself, when he taunts, "Look who's back Anni...see if he still loves you when he finds out what you just did."

Jairus has crossed the room, entering the kitchen just
as Austin finishes the last sentence. I don't say a
word to Austin, as he stands up brushing past me,
running a finger up my arm as he whispers in my ear,
"Tell him, Anni."

Leaving the room, he glares at Jairus who looks a
little dumbstruck.
"Tell me what sweetheart?"
I don't say anything again, a little lost for words that
he's still calling me 'sweetheart'.

Picking up his phone, I shove it against his chest, and
he grabs it as I turn to walk away.
He laughs, "I can't believe I left this here," he
announces, putting it down on the table, and
grabbing my arm to pull me back to him.

I'm still angry at him, even though I don't know why
and I want to pull away but I can't move as his arms
envelope me like he never wants to let me go.

Leaning in, his forehead against mine, his breath in
my face, he taunts, "Did you miss me, sweetheart?"
I let out a little whimper, feeling a rush of warmth run
through my body at having him so close again.
"I missed you, sweetheart. So fucking bad."

He's still staring at me, not moving, and not trying to
kiss me, as though he's waiting for my reply.

Taking a deep breath, I step back and exhale telling him, "I did something bad."
"Bad? Is that what Austin was meaning? Did something happen with you guys?"
"Um...well um..."

"Anni, tell me! I've been in another fucking country for two weeks missing you. At least tell me if you haven't been missing me too."
"I've missed you Jai, but I..."
"What Annika?" he bellows, slamming his fist on the bench.
"Check your phone," I suggest, picking it up and handing it to him again.
"What do you mean? Check my phone?"
"Just check your messages."
I watch as his fingers glide over the screen, and his eyes focus on the text messages I sent to Sara.
He laughs putting his phone down.
"Aren't you mad at me?"
"No, why would I be mad at you."
"Because I guessed your passcode and pretended to be you."

Again he laughs, and leans towards me kissing my forehead, "You made her confess that she was lying all along, just to get at me and telling her to fuck off like that was genius sweetheart."
"So, you're really not mad? You don't hate me?"
"Sweetheart I could never hate you," he muses, smiling at me.
"I'm sure you could."

"Well, maybe," he sniggers, "if something else happened with Austin other than him about to kiss you when I walked in?"

"Well...he slept in my bed last night," I tell him, biting down on my lip.

"And?"

"And nothing...we just slept. I don't want to be with him like that anymore.'

"I'm glad to hear that, so glad sweetheart. What did you get up to whilst I was gone then?" he asks, looking at 'My Little Pony' pyjama pants with a wicked grin.

"Just moped around, wearing these," I reply, grabbing a fist full of the fabric in my hand, "whilst I tried to study for my exams."

"Tried?"

"Yeah, I ended up in tears last night, because I feel like I'm going to fail and Austin comforted me."

"Oh, so something did happen then?"

"No Jairus, nothing happened. He's just being a prick. I think he thought that if Sara was really pregnant, you'd go back to her and he could get back with me."

"Oh OK, so um...have you been wearing these 'pony' pants for two weeks, thinking about the day we nearly kissed?"

"I might have been," I blush, biting down on my lip.

"Oh sweetheart, we better get you out of them then," he laughs, grabbing me around the waist as I jump into his arms.

"Jai, I missed you baby."

"Mmm...I missed you to sweetheart. I love it when you call me baby."

Smiling, I tease him, "Then kiss me, baby."

He doesn't reply, instead crashes his lips to mine in a hungry, soul-shattering kiss. My heart leaps, feeling like it's about to burst out of my chest and fall to the floor at his feet.

Breaking the kiss breathlessly he speaks, "So how about we go get you out of these disgusting pony pants and really say I've missed you?"

"I'd love that, but um..."

"What sweetheart?"

"Shark week just started."

"Oh damn, well I guess pants stay on then whilst I kiss you senseless, sweetheart."

"I like the sound of that baby," I tease, as he puts me down, taking my hand as we head to my bedroom.

His face has a wicked Cheshire cat smirk plastered on it and I giggle feeling the rush of warmth run through my body. I need to find some words to tell him how I feel, but for now, all I want to do is show him how I feel with kisses.

Fifty-Three | Road Tripping

A month and a bit later

Christmas Eve

Throwing the last bag in the boot of Jairus' car, as Austin shuts the door behind us I call out, "Aust, shotgun!"
"Whatever Anni, I don't want to sit in the front anyway," he snaps at me, opening the back door and sliding into the seat.

"So shotgun seat controls the music...is that cool with the driver?"
"Yeah of course sweetheart," Jai replies, lifting my hand up and kissing it.

From the back-seat Austin grunts in disgust, "I've had enough of your sickly sweet love, stop fucking rubbing it in yeah?"
"Sorry man, but she did call shotgun, and I might just forget your sitting in the back when I..."
"Seriously Jairus, don't fucking say anymore. Three hours in the car with you two is going to be bad enough without thinking about you touching her."

"Aust, can you take the stick out of your arse? It's Christmas Eve!"
"Yeah, Anni it's Christmas Eve, that we spend with our families," he taunts with a hint of anger in his tone.

I turn back to look at him in the back seat, as Jairus fiddles with the GPS screen. Scowling at Austin, I mouth to him 'Stop Aust."

He flips me the bird, as I turn around when Jairus asks, "Is this the right address sweetheart?"
"Yeah, that's sad sacks address," I laugh.
With a hand on my thigh, Jairus winks at me sliding the car away from the curb to head to my hometown.

He only takes his hand off my thigh to effortlessly change gears, as we head to Swan Street and the Westgate bridge.
The way Jairus drives amazes me, especially as his parents died in a car accident.
He doesn't let the car take control, never revving the engine before a gear change but slipping into it so effortlessly as we reach the freeway and he glides it up to a hundred and ten.

"You all good sweetheart? You haven't put any music on yet."

"Yeah, I'm fine...just thinking."

"What about?"

"Another year without Alex at Christmas. It's not just hard on my family, but Austin's as well," I reply, turning back to see that Austin has headphones in and is busy playing a game on his Switch.

"Yeah, why's that?"

"Well, um, Amanda...Austin's older sister was his girlfriend."

"Oh shit, that's sad."

"Yeah, they were pretty serious. I think Alex was going to propose to her at Christmas time the year he died."

"Oh sweetheart," Jai drawls, looking across at my tear-stained cheeks, "don't cry, we don't have to talk about it now. Put some music on yeah?"

Nodding, I reach down to my handbag at my feet to take out my prized 'Peter Combe Christmas Album'. Opening the case carefully, I grab the CD out and slide it into the hole in the dash.

'Happy Christmas to you' starts to play through the speakers and I sing along at the top of my lungs, tears streaming down my face.

"Anni, sweetheart, are you sure you're ok?"

"Yeah, Alex loved listening to this with me at Christmas. It always reminds me of him."

Caz May

He gives my thigh a squeeze, edging his hand a little higher and flicking the elastic of my knickers as he winks at me.

"Hey, you tease baby," I taunt, slapping his hand away.
"If I wasn't driving sweetheart, I'd tease you properly," he taunts winking at me and laughing.

Singing along to the music, I think about how much Alex would have liked Jairus. They are so alike, it's uncanny and a smile crosses my face.

Jairus is looking at me out of the corner of his eye, "Is that a smile I see?"
"Yeah, I was just thinking that Alex would have really liked you."
"Yeah, you think he would have approved of me with his little sister?"
"Yeah," I muse, before asking, "can we stop in Ballarat to get a drink? I'm dying for a coffee."
"No worries, sweetheart."

Ten minutes later, Jairus pulls up in the Main Street of Ballarat in front of a coffee shop I've not been to before. Austin has fallen asleep in the backseat.
"Are you coming in baby?"
"Nah, I'll just wait here if you can get me an orange juice."
"Ok," I reply opening my car door when Jairus calls out, "sweetheart do you need some cash?"

347

Leaning my head in the car I reply, "All good baby," before I head inside.

Out of the fridge I grab a Farmers Union Iced Coffee for myself and an orange juice for Jairus.

About to pay, heading up to the counter I spot the lollies, and can't help but grab a pack of Chicos to munch on. They were always a road trip essential in my family.

Back at the car, I throw them at Jai's head, laughing, "Road trip essential cuisine."

"Oh, is that right?" He taunts as I hand him his orange juice.

"Yep, a road trip is not really a road trip if you don't have Chicos and a Farmers Union to wash them down with."

"If you say so sweetheart," he muses kissing my forehead before he starts the car.

The next hour and a half passes by so quickly, I can't believe it when we pull up at the front of Austin's house.

Turning around I shake him slightly to wake him, "Aust, we're home."

He startles, "Huh, what babe?"

"We're home Aust, you slept the whole way."

"Oh right," he mutters, opening his door and racing straight to the boot, tapping on it hastily as Jairus and I both get out of the car.

"Jai, you can wait at the car if you want? I'm just going to say hello to Amanda and Lillie ok?"
"Sure sweetheart," he replies, leaning against the car.

Austin grabs his bag from the boot, as well as an absurd amount of wrapped Christmas gifts.
"Need some help, Aust?"
"Whatever Anni," he jeers, shoving a rather large present into my outstretched arms, as he rushes inside without another word.

Following him to the door, I'm almost bowled over by a super excited Lillie, "Anni, oh my god I've missed you, how's the city?"
Putting the present down by the door I hug her, "Hey Lillie, the city's ok, different I guess."
"Yeah, so um...who's the hottie leaning against the car?" she asks, when Amanda steps up behind her, scoffing.
"Lillie, please, it's none of your business."
"But Mandy you see him yeah?" she turns to look at her older sister like 'do you have eyes?'
"Anni, come on, who is he? Your boyfriend?"
"No Lil, he's just our other roommate."
"Oh, so he's available then?"
"Lillie, he's too old for you," Amanda suggests folding her arms across her chest.

"So? He's gorgeous!" Lillie beams, "Is he single Anni?"
"Um, not exactly."
"Oh...well, whoever his girlfriend is, is a lucky bitch."

"Yeah," I reply feeling myself blush.

"Are you coming over for lunch tomorrow?" Lillie asks with a gleeful tone.

"I guess so, I'll have to ask Mum."

"Ok, well um...I'm going to go catch up with Austin, but tomorrow I want to talk about that hottie," she comments, giving me another hug before she rushes inside.

Amanda looks me and down, a slight smile on her face.

"So Anni, who is he really?"

"Jairus Brooks, he plays for Richmond."

"I thought I recognised him. So, are you together or are you still getting it on with my little brother?"

"I'm kind of with Jairus, yes, but things with Austin have been a little complicated."

"When were they not with you guys?" she laughs.

"I know, are you ok Am? Are you seeing anyone?"

"No, I just can't yet...I still miss Alex so much, as though we lost him yesterday."

"Yeah I know, it's really hard coming back home."

"Yeah, I kind of wanted to stay in the city this year, but Mum wouldn't have it."

"Yeah, anyway I better get going or my Mum will crack it, but hopefully we can chat tomorrow."

"Ok Anni," she replies, kissing my cheek and hugging me.

Walking back to the car, I wave goodbye to her as she turns to go inside.

"Sorry, that took so long Jai."

"All good sweetheart. It seems like you're pretty close with Austin's sisters?"

"Yeah, they're like the sisters I never had."

"Oh," Jairus replies, a little taken aback with a hurt tone.

As he starts to drive the car to drive off, I squeeze his hand that's on the gear knob.

"Jai?"

"Yeah, sweetheart?" he asks softly.

"Just because I'm close with his sister's doesn't mean anything yeah?"

"I know...so which way to your parent's house?"

"Straight down this street, about a kilometre. It's the last house on the left."

Nodding he follows the road, not saying another word, even when we arrive at my parents and they eagerly bound across the verandah to greet us.

Fifty-Four | Family Greetings

Mum is bounding across the verandah the moment Jairus pulls the car into the driveway. She barely gives me a chance to open the car door before she wraps me in a hug, as she cocs excitedly, "Aww....my baby girl, it's so good to have you home."

Dad steps up behind her, "Give her some space Liz, they've just gotten here."
She laughs stepping back, running her hands up and down my arms, "You look thin dear, have you been eating right?"
"Yes, Mum I've been eating fine. I've just been a bit stressed out."

"Ok, dear and who is this lovely gentleman?" she asks as Jairus walks around the back of the car.

"Um, Mum, Dad this is Jairus, my um.... our other roommate."
Jairus bends down kissing Mum on the cheek, "Nice to meet you, Mrs Mathers," he replies so sweetly before nodding at my Dad and shaking his outstretched hand. "Mr Mathers."
"Well, aren't you a dear. Let's get your stuff inside and let you get settled before tea, yes?" Mum suggests, her tone motherly.

Grabbing our suitcases out, Jairus follows us inside, smiling wide like a kid in a candy store. It strikes me as a little odd, but seeing his eyes light up as we pass the Christmas tree and the multitude of Christmas decorations Mum always decks the house out with, I kind of understand.

Squeezing his hand, I ask, "You ok Jai?"

"Yeah sweetheart, it's just been years since I've had Christmas with my foster parents that's all."

"Well, as you can see Christmas vomited here, Mum and Mrs Belvinz go all out."

"I look forward to it."

Mum comes back to the hallway, "Jairus, why don't you head down to the guest room and get settled in."

"Ok thanks," he replies, squeezing my hand again before he heads down the other hallway.

"Second door on the left, dear," Mum calls out to him, before pulling me into the kitchen.

As she starts chopping up vegetables for a salad, she coos at me, "He's gorgeous darling, what's going on with you?"

"He told me he loves me."

"And you don't love him?" She asks like the answer is so blindly obvious.

"I don't know Mum."

"Have you?" She asks, not able to exactly say have you had sex with him.

Blushing I reply, "Mum please...."

"Well, darling, have you or not?"

"No, we've just kissed a lot but haven't, you know, gone all the way."

"So you don't want to be with him?"

"I don't know...things have been complicated with Austin too."

"How so?" She enquires.

"Um...please don't get angry with me Mum, yeah?"

"Why would I, darling?"

"Because I had a pregnancy scare with Austin earlier in the year."

"Oh really?" she replies a little shocked.

"Yeah and since then he's been really clingy and possessive...after all this time he's finally fallen in love with me like I wanted, only now I'm not sure if I feel the same way...I think I'm in love with Jairus but I honestly don't know how I feel."

"You have to do what your heart tells you, honey."

"I don't know what that is Mum."

"I'm sure you will soon enough," she replies in that annoying mother knows best tone like she can read my mind.

"Yeah, I hope so...are we still going to the Belvinz's tomorrow?"

"As always darling," she replies smiling, finishing up the salad.

Turning my head back, I see Jairus coming out from the bedroom in a new shirt with his hair tousled as though he's washed the gel out of it.

His skin looks fresh and a droplet of water from his damp hair has collected at the corner of his mouth. I want to kiss him to lick it off but know a PDA in front

Caz May

of Mum after the conversation we just had probably
isn't the best idea.

Instead, he smiles, stepping up behind me, wrapping
his arms around my waist to hug me from behind,
pressing a kiss to my hair.
"Something smells delicious," he murmurs, still
pressed against my back.
"Mum's famous lasagne," I reply, turning my head
back to look at him, as he lets me go.
Licking his lips, he replies, "Mmm, my fave. Can I help
with anything?"
"Thanks, darling. Could you help Annika set the table
and grab some drinks from the outside fridge?"
"No problems, Mrs Mathers," he nods politely.
"Please, dear, call me Liz," Mum suggests smiling at
Jairus.
"Ok, Liz it is then. Anni lead the way to get these
drinks."
Mum winks at me as we walk away, noticing that
Jairus is again holding my hand with his.

Fifty-Five | Table Talk

As Jairus and I sit down at the table, Mum brings the lasagne over placing it in the middle of the decked out Christmas spread.

Jairus sits next to me, his chair as close to mine as it possibly can be and his thigh is brushing against mine.

I feel exposed, having our skin against each other's with my parent's eyes on us.

I lace my fingers with his, as Dad says our usual grace for the Christmas food we're about to partake in.

Even though we've done a lot more than hold hands in the last few months, the simple touch is making my heart pound and my stomach flutter.

After piling our plates high with food, we all eat in silence for a few minutes before Dad puts his fork down, sighing as he looks towards Jairus.

My heart is pounding, wondering how much my Dad is going to embarrass me.

Instead, he directs his attention to Jairus, who is clearly nervous.

"I've been watching you, young man. You're quite the footballer."

"Thanks," Jairus replies, swallowing hard to try and quell the nervousness I can sense he's feeling.

"Why aren't you spending time with your family at this time of year?"

I see Jairus flinch as he shifts uncomfortably in the chair.
Putting my hand on his thigh, edging it up under the hem of his shorts leg, I squeeze it and he smiles at me, before he replies to Dad, "They..um...passed when I was ten."
"Oh, I'm sorry to hear that son, but it seems as though you turned out alright."
"Yeah...my foster parents were pretty great but I don't see them much now"

Out of the corner of my eye, I see he is clearly upset and agitated by Dad's questions about his past.
About to tell Dad to stop, I take a deep breath in when Dad blurts out, "So Jairus, what's your intentions with my daughter? You seem close."

I feel a deep blush grace my cheeks, wondering if my Dad has developed x-ray vision and can see my hand up Jai's pant leg.

"I don't want to lie to you sir," Jairus replies, swallowing so hard, his Adam's apple juts out and I have to swallow hard to calm myself at how hot that makes me feel.
"Then don't," my Dad snaps, scowling.
"I'm head over boots in love with her," Jairus declares, looking at me smiling wide.

My Dad turns his attention to me, after giving Mum a knowing look, "Annika, do you feel the same way?"
I look towards Mum, annoyed that she hasn't spoken a word this whole dinner.
"I'm not sure Dad," I reply meekly.

"Well, honey...you better make up your mind. A fine young man like this won't wait for you," he informs me, nodding at Jairus as he stands up from his seat, "Excuse me...I have to go and make a phone call."

I look at Jairus, who appears a little dumbstruck by Dad's words.
There is an odd silence in the room, and Mum is like a deer in headlights as she excuses herself to go and do the dishes.

Jairus brushes a stray hair, that's escaped from my ponytail back against my head as he turns his gaze to meet mine, "He's wrong Anni."
"What do you mean?" I ask, gulping.
"I will wait for you, you know I will."
"Jairus, please don't say that."

He stands up holding out his hand to me, "Come on, let's go help your Mum out with the dishes."
We gather up the rest of the plates, taking them to the kitchen and putting them on the sink that Mum has piled high with bubbles.
"Would you like any help with the dishes Liz?"

"No thanks, dear. How about you two go have some time together? I think you need to talk," she replies to Jairus, winking at me.

Jairus takes my hand, squeezing it, sending the warm rush racing through me again as he leads me outside to the patio.

Fifty-Six I Swing Low

Jairus

Once outside on the patio, Anni leads me to sit on the two-person swing seat.
Sighing she wraps her legs underneath her, her already short sundress lifting higher up her thighs, almost exposing her underwear.
I want to edge my hand up underneath it, touch her until she moans, a little payback for her teasing, having her hand up my shorts leg, at the dinner table. But I refrain, knowing that we need to talk, about us.

"So, sweetheart, why did your Mum say we need to talk?"
"Because she likes you and asked me how I feel about you."
"Well, Anni, how do you feel about me?" I ask, hoping she might finally admit that she's in love with me too.
"I don't know Jai, ok" she snaps, gulping as though she doesn't mean her words to sound so harsh,
"coming home just brings all my old memories back."
"Like what? You and Austin?"
"Yeah...we used to come and sit out here after Mum and Dad had gone to bed to talk."

"Just talk?" I ask worriedly as she runs a finger over her lips like she's thinking about more than just talking to Austin.

"No...we um...might have pashed and..." she starts, biting down on her lip as she blushes.

Licking my lips, I smirk at her, "You dirty girl sweetheart."

"Hmmm," she moans, before shifting a little on the swing making it sway.

"And my Dad...well he um..."

"What about him, sweetheart? His questions rattled me a little."

"Yeah, he's pretty protective of me...especially since Alex died."

"Why don't you talk about him?"

"It still hurts, Jai. We were more like twins even though he was two years older than me and Dad was so proud of him...until he got into drugs."

"Drugs really?"

"Yeah, he'd just smoked weed in high school, which Am hated, but after that, he got into Meth and Cocaine. Am tried a bit with him, but she didn't get hooked and was trying to get him to go to rehab and get clean. She really loved him."

"Sounds like it. So your Dad is overprotective now because he's afraid of losing you too?"

"Yeah and he seems to like you. I think he can see what you've achieved this year and he wanted that for Alex."

"What do you mean?"

She shifts across the seat leaning into my side and I wrap an arm around her, kissing her hair.
"He was a ruckman with the warriors here and was looking to get signed with St Kilda before he..."

A sudden thought crashes into my mind. Kissing her forehead, I lift her chin for her eyes to meet mine, "Oh my god Anni, I can't believe I didn't realise the connection before...your brother was amazing."

Her eyes light up, but her mouth turns up at the corner in confusion when she asks, "When did you meet him?"
"At one of the draft pick things I went to a few years back. He kind of came up to me because I was so nervous and told me just to play my best game. I watched him and was in awe."

She laughs sweetly, "Yeah he was a pretty good footballer, but so are you, baby."

"Thanks, sweetheart, but he really inspired me too and when he saw me after he told me, I was a born footballer."
"I'd have to agree with him on that," she smiles, breaking my heart a little.
"Hmmm yeah...I went out for a drink with him after actually."
"Really? When was this?" she asks, sounding worried.
"About two years ago...mid June. He actually mentioned his sister but he called you An."

"Yeah we were An and Al," she replies sweetly, before the concerned tone laces her voice again, "so um, Jai, what else happened that night?"
"I um..met Sara...and was dancing with her and I didn't see him after that."

Tears have now streaked Anni's cheeks, and brushing my finger across them I ask, "Sweetheart what's wrong? I'm sorry I didn't mean to upset you."
"No, you didn't. I...um...think that was the night he overdosed."
"What? Are you serious?"
"Yes...June fifteenth 2015."

The date registers in my mind, and my heart shatters. It is completely uncanny and I feel a mass of guilt rush through me.
"Oh, Anni sweetheart, I'm so sorry. I should have done something."

She shakes her head at me, sobbing "No it's ok...you didn't know and..."

Through her sobs, she lets out a slight giggle, "You probably never thought you'd meet his sister either."

Kissing her forehead, I reply, "No...but I'm glad I did because you're even more amazing than he described you, sweetheart."
"Jai don't," she protests in her sweet innocent way.

Cupping her cheeks in my palms, I bring her lips to mine, kissing her tenderly in a sweet all-consuming kiss that makes my heart pound. She moans, her mouth one with mine as she melts into the kiss. Without a doubt, I can tell how she feels about me, and I will definitely wait for her until she can say the words, but I can't help but wonder if my knowledge about her brother is going to change things. I don't want her to blame me for not helping him.

Breaking the kiss softly I tell her, "Maybe your brother sent me to you."
"Hmmm...maybe, he never really liked me being with Austin."
I laugh and she smiles before she laughs as well.
She edges closer to me, nuzzling against my chest yawning.
Barely a minute passes before she falls asleep and looking down at her sleeping figure in my arms, I feel overwhelmed with how much I love her.
She takes all the fear from my past away, takes away the fear that I can't be loved, making me wonder that maybe even though she can't seem to let me into her heart that we're meant to be.

Fifty-Seven | Giving Gifts

Waking up on Christmas morning is so different as an adult than it was as a kid. Alex used to come in at the crack of dawn to shake me awake, eager to open gifts with our bleary-eyed parents watching as they downed coffee, that I found out later was more whiskey than coffee.

We'd sit around the tree, playing the 'Peter Combe Christmas Album' loud enough to wake the neighbours as we tore into the pretty paper of our presents.
Alex was notorious for shaking his presents before ripping into them.

One Christmas when he was seven, he shook his present so hard, squeezing it as well, that he broke it and opening it he found his brand new remote control car had no antenna as he'd snapped it off.
He burst into tears, throwing it across the room.
I picked it up, taking it back over to him and told him we could still play with it.
He laughed at me and told me I could have it. I'd been so happy that he wanted to give me his toy, I didn't care it was broken.

Tears sting my eyes, as I wake on this Christmas morning, thinking about another year without him makes my heart ache. I think about everything that

could have been different if he hadn't overdosed,
about how we would've been celebrating his
recovery and his wedding to Amanda.
My heart also aches because my big brother can't be
at my own wedding, whenever that is going to be,
and it hurts like hell.
I could be mad at Jairus for not doing something that
night to stop my brother from making the stupid
decision he did, but it isn't Jairus' fault.
He didn't know me, and he'd only just met Alex,
having no idea of his history.

Wiping my arm across my tear stained cheeks, I try to
focus on thinking about what happened after my
conversation with Jairus on the swing seat. I can't
remember getting to bed for the night.
All I can remember is the conversation with Jairus
about Alex and the kiss we'd shared after that made
my heart pound like it was going to escape my chest.
After the conversation about Alex and his words at
the dinner table, about waiting for me to tell him
how I feel, I'm overwhelmed with emotions.

Sitting up in bed, I stretch my arms above my head,
yawning when Jairus walks into the room, with only a
towel around his waist.

"Morning sweetheart, how'd you sleep?"
"Good, um..." I stutter, looking down at my chest
realising I'm only wearing underwear, "last night did
we um, you know?"

"No sweetheart," he laughs deeply, winking at me, "I just carried you to bed and helped you out of your dress. You were half asleep."

"Ok...but the convo about Alex? I didn't dream that?"

"Nope, all true sweetheart," he replies sitting on the bed and pressing a kiss to my forehead.

I look at him lustfully, my eyes running up and down his bare chest.

"Mmm sweetheart, you tease me with that look."

My gaze wanders to the tent rising at the front of the towel and to tease him more I graze my fingers across it.

Grabbing the edge of the towel I give it a tug, pulling it back to expose him.

Touching him, he lets out a guttural moan.

"Sweetheart," he drawls, smirking before he dives at me, pushing me down on the bed as his kiss lands on my lips, hard and teasingly.

Pulling back a moment later, he practically moans, "God sweetheart, I want you so bad but not here in your parent's house."

Sitting up again he pulls the towel over himself and I laugh at his attempt to cover up how kissing me makes his body react.

"You better put some clothes on, before I can't help myself," he teases, winking at me as he stands up and shuffles back to the bathroom.

Getting out of bed, I fish through my suitcase deciding on an outfit of skimpy denim shorts and a red singlet with a camisole bra in it.

Unclasping my bra, I let it fall to the floor, about to slip the singlet over my head when Jairus comes back into the room wearing jeans and a v-neck olive green t-shirt that brings out his eyes.

"Is that what you're wearing sweetheart?" he laughs, stepping up to me and grabbing me around the waist.

"No, you dingbat!" I laugh, trying to pull the singlet over my head.

He bends down to kiss across the top of my breast, "Mmm, you're the best Christmas gift."

Wriggling in his arms I protest, "Baby stop, the door is open!"

"Oh shit," he laughs stepping back and helping me put the singlet on before he kisses me.

"Jai, please...I don't want my parents to catch us pashing."

"Why not Anni? Clearly, your parents wouldn't care if we were together."

"I know, but I...I don't like PDA's in front of them. It's just awkward."

"Fine," he snaps, obviously a little upset.

"You know we're going to Austin's house, yeah?"

"Yeah, and I'm not going to sit back and make him think you're not mine Anni."

"Jai, baby, please, it's going to be super awkward as it is."

"Why is that?"

"Because Lillie, his little sister thinks you're hot and his parents don't know that we aren't together anymore."

He doesn't reply, walking out, leaving me confused and worried about the day ahead. I hear him greet Mum, and say, 'yeah sure we can take my car.'

~~

Fifteen minutes later, with gifts in our arms, we're on the Belvinz's doorstep pressing the doorbell. Lillie opens it, screaming gleefully, "Merry Christmas!" Taking some of the presents she ushers us inside.

She eyes Jairus, as he follows me inside and I turn to him giving him a 'see what I mean' look. He smirks at me, before winking at Lillie. She yelps in delight, running off to put the gifts under the tree.

Mum and Dad have gone M.I.A, off to speak to Austin's parents and organise lunch.

Lillie comes running back to pull my arm, dragging me into the lounge room.

"Oh Anni, you look gorgeous. What makeup do you wear?"

I look back at Jairus, who is standing against the archway uncomfortably, "Um, not much at all, if any Lillie. Why?"

"Because you always look so pretty, and I think Mr Hot stuff over there likes you."

I beckon Jairus over, as I sit on one of the leather three seater couches.

He sits next to me, his thigh brushing mine and I'm
thankful for the denim he's wearing.
"Um...Jai meet Lillie."
He laughs, extending a hand for her to shake, "Hi
Lillie, ripper to meet you."
She doesn't shake his hand but bends down to kiss
his cheek. "It's great to meet you too. You're so hot!"
"Um, thanks, I guess."

I see Amanda walk into the room, scoffing at her little
sisters over the top behaviour, "Leave the poor guy
alone Lillie. He's here with Anni yeah?"
She turns to look at her sister and then back at Jairus
and me.

"Really? But I thought you weren't together? Austin
said last night that he's in love with you Anni."

I try to speak but I'm completely tongue-tied,
annoyed that Austin had to blab to his little sister
about how he feels about me.
"Um Lillie, things are a bit complicated, ok?"
She stands up, scoffing as she heads down the
hallway, brushing past Amanda and scowling at her.

"Sorry about my little sister Jairus. She's pretty close
to her older brother and wants Anni to be her sister
in law. I'm obviously not good enough."
"All good," Jairus replies, grabbing my hand and
squeezing it.
"So, tell me, Anni, what's changed with you?"

"Well, Austin finally fell in love with me, but I don't think I feel the same way you know?" I reply to Amanda as she sits down in the single lounge chair.

"Yeah, love is a complicated thing. I'm still so in love with Alex...I can't let anyone else in."

"Has there been others?"

"Yeah, a few guys but I always break it off before I get too attached."

Jairus is looking between us like his heart is breaking and it makes my heart beat faster.

"Oh Am, Al wouldn't want that for you. You know how much he loved you, he'd want you to be happy."

"I know, and I will be. You know what else would've made him happy?"

"I can guess," I laugh, squeezing Jairus' thigh.

Amanda laughs, "Yeah, you not being with my little brother."

"So you meant that last night? Your brother didn't like you and Austin together?" Jairus asks.

"No, I honestly don't know why."

"Me either, but anyway are you two together?" Amanda asks, not directing her question at either one of us.

Jairus replies, "You'd have to ask Anni that, but I'm head over boots in love with her."

Amanda smiles, laughing, "I'll let my little sister know you're taken then."

We all laugh when the air becomes thick with Austin's entrance to the room.

"Merry Christmas Anni, Jairus," he says, stumbling on Jairus' name like it's poison on his lips.

He saunters over to the couch, pulling me up from it
as he hugs me super tight. Whispering in my ear,
"Merry fucking Christmas, babe. I love you."
I pull back, "Aust, let me go, you're suffocating me."
"Sorry babe, so are we opening presents now or after
lunch?"
Amanda stands up, "I'll go check with the old fella,
but I'm guessing now like usual."

Watching her walk away, I sit back down next to
Jairus. "You ok, baby?"
"Yeah, I um...just didn't realise it would be so
awkward."
"I'm sorry," I apologise leaning into his side, "Better?"
"Yeah," he replies kissing my forehead.

 I hear Austin scoff, as the sound of our parents,
Amanda and Lille coming back into the room breaks
the awkward silence.

We begin handing out gifts to each other, happily
opening them and I revel in how happy I feel. Austin
smiles at me, as he hands me a small present that
looks like a box.
"Open it please babe, I want to put it on you."
I shift uncomfortably, extracting myself from Jairus'
arm around me.
 My heart is pounding and not in a good way.
Ripping the paper off, just as I suspected inside is a
small velvet box.
Flipping the lid open I find a pendant, a half of a best
friend heart pendant.

Austin is smiling oddly at me, "Babe, do you like it?" he asks, as I take it out holding it up.

"Aust, I...I don't know what to say."
"Can I put it on you?" he asks, moving closer to the couch.
I turn around handing it to him, and he places it around my neck.
I press a quick kiss to the side of his mouth and he smiles.
Edging back on the couch I look towards Jairus, who has gone to get a present from under the tree. He looks so sad as he hands it to me, "Merry Christmas, sweetheart," he says unenthusiastically sitting back down next to me.
Ripping the paper open, my heart lurches forward in my chest at his thoughtful gift. He's given me a special edition copy of a book by my favourite author I've been eyeing off. I fall across his lap hugging him.

"I'm sorry it's so lame compared to Austin's gift."
 "It's not lame Jai...it's sweet that you remembered."
Hugging him again, he whispers in my ear, "I love you Annika...please tell me you love me too?"
Looking up at him, my mouth opens, the words on the tip of my tongue.
 I can't say them, I can't say them now, sitting in the Belvinz's lounge room with Austin staring at me but I'm almost a hundred percent certain that I feel them.

Fifty-Eight | Past Memories
Austin

It's after midnight, when I sneak into the Mather's backyard through the side gate, hoping that Anni is sleeping in her old room.

Luckily, it's a moonlight night, and I can see clearly as I tiptoe around the house to her room. The curtains are billowing in the slight breeze, which means the window is open. Sliding it across as quietly as possible, I smile finding that it still doesn't have a flyscreen.

As I'd hoped Anni is sprawled out in the middle of her double bed.
I take a moment to glance around her room, which still hasn't changed from years ago. The walls are still painted lilac purple, and her furniture has not moved.

Reaching the bed, I pull back the covers climbing in beside her and draping an arm over her waist. She moans, shifting in my arms.

"Mmm, baby, you can t be in here," she mutters turning to face me.

"Baby huh?"
"Austin, what are you doing?"
"I missed you, babe. I snuck in."
"You need to go Austin, if....if..."

I press a finger to her lips, "I'm not going anywhere until you agree to sneak out with me, for old times' sake."
"Come on Aust, it's the middle of the night and we have to head back to the city tomorrow....well today actually."
"Please babe," I beg, starting to tickle her.
"Ok Aust, ok," she giggles, freeing herself from my arms and sliding out of the bed.
"Mmm, babe, your arse looks hot in those knickers."
"Stop, Austin, please."
"Fine, just put some shorts on. It's still hot outside."

She dresses quickly, climbing out the window with me holding her hand.

"Why is your Dad's ute here? Where are we going, Aust?"
 "Bunny bashing Anni," I laugh, as she gets in.

Sliding into the driver's seat, I turn the ignition when she replies, "Really Aust?"
"Yeah, you said you missed the old times, so I'm bringing them back."
She doesn't reply, even as we head down the end of the road, through the gates and into the paddock that isn't owned by anyone in town that I know of.

Halfway down the dirt road, I turn the ute into a clearing and park.

"This isn't bunny bashing Austin, seriously what are you doing bringing me out here in the middle of the night?"

"Get out of the ute and you'll find out babe," I reply eagerly, racing around to the back of the ute to flip the tailgate down.

Anni stops at the tailgate with her hands on her hips, looking at the picnic basket and blankets in the back of the ute.

"Aust," she drawls, making my insides flip-flop with how she utters my name.

Grabbing her by the waist, I hoist her up to sit on the tailgate, stepping in between her legs.

"Annika, I love you. I'm sorry it's taken me so long to realise it."

"Aust I....I..."

"I wanted to bring you out here to look at the stars like the first time we were together, so you can see that we're meant to be."

She doesn't reply, a hint of a smile trying to cross her lips as she remembers our first time. Smiling back at her I step back pressing my hands into the tailgate to sit next to her.

Brushing a stray hair from her cheek, caressing it with my finger, I lean closer pressing my forehead against hers.

Caz May

"You're so beautiful Annika, it's always been you,
only you. I love you so fucking much."
She takes a deep breath in, her lips parting before
she pulls back, just as I'm about to kiss her.
"Aust, don't please," she begs, jumping down off the
tailgate, "I can't kiss you because I don't feel that way
about you anymore. Please take me home."

My heart shatters, as she gets in the ute, slamming
the door hard.

I've lost her, I've lost the only girl I'd ever actually
loved because I was too afraid to admit to her how I
feel and now it's too late.
She's fallen in love with someone else and I hate to
admit to myself that maybe he is good for her.

Fifty-Nine | Wait! What!

Bella

Being the first one home, the house feels empty after spending time with my Mum and sister over Christmas. It had been so amazing to get away for a few days, to not think about work, or how my relationship with Jace is going down the toilet.

We've not slept together since he just up and left our party a few months ago. I can't help that every time he tries to touch me, I practically flinch and my muff stays as dry as a desert.

It's partly because I know he'd cheated on me, but also because I'd cheated on him again, and with Austin.

Austin has always been Anni's, so even though, I like every other girl with eyes, find him as gorgeous as fuck, I'd never thought of doing the dirty with him until the night of the party.
It's now pretty much all I think about, even though we've barely seen each other or spoken to each other in the last few months, I want Austin in my bed again.

Cuddling up in bed, I clutch the pillows, about to relieve myself of the sexual tension pent up in my core when the bedroom door flies open.

"Oh shit Bel, I'm sorry I didn't know you were home." Pulling out my hand, hoping Anni didn't see I had it down my underwear I sit up, "All good Anni, how was your Christmas?"
"Um good I guess, yours?"
"Really great, I didn't want to come home, but I've got work tomorrow."

"Oh, really that sucks."
"Yeah tell me about it."

Sitting on the edge of the bed she asks, "So Bel, what else is new? I feel like we haven't spoken for months."
"Yeah, I know. I was actually just thinking about that and I need to tell you something."
"Um, yeah ok."
"I fucked Austin."
"What? When?"
"The night of the party, when I thought you were fucking Blondie."
"Why didn't you tell me, Bel?"
"I don't know. It just happened. He was really upset that you'd basically thrown yourself at Blondie and we were drunk."
"Fuck Bel, that's no excuse! You always seem to get naked with the wrong guy when you're drunk."

"I know, but things are really shit with Jace. We haven't slept together in months."

"Still Bel, that's no reason to fuck my best friend!"

"I know Anni, ok? I'm sorry."

"Whatever Bel, you need to sort things out. If you want Austin then fine, be with him, but I don't want you to keep secrets from me."

"Wait? What? How are you so cool about this Anni?"

"Well, um my Christmas was eye-opening."

"How so? Did you finally sleep with Blondie?"

"No, but he told me something that made me realise how I feel about him.'

"What? How do you feel about him, Anni?" I taunt her giving her tell me bitch eyes. I'm eager to hear what's changed her mind, what's made her realise that she's been in love with Jairus for months.

"Well, he met Alex the night he overdosed and told Jai how amazing his baby sister was. It just seems so serendipitous that Jai came into my life you know?"

"Wow Anni, that's crazy. So, did you tell him how you feel?"

"No, I didn't but Bel....god I can't believe I'm saying this...I'm absolutely head over heels in love with Jairus."

"You need to tell him, Anni. You know he's crazy in love with you."

"Yeah, but I need to actually tell Austin first."

"He already knows Anni."

"Yeah, that's probably true, but I still need to actually tell him. He's still my best friend."

"Yeah, I know."

She laughs, "So you and Aust? How was it?"
"Damn good actually," I laugh, "But you'd know that."
"Yeah, I'm kind of scared about sleeping with Jairus."
"Why? It's not like it's your first time Anni."
"Yeah I know, but you know what I mean."

"Yeah, I do, but I don't doubt it will be beyond
amazing. Just let yourself feel."

She nods, standing up to start unpacking her suitcase
and I slide out of bed, pulling on my leggings from
beside the bed.
"I'm going to order a pizza, you good with that?"
"Yeah, sounds good, check with the boys if they
haven't killed each other."

Laughing I grab my phone, leaving the bedroom and
heading to the lounge room. I find Austin and Blondie
sitting on the couch engrossed in playing a video
game together, and call out to Anni, "Bitch get in
here, you won't believe your eyes!"

"What Bel?" she calls out as she comes running out
of the bedroom.

She laughs, "Well boys will be boys, I guess. Just
order the pizza and they'll eat if they're hungry."

Dialling the pizza shop, I nearly choke on the order
when Anni goes over to sit on the couch next to
Blondie. She kisses his cheek and still frantically

pressing the controller buttons he turns his head to kiss her lips, whilst Austin looks across at them. The heartbreak he feels is written all over his face, and I smile at him, nodding my head to tell him to follow me to the bedroom.

He stands up, dropping the controller on the floor, scoffing at Anni and Blondie who are still joined by the lips.

When he reaches me standing in the hallway, he leans in to whisper in my ear, "What Bel?"

"Up for a quickie before the pizza arrives?"

"Are you serious?"

"Yes, Austin, I wanna fuck."

He grabs my hand, pulling me down the hallway to his bedroom.

It's wrong to take advantage of his heartbreak, but I also know that Austin will never say 'no' to a quick fuck, no matter who it's with. Part of me also wonders if I should just forget about relationships too and just engage in some harmless casual sex.

Sixty | Hearts Shatter

I've been avoiding Austin since we got back from our parents, and since he was oddly playing video games with Jairus on the couch.
He's disappeared with Bella again, and my mind definitely wonders if they've hooked up again.

Jairus had to head back to training as pre-season is fast approaching and Bella is working extra shifts, so it's only Austin and me home again like old times.
He's busy playing his Switch when I sit on the couch next to him clutching my iced coffee carton in my palms.
"Aust, can we talk?"

Pressing pause he turns to look at me, which I find a little odd as he never pauses his game for anyone.
"Yeah, I guess. What's up, babe?"
"I need to tell you something, Aust."

His eyes graze over my collarbone, and up my neck before locking on mine.
"You're not wearing your necklace anymore."
"Um, yeah I took it off because um..."
"What Anni?"
"You know what I'm going to say, Aust."
"Yeah, but I want to hear you say it."
"Ok...well um, I'm in love with Jairus."

"Yeah, I know," he replies pressing play to go back to his game.

Lightly I brush his arm, and he spits at me, "Don't touch me, Annika."

"Aust I'm sorry ok, I can't help that I fell in love with him and not you."

He again pauses the game, "Yeah well I'm sorry I fell in love with you too. You've broken my heart, Annika."

"I'm sorry Aust ok? Please don't hate me."

"I could never hate you, Anni, ok? But you've got no idea how much it hurts to know you don't feel the same way about me after all we've been through."

"Aust, I...I" I stammer as tears start to fall down my cheeks.

"Anni, please don't pretend like you give a shit, ok? I was there for you when Alex died, I gave you my virginity and to be honest you've had my heart since then. I was just too fucking stupid to realise it."

"Don't you dare bring Alex into this. You know he never wanted us together because of your reputation. He didn't want you to break my heart."

"What? So, it's ok to break mine because your dead brother told you to?"

Standing up I throw my half-full iced coffee on the floor, not caring as it sloshes all over the floor, "I can't believe you just said that. Fucking hell Austin! I hate you!"

"You couldn't hate anyone Anni."

"Don't call me that, you don't get to call me that anymore. And you know what?"

"What Anni?" he taunts, smirking at me.

"Jairus asked me to move out with him."

"Good, fuck off then!"

"I will! I'm already gone!"

"Good, fuck off already!"

"Fuck you Austin."

"Already have babe."

"Ahhh, you're such a..." I start, not able to think of a single insult to hurl at him, instead, I put my hand into my pocket taking out the necklace throwing it back at him as I leave the room.

Grabbing my keys and purse, I rush out the door straight to the tram stop.

Sitting on the tram, I send a text to Jairus.

Anni: baby, my answer is yes
Jai: awww sweetheart I love you
Anni: I'm going out....had a fight with Austin...
Jai: you ok?
Anni: yeah but I think I just lost my best friend
Jai: Oh sweetheart I'm sorry...just when the dill was growing on me.
Anni: yeah I noticed...
Jai: I'm heading home in ten.
Anni: I'll be there soon. I just need to get something
Jai: ok sweetheart xxxx

Jumping off the tram, I walk into Bra's and things, feeling a little overwhelmed by all the underwear that is clearly way more than I can afford.

"Hi Miss, can I help you with something?"
"I um...was looking for something to wear tonight."
"Is it a special occasion?"
"Kind of...it's um...my first time with someone new."
"Oh, so what were you looking for?"
"Something sexy I guess," I reply feeling myself blush.

The sales assistant looks around, before holding up a red halter neck lace teddy that dips in a V at the front that will graze my belly button.
At the back, it scoops across the top of the butt into a heart-shaped g-string.
"How's this?"
"Perfect, is it ok if I wear it out of the store?"

"Sure, is size ten right?"
"Yeah, maybe a twelve to be sure."
"Hmmm yes, here, try the twelve first," she replies grabbing it and pointing in the direction of the change room.
The moment I strip from my clothes and underwear to put it on, I know it's the perfect size.
"Is it the right size dear?"
"Yes, it's perfect," I reply sliding the curtain open with one hand as I hold the halter neck ribbon around my neck with the other.

"You look amazing dear, let me help you tie that," she replies as I spin around and nervously let go of the ribbon as she ties it easily.

"Thanks, are you sure it's ok to leave wearing it?"

"Of course dear," she replies, unpinning the tag.

"How much is it?" I ask taking in a deep breath, ready to walk away heartbroken at not being able to afford it.

"It's a hundred dollars dear, but I'll give it to you for fifty."

"Oh no, you don't have to do that."

"Red is your colour dear, and you look amazing in it. It's fine. Get dressed and I'll put it through for you."

Putting my shorts and t-shirt back on, I smile at myself in the mirror, excited to finally tell Jairus how I feel about him.

After paying I leave the store, my stomach fluttering at the thought of finally giving Jairus everything.

Sixty-One | The Inside

Jairus

Even though Austin is home, I'm lying on my bed in just my boxers staring at the ceiling and thinking about Anni.
Spending Christmas with her family had been amazing, and had made me fall even more in love with her.

It was weird, but on the way home Austin seemed to have lost the stick up his arse and was actually nice to me. I can see my being with Anni still gets to him, but he seems to have calmed his tits a bit and isn't as hostile towards me.

My thoughts are broken when I look up to find Anni standing in my door jamb, looking absolutely gorgeous in her skimpy denim shorts and a white t-shirt that bares the outline of red underwear that makes my mouth water.

"Baby, my room in five yeah?"
"Um, yeah ok. Is everything ok?"
"Better than ok," she replies turning away to head down the hallway towards her room.

Immediately I jump out of the bed, not giving her even a minute before I step up behind her, wrapping my arms around her waist.
Beneath my fingers, the fabric of her t-shirt doesn't hide the fact that she's wearing something lacy underneath.

Walking towards her bedroom, she giggles when I ask, "Sweetheart, what are you wearing underneath your clothes?"

Reaching the bedroom, she wiggles out of my arms, pulling my arm to drag me into the room. Slamming the door behind us, I look her up and down, eager to find out what present she's hiding.
"Undress me and find out baby," she taunts, holding her arms above her head. Capturing her arms with mine as I step closer to her, I kiss her hard, loving the little moan she can't help but let escape from her lips.

"Jai, make me yours," she begs breaking the kiss.
"Uh-uh sweetheart, you know I can't do that yet, unless you have something to say to me?"

She's silent, but her soft blue eyes darken as I lift her t-shirt over her head, practically drooling when my eyes gaze over the red lace that dips all the way to her belly.

"God sweetheart, you're beautiful," I groan, unbuttoning her skimpy denim shorts and pushing them over her hips to the floor.

The lace of the red teddy looks delectable against her skin, I want to rip it off her body and taste her. She giggles again, turning around to show me the back and my cock springs to attention at the heart-shaped g-string back that accentuates her curvy arse. Grabbing her by the waist, I pull her back against my body.

"Do you feel what you do to me, sweetheart?"

"Mmm...your cock is hard as fuck baby," she teases, turning her head back to kiss me as she grinds her hot arse against me.

"And Jai, I want your cock inside me."

"Oh, really sweetheart, do you have something to tell me?"

"Maybe," she teases turning around to face me.

Again, I smash a kiss to her lips, sneakily untying the ribbon around her neck as I deepen the kiss.

The front of the teddy falls exposing her breasts and without warning I take one in my mouth, licking and biting the sensitive bud.

Her head tips back, as pleasure rushes through her.

"Tell me how you feel about me sweetheart, unless you want me to stop," I taunt, locking my eyes on hers.

"Don't stop baby, please don't stop!" She moans.

"Three words, sweetheart. Three words and I won't stop until you scream out my name with my cock inside you."

She locks her eyes on mine, takes a deep breath in and exhales, "I...I...love you Jairus Kingsly Brooks."

"Say it again sweetheart, just to make sure I heard you right."

"I love you Jairus."

"God Annika, I love you so fucking much."

"Show me how much then?" She asks teasingly.

Not replying with words, I kiss her so passionately my heart is about to burst with the rush of love coursing through me.

Picking her up by the waist I lay her down on the bed, kissing down her body until I reach her stomach.

"So, I seem to remember that if I touch you here you squirm in pleasure, yes sweetheart?" I ask, grazing my hand over her hips that buck up as she moans.

"Mmm, baby please," she begs, as I pull the teddy from her body, discarding it to the floor.

She kicks her thongs off, laughing before she pulls me down to kiss me like she's never going to kiss me again.

My dick is straining against the fabric of my boxers, pressing against her belly as she deepens the kiss, taking my mouth and tongue as hers.

Breathless, I pull back, "God Annika, sweetheart I want you so bad. Tell me again how you feel about me."

"I love you Jairus, so please make love to me now."

"Mmm," I moan, yanking my boxers down and kicking them off when they land at my feet.

"Jai, baby please," she begs in a sexy tone.

"Do you have a franger?"

She shakes her head, "No, I just want you Jai, inside me, nothing between us."

"Are you sure, sweetheart?"

"Yes," she replies pulling me down to kiss her lips again as I slide inside her.

Her hips buck to meet mine the moment I enter her, and she moans, panting as I thrust in and out of her drenched core.

Wrapping her legs around my arse, she pulls me deeper inside, rocking her hips to meet every thrust. I revel in the sound of flesh against flesh, our bodies finally becoming one.

"God Annika...Fuck!" I scream out, plunging my cock even deeper inside, making her moan.

"Mmm Jairus, I..."

"Come for me sweetheart, I wanna see you come with my cock buried inside you."

Her hand reaches down between our bodies, touching her sensitive bud as I pound into her hard again. She moans, my name on her lips, as I continue thrusting harder, deeper, "Fuck Annika, you're made for me," I groan, feeling her tightening around my cock, her climaxing looming.

The moan she makes as her climax rocks through her body moments later is the most exquisite sound I've ever heard.

"Jai, Jai, oh fuck, oh God!" She screams out, riding out the ecstasy of her release as I shudder, releasing my load into her, screaming out, "Annika fuck I...I love you!"

We lay there for a moment, our bodies still one.

Pressing a kiss to her forehead, I roll off her spent body to lay next to her and pull her close.

"Sweetheart, that was phenomenal."

"Really? It was that good for you too?"

"Are you kidding sweetheart?"

"No, I..."

"Annika, that was seriously some of the best sex, I've ever had."

"Yeah, it was pretty amazing."

"You have no idea what it felt like to finally be inside you, sweetheart. I love you so much."

"I love you too Jai, and I'm sorry it took me so long to tell you."

"It's ok sweetheart, it was all the more amazing hearing you say it," I tell her before kissing her tenderly, entangling my legs with hers and pulling her body as close as possible to mine again.

There is only one thing I need now, and I already have an idea running through my mind. But firstly, I have to find a place to call our own.

Sixty-Two | Goodbye Pain

January is upon us quicker than I thought possible. Jairus has been off looking for a new place for us to move into, not telling me anything about where it is or when we are moving out.

The summer is already scorchingly hot, reaching the high thirty's every day for the first couple of weeks of January.
Our apartment has no air conditioning, so to keep cool I'm lying on my bed, in my underwear with the fan blowing a breeze directly onto to my face as I read a book.

Jairus comes in wearing his footy shorts and a white loose t-shirt. Underneath I can see the outline of his abs, and as he comes closer to the bed I lick my lips, thinking about licking them.

Lifting his t-shirt off, he dives towards the bed kissing me as a greeting.
"Mmm, hello to you to baby," I tease.
"Hey sweetheart, do you want some good news?"
"Yeah, why wouldn't I?"
"I found it, the perfect house."
"Really? Where?"

"Yep, South Yarra, and we can move in next week, as it's in the final stages of lockup."

"What? Next week?"

"Yep, it's brand spanking new and it's going to be ours. The loan is all approved, and draw down will go through tomorrow. It's happening sweetheart."

"That's amazing. I guess, I better start packing then."

"Yeah, but we've got all week for that. I'd rather just be with you right now. I feel like we've hardly spent any time together lately."

"Mmm yeah, but you might get sick of me soon."

"Never sweetheart, plus it will be just us in our house and I plan on having my wicked way with you in every room."

"Mmm...sounds amazing baby," I reply, laughing as I lean forward pressing my lips to his Adam's apple and running my tongue down his abs.

"Oh really? It's like that is it sweetheart?" He taunts, kissing me hard, biting my lip and moaning as he deepens the kiss.

Mere minutes later we are naked, our bodies locking together in celebration of taking the next step in our lives.

~~

The next week flies by. I've thrown all my clothes haphazardly into three suitcases, and packed up all my books and other personal possessions into a grand total of ten boxes.

It's a Saturday, the hottest summer day so far, Jairus has sweat dripping down his brow as he loads up the car with all of our belongings.

"Are you ready sweetheart? he asks, leaning against the car with his arms folded across his chest.

"Yeah, I just need a minute to say goodbye to Bella and Austin."

"Ok, take your time."

Austin and Bella are both inside, on the couch, seeming a little cozy.

Tears are stinging my eyes as I step up to the couch.

"I'm going to miss you guys," I sob through tears.

Surprisingly after our fight a few weeks earlier, Austin stands up to hug me, a whimper escaping his lips as he pulls me tight against his chest.

"Goodbye Anni, I'm sorry for everything."

"I'm sorry to Aust, can we still be friends?"

"I don't know. You broke my heart, and even though I'm sorry, I'm not sure."

Pulling back from his hug, I watch him walk away, feeling guilty for causing him so much pain and my heart is breaking as it feels like I truly have lost my best friend.

Bella is sobbing when she stands up.

"Bel, what's happening with you and Jace?"

"Let's not talk about it now. We'll catch up for a coffee when you're settled into your new place."

"Ok, I'm going to miss you so much, Bel."

"Me to girl but living with Blondie won't be so bad, especially having the place all to yourselves." She winks at me.

"Oh yeah," I laugh, "So you'll text me about the coffee catch up yeah?"

"Yeah, Anni I will, just get going yeah, before I'm more of a blubbering mess."

I pull her into a hug, "You already are a blubbering mess, Bel."

"Yeah, well so are you," she jeers, laughing slightly.

"Bel, I'm so glad you crashed into our house last year."

"Me too Anni, now get going, girl. Your hot as fuck man is waiting for you," she laughs, slapping me on the butt as I leave.

Waving and blowing her a kiss, I leave the house and run to Jairus, who is smiling wide when he sees me.

Hugging me tightly, pressing a kiss to my forehead he asks, "Ready to go home sweetheart?"

"Definitely baby," I reply, kissing him, the amazing man I've fallen in love with when he'd showed me his charming side.

Sixty-Three | High Rise

Driving away from the Richmond apartment feels so final like a part of my life is ending.

I feel shattered that I've lost Austin, and feel like I'm going to lose Bella as well. Having her living with me had made us even closer friends, and saying goodbye feels like forever.

It isn't even that far between Richmond and South Yarra, but in slow-moving Saturday traffic, it feels like the longest drive ever.

"Sweetheart, you ok? Why are you pouting?"

"I don't know, I feel like part of my life is over. I miss Bel and Aust already."

"Did you sort things out with Austin?"

"No, and I feel wretched about it, like I've lost another part of me and that part of my life is gone forever."

"It might be sweetheart, but our life together is just beginning," Jairus replies, squeezing my thigh as he looks over at me.

"Yeah that's true, I can't wait for our life together to begin."

"Me either sweetheart," he smirks, turning off the road into an underground carpark below a massive high-rise apartment building.
Pulling into a carpark, he shuts off the engine, turning to look at me.
"Are you ready sweetheart?"
"Am I ready for what? Living with you?"
"Well, that yes but I meant are you ready to see our penthouse?"

"Penthouse? As in the whole entire top floor of this apartment building?"
"You said it, sweetheart," he laughs, getting out of the car and coming around to my side to open my door before I even have a moment to process his words.

He kisses me sweetly, before taking my hand to lead me to the elevator.
I hear the beep of the car locking as the doors of the elevator slide open.
My eyes boggle at the lavish inside, gold railings in the middle of a floor to ceiling mirrors.

"Do the honours sweetheart," Jairus suggests nodding at the button panel that has a 'P' for penthouse on the very top.
Giggling, I press the button, noticing that there are twelve floors before the penthouse on the thirteenth floor.

"Number thirteen huh baby?"

"Yep, you know me too well. So have you ever kissed someone in an elevator sweetheart?"

"No, but I'm guessing you're going to change that right now."

"Damn right, sweetheart," he replies pushing my back against the gold railing and smashing his lips to mine in a heated kiss.

The elevator ride to the top is smooth and a lot quicker than I think it would be.

When the doors slide open there is a small open hallway.

In front of the elevator is a double door, painted white with gold handles and a scan pad for keyless entry.

Jairus steps up to it, dragging me to stand beside him, as he scans a card against the reader and depresses the handle. The door makes a click sound and swings open.

He again drags me inside closing the door behind us. The sight before me is beyond anything I ever expected.

To the right is a large open plan kitchen, with black shiny appliances and a huge island bench.

To the left is a sunken lounge room, with an almost cinema-sized screen on the wall. Next to the screen, is a cube bookshelf wall that leads to the rest of the rooms.

I can see in front of me, there is a dining room, that leads out onto a balcony, but I want to explore the bedrooms and bathrooms.

Jairus is standing next to me, smiling wide.

Eagerly I ask, "Jairus is this really our house?"

"It will be sweetheart. We have a mortgage still," he laughs.

"I know but Jai, it's amazing."

"Wait until you see the bathroom and the master suite."

"If these rooms are anything to go by, I'm sure they are lavish."

Taking my hand, he smirks, walking me through the house behind the cube bookshelf. There are two other bedrooms and a small bathroom that has a simple walk in shower and a corner spa bath.

My mouth gapes open when we reach the master suite, at the end of the hallway.

To one side is a king size bed, next to a massive floor to ceiling window with the most amazing view of the city.

On the other side is a huge walk in with drawers, shoe racks and so much hanging space, I could open my own boutique selling his and hers outfits.

On the other side is an ensuite with double sinks, an open double shower equipped with rain shower heads and handhelds as well.

Between the sink and shower is an in-wall toilet and the walls are covered in a soft pastel green tile.

As my eyes scan the room Jairus steps up behind me, his fingers running along the elastic of my skirt.

"Told you it was amazing."

"You got that right," I beam.

"So, how about we make a start on fucking in every room?" He suggests pushing my skirt to the floor.
"Mmmm sounds like a hot idea," I taunt, turning around in his arms.
"Tell me where first sweetheart," he demands, a teasing tone in his voice.

I don't reply, instead, I pull him back towards the bed. Smirking he sits down on the edge, pulling me down to straddle him.
"Annika, sweetheart you're so fucking beautiful."
"Jairus, baby, you're so fucking handsome," I reply loving the sweet smile that crosses his lips before he kisses me.

Grinding against him, we kiss frantically. My heart is pounding so hard, my breathing rapid, when I break the kiss to lift my t-shirt off.
"Mmmm, "Jairus murmurs, reaching around my back to unclasp my bra.
It falls down my arms and he grabs it, throwing it behind us.

"Beautiful," he drawls, kissing the sensitive skin of my neck, following his lips with his tongue as he reaches my collarbone.
When he reaches my breasts I moan, tipping my head back as a rush of pleasure courses through me when he takes turns licking and sucking each breast.
"Tell me how you feel about me again, sweetheart," he taunts, smirking again.

"I love you Jairus," I reply, sliding my hands under the hem of his t-shirt.

"God, I love you to Annika. And when you touch me, I feel so alive."

He lifts his shirt over his head, before smashing a kiss to my lips and pulling me down onto the bed.

This time breaking the kiss, I whisper in his ear, "I want to ride your cock baby."

He groans, reaching down between us to unbutton his jeans and free his cock from the confines of his boxers.

"Oh sweetheart," he drawls with the hottest smirk ever on his face.

Laughing, I stand up on the bed, looking down at him as I slide my knickers down my legs before kicking them to the floor.

Below me he's wriggling out of his jeans, yanking them and his boxers off, kicking them to the floor when they reach his ankles.

"Come here, sweetheart" he requests, his tone teasing when he continues, "come and ride my pony."

Laughing I sit back down in his lap pulling him up so our chests are together. With my forehead against his, I whisper "I love you, baby."

He whispers back, his breath warm, "I love you too, sweetheart."

Shifting my body a bit, as I kiss him I impale myself on him, rocking up and down. His arms wrap around me, and I wrap mine around him. Our bodies can't get any closer, our skin is touching everywhere.

"Jai, baby, god so good," I drawl out huskily, giving him a teasing kiss as I grind on his cock inside me.

"Mmm, Anni, sweetheart, you riding my cock is seriously amazing."

I bounce my body up and down on his length, his hard cock hitting my insides, filling me completely. I've had cowgirl sex before but it's never felt so damn amazing, as having Jairus' cock inside me. It's like pure ecstasy.

Quickly, I increase my pace, screaming out, "Fuck Jairus, I'm coming, I love you!" My climax rips through my body, sudden and fierce. I shiver, riding his cock harder, desperate to milk his release as well. Shuddering from the ecstasy of my release, I feel him explode inside me, as he calls out, "I love you, Annika. Fuck! I love you."

Climbing off his lap, we lie down together, diving under the covers of our king size bed, entangling our legs, pulling our bodies close together again.

His arms wrap around me, as he presses a sweet kiss to my lips.

Sixty-Four | Coffee Gossip

It's strange going out into the city during the day.
Even though we lived so close to the CBD we rarely
go there.
Bella is finishing work at one, so I ask her to meet me
at Gloria Jeans on Elizabeth street.

Walking in I'm happy to find the couches near the
window are free.
As I sit down my phone pings with a message.
Bella: be there in five. Order for me.
Anni: no worries Bel. :)

Grabbing my purse, I walk up to the counter, ordering
a caramel latte for Bella and an Iced coffee for myself.

As I'm about to walk back to the table, Bella walks in
and I race over to hug her.

"Hey Bel," I beam.
"Hey Anni, don't break me yeah?" She laughs, as we
sit down.
"Sorry Bel, I've just missed you so much."
"Yeah, I know Anni, I've missed you too but it's only
been like two weeks."
"It feels like a lifetime."

"Yeah, I get you. So what's it like?"

"What Bel?"

"Living the high life, Anni? You're living in a penthouse for fuck's sake."

"It's amazing Bel, so surreal."

"I bet," she smiles, as our coffees are brought over to the table.

Taking a sip of my iced coffee as Bella sips her caramel latte, I feel like she wants to tell me something but is holding back.

"How's Austin?" I ask after she's put her coffee back down in case she spits it everywhere.

"He's still heartbroken but ok."

"That's good, I guess, I miss him."

"Yeah well he won't admit it but he misses you, even just as his friend."

"Yeah, so what happened with Jace?"

She hangs her head low, taking another sip of her coffee before she sighs and replies, "I told him about sleeping with Austin and he lost it.

"Oh my god, Bel! You told him that?"

"Yeah, I felt horrible that I'd cheated on him again. It's really over this time," she sniffs, holding back tears.

"I'm sorry Bel."

"I'm ok. I just need some space to sort out how I feel. I moved all my stuff out last week when I told him."

"Really, so you've moved into my room?"

"Yeah, I hope that's ok? Austin didn't want that room anymore."

"It's fine Bel. So are you sure about the space thing?"

"Yeah, why?"

"Because Jai told me his best friend, you know Travis thought you were hot. He apparently wants Jai to set you up."

"Really?"

"Yeah. I can give him your number if you want."

"Yeah ok, I guess" she replies downing the rest of her coffee and smiling slightly, "Maybe, I'll get my happy ever after with my own hottie."

I laugh, "Yeah maybe, have you been with Austin again?"

"Would it be bad if I have?" She replies blushing, telling me the answer before I probe her for more.

"Well, kinda Bel, have you or not?"

"Yes, but it's just sex, Anni. He's still in love with you. I caught him looking at photos of you the other day and he was crying."

"Let me guess, you made him feel better?"

"Yeah," she laughs, blushing again and I wonder if she's lying that it's just about the sex between them.

"Bel, you're so bad, girl."

She laughs, "I know, I know, so how's the sex with Blondie? I know you've obviously slept with him so don't deny it, Anni."

"Roommates don't fuck and tell Bel," I taunt, laughing before I take a sip of my iced coffee.

"We aren't roommates anymore Anni. So spill girl!"

"Fine," I snap, laughing, "it's off the charts, Bella. I never thought sex could be so amazing."

Her smile is wide, "Sounds like Blondies the one then, huh?"

"Yeah, I think so. I love him so much Bel," I confess.

"I'm glad you've found someone Anni. Austin was never the right guy for you."

"Why do you say that?"

"Because Anni, I just know."

"Bel, tell me!"

"Ok well, that night last year wasn't the first time I'd kissed Austin."

"What?" I snap, my mouth falling to the floor.

"Yeah before he got with you, we got drunk together one night and we kissed and we..."

"Let me guess, you fucked him then too?" I snap, feeling anger rising in my chest at both of them for lying to me.

"No, I didn't. You were his first. He was lusting after you even then. I think he was just my friend to try and get with you, Anni."

"God Bel, I'm kind of shocked, but tell me this then...do you have feelings for Austin?"

"Now, no...but back then, yes I did."

"I'm sorry Bel, I had no idea."

"Don't worry about it Anni, it's in the past."

"Yeah, I guess. But be careful Bel yeah? I don't want to see you get hurt."

"I'm a big girl Anni, and I'm glad we're friends."

"Me too Bel," I smile, downing the rest of my iced coffee before I stand up, "I got to go meet Jai at training. I forgot my swipe card, so can't get in the house."

She laughs, and stands up too, "Not house Anni, penthouse!"

"Ok, penthouse. You'll have to come over one day."

"Sounds great, I love you, Anni," she replies, hugging me again.

"I love you too Bella, say Hi to Aust for me please."

"I will," she replies, as I walk out, waving to her.

As I head to the train station to go and meet Jairus I can't help but think about the mistake Bella is making. Telling me she doesn't have feelings for Austin isn't sitting right with me, as Bella was never good at hiding how she feels.

If things weren't strained between Austin and myself, I'd tell him to back off, but it wasn't my place and they needed to work it out for themselves.

~~

Arriving at Jairus' training session, he's walking out with Travis.

They bro-hug and Jairus rushes over to hug me.

"Hey sweetheart, how was your coffee date? You look a little down."
"It was great...but..."
"What sweetheart?" he asks, unlocking the car and throwing his bag into the backseat.

Sliding in together, I sigh as he starts the engine. "Tell me, sweetheart, I hate seeing you upset."
"Bella and Austin slept together again."
"Sorry what? What do you mean by again?"

I bite my lip, realising I haven't actually told Jairus about what happened the night of the party.
"They um...slept together that night we had the party and have been since."

"God, what a tool."
"No...he's not but she told me that she nearly slept with him in year eleven before we got together and that she had feelings for him."
"Woah, sweetheart that's a lot to take in, but it's not for you to worry about."
"I know, but I'm worried she's going to get hurt."
"Yeah, I know sweetheart, but leave it be, yeah?"
"I will. When did you get so wise, baby?"

He laughs, "Don't know."
He smiles at me, and I know exactly what thoughts are running through his mind without him even having to say the words.

Biting my lip I think for a moment, "Kitchen bench or spa bath?"

He licks his lips, smirking at me as we turn into the parking garage of the penthouse.

When he replies, "Both, sweetheart," in a teasing tone, a rush of desire hits my core soaking my skimpy undies.

The moment he cuts the engine, we're out of the car, in the elevator and racing up to our penthouse with our lips locked.
Having the penthouse to ourselves definitely has its perks.

Sixty-Five | Date Night

Jairus

After coming home from training the other night I'd taken Anni in the spa bath first, amidst a mountain of bubbles.

We got clean and then dirty as fuck before moving to the kitchen where I took her on the bench, loving how since we'd moved into the penthouse she showed absolutely no inhibitions when we were having sex.

She has no idea how crazy she makes me feel, and no idea how much I love her.

I've had the idea tumbling around in my head for weeks, and I want to make it so special that she'll never forget it.

The first time the thought entered my head was Christmas and stepping into our walk-in watching her getting dressed my mind wanders back.

After I'd walked out of Anni's room, I was greeted by her Mum asking if we could take my car.

Replying 'yeah sure we can take my car' she called out to Anni, who came rushing out of her room smiling at me sweetly.

I threw Anni the keys and excused myself to go to the bathroom.
My stomach was in knots, for one I knew being in Austin's family's house was going to be awkward as fuck, but also because after the night before I knew there was something else I needed to do before we left.

Walking out into the kitchen, I found her Dad putting drinks into an esky from the outside fridge. Taking a deep breath, I stepped a little closer to him before opening my mouth and then shutting it in nervousness.

"Hello Jairus, are you ok son?" he asks, flipping the lid of the esky closed.
"Um, yep, I um wanted to talk to you about something."

He smiled wide at me like he knew what I was going to say.
"Ask away son," he replies, closing the fridge and picking up the esky in one hand.

"I would...um..." I started, swallowing the lump in my throat, "like your permission to ask Annika to marry me?"

His smile grew wider, and he dropped the esky to the ground before hugging me.

"I'm guessing that's a yes?"

"Yes, Jairus, you have my permission. I can see how much you love her."

"I just hope she says yes," I reply a little forlorn, as he picks up the esky again and I follow him inside.

"She's in love with you Jairus."

"How do you know Mr Mathers?"

"Please son, Ali is fine, and trust me, I know my daughter. She loves you and I'm glad she's found someone worthy of her."

"I'm sorry, worthy of her? Didn't you approve of her with Austin?"

"No, son I didn't. That boy might practically be family already, but his head is in the god damned clouds. My girl deserves someone who can take care of her."

"I'm glad you think I'm worthy. I love her so much."

"I know son and she loves you. Just give her a bit more time to realise how she feels before asking her the big question."

"I will," I smile as he walks out to the car and I follow a few moments later.

Getting in the car, I drive back over to Austin's house, mentally preparing myself for a day of awkwardness whilst starting to think about the perfect proposal.

Anni turns around after slipping on a cute baby blue sundress with a scoop neckline.
It makes her blue eyes sparkle.
"Hey baby," she smiles sweetly, "can you zip me up?"
I step closer, running my hand across the small of her back, as I zip the back of the dress up.
Wrapping my arms around her waist, grazing them over her stomach I whisper in her ear, "I can't wait to unzip this cute dress later, sweetheart."

She turns in my arms, kissing me sweetly.

With her forehead against mine, her breath in my face, she asks, "What room is it tonight baby?"
"You'll have to wait to find out sweetheart. It could be the shower, or the dining table or maybe even the balcony."
"You tease, baby," she smiles, stepping back from me and sliding her feet into her slip-on sandals, "but won't someone see us if we're out on the balcony?"
"Sweetheart, we're thirteen stories up and it will be dark, plus it might be the shower or the dining table."

Smiling she takes my hand, "Should I bring a jacket?"
"Yeah, put that cute white cardi on," I reply, knowing it's the perfect addition to her outfit and the last place I saw it was on the coat rack by the door.
"Oh yes, that's perfect," she beams, dropping my hand as she runs towards the front door.

As she slips it on, I check in the pocket inside my jacket, making sure the little box is still there and not obviously.

"Ready sweetheart?" I ask, taking her hand and dangling the car keys in the other.

"Yep, where are we going anyway? Terrace?"

"No, sweetheart, somewhere even more special," I inform her as we get in the elevator.

She lets out an excited yelp and I can't help but smile, before smashing my lips to hers in our usual elevator style.

~~

Stopping at the bottom of the Eureka Skydeck, ready to go up to 89 Anni giggles excitedly as she clutches my hand.

"Are you serious Jai?"

"Yeah sweetheart, we haven't gone on enough dates."

"But this is like one of the most expensive restaurants in the city."

"Sweetheart, you know you don't have to worry about having the money yeah?"

"I know, but I don't want you to spend a ridiculous amount of money on me either. I'd be happy with Macca's."

I smile at her, and the look on her face tells me she's dead serious.

It hits me that I'm about to make a decision that isn't the right one.

Proposing to her at some fancy restaurant isn't the right thing to do.

She's at the elevator, about to press the call button, when I ask her, "Anni, do you just want to get Macca's and go home?"

She pouts, "Yeah sounds more like my style, baby."

Taking her hand, I lead her to walk along Riverside Quay.

"Sweetheart, can I tell you something?"

"Yeah, anything baby."

"Your support coming to my games means the world, and I'm so glad we can just spend time together without it having to be some big fancy night out."

She laughs. "Well baby, for one thing, why wouldn't I want to watch you doing what you love in those hot as shorts and two I don't care where I am as long as I'm with you.

"You know preseason starts in like two weeks, yeah?"

"Yeah, and I'll be there every game I can, Jairus."

"I know sweetheart, so what's your Macca's favourite?" I ask as we walk inside.

"Quarter Pounder, fries, a chocolate shake and a caramel sundae," she ravels off her order, licking her lips after.

She finds a seat, and I order, getting the exact same order for myself. Once it's all on the tray, I slide into the booth across from her.

"You got the same thing?"

"Yep, it sounded delicious."

"Definitely, Sundae first, and you have to dip your fries in it."

"What? Dip your fries in the ice cream?"

"Yes! You've never done that?"

"No! That's weird sweetheart, I don't know if I can be with you now I know this weird fetish of yours," I tease.

"Not funny baby, just try it!"

"Ok, I'll try it, but don't blame me if I spit ice cream all over your dress."

Lifting the lid off the sundae I take a fry and dip it in the ice cream, watching as Anni does the same.

On the end of her fry is a chunk of ice cream.

Putting the fry in her mouth a delicious moan escapes her lips before she licks them.

I put the fry I'm still holding in my hand slowly into my mouth, and find it actually tastes rather nice.

"So, is it horrible?"

"Um, no, rather nice actually, but I'm wishing we got this take away because that moan you just made sweetheart has me craving you for dessert instead of this sundae."

"Eat up then baby, our balcony awaits," she taunts, driving my desire for her even higher.

~~

As usual, the moment we step into the elevator we are madly kissing, stumbling to our front door without parting.

Every kiss makes me crave her, the taste of her lips on mine and the way her body responds to my touch is addictive.

h Caz May

Once inside she turns her back to me, "Unzip me, baby?"
I comply with her request, watching as the fabric of her dress falls to the floor and she kicks off her sandals.
She grabs my shoulders, helping me shrug off my jacket before her hands run up my abs, underneath my t-shirt.
Rolling the fabric up from the hem she smirks as I pull it over my head.

She bends down to lick from the waistband of my jeans, all the way to my lips without kissing me.
Her face is so close to mine when she drawls, "Take me on the balcony baby."
"God, Annika," I groan, lifting her by the arse into my arms.
She wraps her legs around me as I kiss her hard and walk backwards to the sliding glass door that leads to our small balcony.
Still kissing her, I reach down to slide the door open.
She breaks the kiss though, panting and smiling wickedly at me.

"Baby, you have too many clothes on," she teases fumbling with my belt before dakking me.
Stepping out of my black jeans, I kiss her furiously again and she steps back towards the glass railing.

Her lips leave mine and she hisses out a panicked whimper when her arse hits the railing.

419

"I won't let you fall, sweetheart," I promise, kissing her again as I wrap my arms around her waist, pulling her body against mine.

Already my dick is aching for release, straining against the y-front boxers I'm wearing. Her only clothing is a skimpy barely there white lace g-string and a nude strapless bra that pushes her cleavage up.

"Baby," she drawls, breaking the kiss again.
"Mmm, yes sweetheart?"
"I want you," she moans.
"Yeah, I'm just enjoying the view."
She laughs so sweetly it makes my heart melt.
"And I'm not sure which view is better? You in underwear, or the city skyline at night?"
"I'd have to say the city," she suggests cheekily.
"I was actually thinking you in underwear sweetheart," I drawl, pushing my boxers to my knees as I step back towards the window.
Pulling her with me, she jumps into my arms again, wrapping her arms around my neck.
Her kiss meets the sensitive skin under my ear, and she whispers, "I can feel your cock teasing me baby."
"Let me in then sweetheart," I whisper into her ear.
"I don't want to let you go though," she laughs.
"Then don't sweetheart," I taunt, my hands grabbing the elastic of her g-string around her arse and peeling it off her, ripping the lace.
"Mmm, that's better," she moans bearing down onto my aching cock.

For a moment we don't move, just enjoying the feeling of being together again, but then she kisses me zealously rocking her pelvis against me.
Deepening the kiss with my tongue lacing with hers I grab her arse and turn us around so her arse is up against the glass instead.

A carnal moan escapes her lips as I drive into her soaking core.
Her breathing becomes panting and her moans increase.
"Jai, I... Jai...oh...god....baby.... oh!"
"Mmm...Anni...sweetheart...god...oh fuck!" I scream out, my release hard and fast as her body shudders with me, her climax a wave we ride together.

I press a kiss to her forehead, as she slides her legs to the floor, "I love you, Annika, I can't ever get enough of you."
"Likewise, Jairus," she replies, giving me a sweet kiss as she takes my hand, "So tomorrow night?"
"Maybe the dining table?"
"Mmm...best dessert ever," she smiles, as we go inside towards our bedroom.

There is no doubt in my mind that Annika is my forever love.
She supports me in everything and I know the perfect time to ask her to be mine forever is only a few weeks away.

Sixty-Six | Only You

Jairus

The last few weeks have flown by, February was like a blip on the radar and it's already the final pre-season match.

It feels beyond surreal after the ripper 2017 season, that at the start of the 2018 season we are playing the pre-season grand final.

As always Anni is behind the goals, doing the honours of waving the flag whenever we score.
She's been at every pre-season game, as Uni is starting back a little later this year and Dana has given her the job of waving the flag.

It makes me smile so wide when I kick a goal. She's waves it higher and screams out, "Jai my man, I love you!"

I'm super nervous to play today, as my stomach is doing flip flops, not able to focus on anything but my plan for after the game.
In my mind I have it all planned out, and we have to win or it just won't be the same.

In the rooms, Trav is firing us all up, barking direction only he as the new captain can. His arm is around my back as we huddle together.

Our other arms in the middle, hands on top of each other's as we roar out 'go Tigers' before moving off to finish preparing to run out.

"You good man?" Travis asks as he adjusts his boot.

"Nah, I'm so fucking nervous man."

"About the game or after?"

"Well, both, we have to win or my whole plan goes out the window."

"Trust me, man, we've got this in the bag."

"I hope so, but I'm scared she'll say no because of the spectacle."

"Are you kidding me, man?"

"No, you know how shy she is sometimes."

"Yeah, but not around you, and she loves you fucktard. She's not going to say no!"

"Yeah," I reply shaking my head, "let's get our game on, Captain."

He smiles, "It's so weird you calling me captain."

"I know right, best man sounds better," I laugh.

"You know I will be...God, Jai you're going to be getting married. Hearts all over Melbourne will shatter, man."

Laughing I reply, "Yeah but you're still available."

"Not funny man, you know I'm jealous as fuck you found the perfect girl."

"You'll find your girl Trav, when you stop being such a tool."

"Harsh words man, but yeah...anyway come on we gotta go smash the Hawks."

I follow, as our captain and my best friend signals us to run out.

There's a strange buzz around the ground as we start warm ups.

Seeing Anni in the crowd, I blow her a kiss, laughing when she waves the flag high.

On one side is the Tigers logo with 'Go Tigers' underneath it and on the other side in the team colours with a red heart in the middle are the words 'Annika 🩶's Jairus'.

My smile is wide, as I run up to the barrier, leaning over it to kiss her.

"I love you too, sweetheart."

"Play hard baby!"

"Always sweetheart," I tease running back off to the middle of the ground for ball up.

~~

The final siren rings out signalling our easy twenty-point win.

Waving to the crowd, we run back down to the rooms celebrating our win in the usual way.

There are fifteen minutes before we have to head back out for the presentation and I bail Trav up to speak to him about the plan.

"Is everything sorted Trav?"
"Yes, man, stop worrying. You know it's going to be sickeningly perfect."

"I'm so nervous though, it's different to everyone watching me play."
"Yeah but you've got it, man. Just focus on her and it will be awesome," he replies patting me on the back and pulling me into a bro hug.

Out on the stage five minutes later, we are lined up as a team behind the microphone.
Travis accepts the trophy, holding it up as he steps up to the mic, "Damn Tigers, it's an honour to accept this as Captain for this upcoming season and I'm so glad to be able to play with these guys again this year, but today, before we get all the official medals presented, a teammate, my best friend Jairus has something special planned."

My heart is pounding in my chest, as the song *'Deep end'* by Daughtry blares out of the speakers.

Stepping up beside Travis, I take a deep breath to calm myself when he says, "Is there a girl by the name of Annika Mathers out there in the crowd?"

The camera that displays what's happening around
the ground on the big screens, pans around until
Anni is on the screen.
Her smile is so wide and her cheeks are crimson.

"Annika come up here girl, Jai needs to ask you
something."

Anni jumps the barrier running onto the field, up
onto the stage and straight into my arms.
She hugs me before kissing me softly.
I hear the crowd cheering as she stretches up on her
tiptoes to whisper 'yes' in my ear.

Stepping back from her hug, I drop to my knee in
front of her.

Trav hands me the microphone and looking up at her,
I take a deep breath, holding the microphone close to
my lips.
The smile doesn't leave her face when I speak,
"Annika Elizabeth Mathers, it's always been only you.
You're meant to be mine. I was sent from the
heavens to love you and I want to dive into the deep
end with you, sweetheart. Will you marry me?"
Her reply as I stand up holding the microphone
towards her lips is a sweet, "Yes, of course, I'll marry
you Jairus."
I hand Travis the microphone back and he gives me a
medal that I put around her neck before kissing her.

The applause and cheering erupt around the ground as I whisper in her ear, "I'll give you a proper ring when we celebrate later sweetheart."

Kissing her, not caring that the whole crowd at the Melbourne Cricket Ground is watching, I hear Travis speaking in the background, "Well there you have it. Jai the man is officially off the market ladies, but I'm still single, so hit me up and get ready for another great season and a wedding!"

Breaking our kiss, I look up at the big screen to see a heart around the camera shot of Anni and I kissing with the words 'She said yes!' above it.

At that moment my heart damn near explodes, Anni has indeed said yes and I can't wait to celebrate our engagement and more importantly our wedding. I've fallen in the deep end, fallen deeply in love with her and I'm ready for forever with her by my side. Now all I want is to get out of this football oval to go and show her how forever is going to feel.

Sixty-Seven | Lyrical Copulation

Jairus

The medal presentation feels like it's taking a month of Sundays. Anni stays up on the stage with us, standing next to me holding my hand as though she is proud to be mine.
The feeling is completely mutual.

After the game, down in the club rooms, Travis makes a toast to us.
Everyone, including the cheer squad is there.
"Well Jai my man, my best mate, I'm so happy for you and Anni here. The first time you told me about your girl, I knew you'd fallen hard for her and you're a lucky bugger that she loves you back, so Congrats man!" he announces, hugging me and Anni.

The team cheers, before they all hug me in turn.
Dana steps up last, looking a little down when she coos, "Congrats Jai!" She kisses my cheek, blushing.
Anni squeezes my hand, as I smile back at Dana, "Thanks, Dan, no hard feelings yeah?"
"No, of course not. I just want you to happy," she replies sadly, before turning to Anni, "Congrats Annika, you're seriously lucky to snag this guy."
"Thanks, Dana, I know he's pretty amazing," Anni replies, stretching up on her tiptoes to turn my face to hers as she presses a kiss to my lips.

Dana sighs as she walks away.
"Sweetheart, that was a little mean."
"You're mine Jai, and I know Dana has a mega crush
on you, so..."
"Yeah, I know, but I've only got eyes for you."

She giggles, kissing me again when Travis elbows me
in the side, "Mate, you need to get out of here, find a
room and celebrate your engagement alone before
we all chunder."
"Ready sweetheart?" I ask.
"Yeah, more than ready," she replies taking my hand.

Quickly I grab my bag, pulling on my jeans over my
footy shorts.
Anni laughs as I strip off my Guernsey, shoving it in
my bag and replacing it with a chambray shirt.

She licks her lips like she's thinking about undressing
me.
Slinging my bag over my shoulder I tease, "Later
sweetheart, you can have me for dessert."
"Mmm, can we have dessert now then?"

"No sweetheart, we have dinner plans at Terrace."
Getting in the car, she huffs, "Why Terrace baby?"
"Because the night I took you there was when I
realised that I was falling in love with you."
She doesn't reply at first, instead laces her hand with
mine over the gear knob and smiles at me.

"Baby?" she asks softly.

"Yeah, sweetheart?"

"I think I loved you from the first time you kissed me that day."

"I know sweetheart, but sometimes words are hard to say."

"Yeah," she muses, as I slide the car into the carpark underneath Terrace.

Once inside, we are ushered to a table on the rooftop.
In the middle, the number thirteen is the table number and Anni laughs.

"Did you ask for table thirteen, baby?"

"To be honest no, but it's perfect, just like you sweetheart," I reply pulling out her chair for her to sit down, before taking my own seat opposite.

We order as soon as the waiter is at the table, knowing exactly what we want from last time and standing up, I fish the small velvet box out of my jeans pocket.
Again I get down on one knee, opening the box, holding it up to her.

"Sweetheart, I know you've already said yes, but to make it official will you accept this ring?"

"Yes, Jai, yes, it's...it's stunning! It must have cost you a fortune," she beams as I slip it on her finger before kissing it and standing up.

"Only a month salary, but it's worth every cent seeing the smile on your face and how perfect it is on your finger."

"But Jai, that's like 20,000 dollars!"

"Yeah I know but for you sweetheart, I'd pay so much more. You're meant to be mine."

Our food is brought to the table, and I watch as she eats, shifting in her seat like she's uncomfortable.

"Sweetheart, are you ok?"

"Yeah, I um...as much as this dinner is super nice, I kind of just want to go home and be yours in celebration."

"Yeah, eat quickly then sweetheart," I smile, taking a couple final bites of my steak.

~~

Driving home feels like forever when all I want to do was make love to Anni, my beautiful fiancée'.

Gunning the car, I silently pray for no cops to be around as I speed down St Kilda Road.

"Jai, you'll get a speeding fine!"

"Don't care, sweetheart, I want to get home like now!"

She laughs, as we turn into the carpark and I slide the car into our parking spot, cutting the engine the moment the car stops.

I'm out of the car like a rocket, helping her out and dragging her to the elevator where, as usual I smash my lips against hers.

Teasingly, as we reach the front door, I run my hands up the back of the oversized sweater she's wearing with her white leggings.

I press my arse against the scan pad, as the card is in there to open the door. Hearing it click, I reach behind and depress the handle.

It closes behind us, as Anni jumps into my arms, kissing me so fiercely my heart pounds a hundred miles an hour.

Breathless she breaks the kiss, her forehead against mine when she asks, "How did you know I was going to say yes?"

"I didn't sweetheart but it doesn't matter now because you're mine forever."

"Mmm, forever sounds wonderful."

"Oh yeah, sweetheart and tonight I'm going to show you again just how much I love you and exactly what forever feels like."

Her breath hitches in her chest, as she lifts her arms over her head before jumping to the floor.

Lifting the sweater over her head, I moan seeing she is only wearing a crop top bralette.

"Make love to me Jairus," she drawls, slipping the bralette straps down her arms. I watch the fabric fall away exposing her breasts, taking one in my mouth and teasing the bud, biting it between my teeth, making her moan.

Taking the other one in my mouth, I run a finger along the elastic of her white leggings, pushing them to the floor with her skimpy underwear too, before I look up at her, "Annika, you're so fucking beautiful. Every fucking centimetre of your body is so perfect."
"Jai baby, please touch me," she moans, biting her lip and blushing.
"I'm going to do more than touch you sweetheart, but you have to help me get undressed first," I tease, running a finger along her wet core, flicking it over her clit, making her let out a hot pleasure filled whimper.

Her fingers find the button of my jeans, and she makes quick work of dakking me, pushing my jeans to my ankles, along with my footy shorts. She's about to push my red boxers to the floor when I capture her hands in mine.
"Uh-uh sweetheart, I'm going to make you cum first and then you can finish getting me naked."
"Mmm, but baby..." she muses, fumbling with the buttons of my shirt and trying to push my shirt off.

"Sweetheart," I muse before kissing her hard, plunging a finger inside her, making her moan against my lips.

"Jai, baby please...make love to me now...here...now," she begs, pressing her body against mine.
"Oh really, right here, right now?"

"Yes," she hisses as I tease her again brushing my fingers above her clit, before lifting her into my arms, carrying her over to the sunken couch.

Dropping her down, she stretches out and I lean over her body smirking at her, "What do you want sweetheart?" I taunt.
"A kiss...here," she teases, touching her clit and moaning.
"Mmmm, best dessert ever," I growl, before licking down from between her breasts, over her stomach and hips.
They buck in response and smiling I spread her legs wide licking up her thigh, before pressing my lips against her clit.

She again moans, as my tongue circles her clit before I delve inside her wet folds, tasting every drop of her delicious honey.
"Jai, baby...fuck that feels good," she moans, her hips lifting on the couch as I tease her with my tongue more.
Looking up at her for a moment I groan, "you taste so fucking delicious sweetheart, cum for me yeah?"

Again I lick over her clit, and she lets out a loud as moan, her body shaking as the pleasure of her climax rocks through her.
Stretching over her naked body, I lick my lips smirking at her when I tease, "Fuck I love making you cum, sweetheart."

"Mmmm, can you kiss me here now baby?" She taunts running a finger along her lips.
"Oh yeah?" I laugh smashing my lips against hers, lacing my tongue with hers so she can taste herself on my tongue.

I can't help but let out a deep groan against her lips when she grabs my cock in her palm, stroking her fingers up and down the growing length teasingly.
Breaking the kiss, she taunts, "my turn now baby."
She daks me, ripping the side of my boxers in the process of yanking them to my knees.

She sits up, pushing her hands against my bare chest so I'm on my knees.
Her sweet blue eyes look up at me as she takes my hard cock in her mouth, running her tongue up and down the length furiously.
She teases the tip, licking the pre-cum that I can feel spurting out.
Grabbing her hair, freeing it from the bun on top of her head, I pull her mouth off my cock, "Sweetheart that feels beyond amazing, but I want to bury myself inside you, so bad."

She smirks at me grabbing my shoulders to push my shirt off.
I shrug out of it, throwing it behind me, before pushing my body back over hers and kissing her passionately again.

My cock is grazing her entrance, her hips rising to meet mine, eager for me to slide inside her waiting body.

"Jai baby, you're so handsome," she muses, licking her lips and biting down on them as I plunge inside her hard.

Her moans are carnal as I thrust deep, before almost withdrawing completely before plunging inside her, deeper again.

"Mmmm...god...Annika...fuck..." I groan, pounding into to her so hard, I'm afraid I'm going to break her.

She moans louder, as I push even deeper into her. Her hands find my cheeks bringing her lips to mine for a hot, heart-shattering kiss. Her legs wrap around my arse, not letting me move as she comes apart beneath me.

Her body shakes as her climax takes over and I lose myself in her, coming undone and collapsing against her chest.

I feel her kiss against my hair, as she whispers, "Jairus, baby, that was even more incredible than the first time we had sex."

Looking down at her, as I lay down beside her, I reply, "Sweetheart, every time I make love to you is incredible and I'm so glad I can make love to every day for the rest of our lives."

"Every day?" She asks with a hint of laughter in her tone.

"Well, I guess not every day, shark week will interrupt us," I laugh, biting my lip when I think about the last time shark week interrupted us being together, "um sweetheart, when was the last time you had shark week?"

She doesn't hesitate in replying, "When you came back from Hong Kong, why?"
"You're not pregnant, are you?"
She laughs sweetly, and I'm not sure whether to laugh back or not.

"No, I'm on the pill baby, and I've been skipping the sugar pills so I don't have shark week."
"Oh ok," I mutter, kind of feeling upset that she isn't pregnant and didn't tell me that she's on the pill.
"Sorry baby, I should have told you."
"It's ok, I kind of want you all to myself for a little longer."
"Yeah," she muses kissing me tenderly as I wrap an arm around her waist, scooping her into my arms.

Standing up I carry her bridal style towards our bedroom.
"Baby what are you doing?" She laughs.
"Practicing for our wedding night, fiancée," I tease throwing her down on the bed, before stretching over her to kiss her again.

"Mmm, I know something else we can practice," she teases, diving under the covers and beckoning me towards her with a finger.

"Oh, really sweetheart? We've got forever to get that right," I tease getting under the covers with her and pulling her body against mine.

"I love you Jairus," she muses, making my heart soar.

"I love you to Annika, forever."

I press a kiss to her lips, my heart pounding hard in my chest, so happy that I have forever to kiss her. She is my everything.

Caz May

Epilogue | White Dress

Six Months later

Carrying a rather large suit bag down Bridge road
towards my car in the middle of winter is a
challenge.
The day is bitterly cold, the coldest August day
we've had in years, so cold that even trying on
my wedding dress in the shop I shivered.

The shivers in the shop, I know weren't just from
the cold though, it's the excitement that in four
months' time, I'm going to be marrying Jairus.

My heart aches a little, as I haven't spoken to
Austin since I moved in with Jairus in January
and I miss having my best friend around.

The rain has started to pelt down, so awkwardly
not looking where I'm going I start to run
towards my car.
Nearly falling face down on the footpath, I bump
into someone.

"Anni, is that you?"

I look up, coming face to face with Austin.

"Hi Austin," I reply, shaking my head to make sure he really is standing in front of me.

He doesn't say 'hi' back, instead states a question, "So Bella wasn't lying then?"

"No Aust, I'm marrying Jairus in December and I'm sorry I didn't tell you."

"Yeah, you could have told me, Annika. I...I..."

"I thought you'd not want to know," I say apologetically.

"How can you say that Annika? You were my best friend. I still love you and the fact you're going to be wearing that white dress whilst you marry someone else really hurts...more than you'll ever know."

"I'm sorry Austin, I really am."

"Yeah so am I Annika, but I hope you're happy."

I smile at him, "I am Aust...I really am but I gotta go. Take care."

I think about hugging him, and for a moment I think he's going to kiss my cheek, but instead, he smiles walking away as I unlock the car.

Laying my wedding dress on the back seat, I watch him walk away and my heart breaks all over again, just like the day I said goodbye to him six months earlier.

Getting in the car, I make a mental note to ask Bella if I should make amends by inviting him to the wedding.

I want my best friend back because without him life just isn't the same.
Roommates do kiss and tell, but friends don't say goodbye.

THE END

Australian Slang Glossary

Ute-Truck

Bludger- someone lazy, doesn't do much and possibly relies on social security benefits

Ripper- something really good/great

Ridgy-Didge- Cool

Bonzer-Great, awesome

Pash/ing/ed- to kiss/make out

Arvo- afternoon

Chunder- Vomit, throw up

Gobby- Blowjob

Aussie Kiss- going down on a girl

Daks- pants/trousers/underwear

Undies/Knickers/Jocks-underwear (female knickers, male Jocks, undies both)

Dakking- to pull someone daks down (see above)

Thongs- Footwear, otherwise known as flip flops

Esky- Cooler-you keep drinks cool in it

Dunny- toilet

Bogan-white trash/trailer trash

Old Fella- Your father/Dad

Franger- Condom, Trojan etc

Milo- a malt chocolate powered drink mix (can be made hot or cold)

Macca's-MacDonalds

Fair Dinkum- used to emphasise or seek confirmation of the genuineness or truth of something

Shark Week- A woman's monthly cycle

Stuffed if I know- *a nicer way to say fucked if I know*

That will barely cover your mappa Tassie- that will barely cover your vagina

AFL- Australian Rules Football

Playlists

Annika

Austin

Jairus

Bella

Acknowledgments

an't believe I'm typing this, you know actually writing
knowledgments for my first published book. But it's happening!
, let's get straight to it!

rstly, I'd like to give a big shout out, huge thanks and hugs to my
w writing buddy, Joey Sims. Her help in beta reading, editing
d being someone to bounce ideas off has been so amazing. Not
ly that, she's helped me with her knowledge of self-publishing
d given me confidence to get my writing out there. Joey, I know
e haven't met in person, but I'm forever grateful for you and the
endship you've given me these past months. We're on this
riting journey together and that makes it so much better, to
are it with such a great friend.

f course, I can't forget my best friend Bianca, who this book is
so dedicated to. We've been best friends for over twenty years
d she has always supported my writing, encouraging me in
ery step of this journey. Her help in the final editing stage,
ling me that I've done well makes me so happy. Some of the
sis for Annika and Bella's friendship is based on our lives and
endship. B, I truly can't thank you enough for always being my
ggest fan. I love you!

d yes, I need to thank my own loveable bearded hero, my
sband Cam. I think he has a bit of Jairus in him, always teasing
e, but I know he loves me and supports me in anything I want to
. Life wouldn't be the same without him by my side, working
rd and encouraging me, plus letting me use the credit card to
y this, that and everything.

Cam, you're my rock, my better half (most of the time) and you'll forever be my one and only, Always only you.

Nearly at the end, I also need to thank my amazing Mum. She's helped me navigate the whole setup process for self-publishing from a business perspective, and even though she hasn't read my work as yet she constantly praises me, encourages me and forces me to use the logical part of my brain which I often switch off when in the thick of writing a book. Mum, if you ever do read my books, I'm sorry I'm not as innocent as you think I am, and yes, I did sneakily read Mills and Boon romance books when I twelve. I love you mummy, you will always be an inspiration and guiding light in my life.

And lastly, thank you to all of you who have now read my book, c I've met on Wattpad or Instagram. There are too many of you to name, but if we've had a Direct Message chat or you've followed me and liked my content, this book is for you.
Your support is what keeps me writing!
And I don't want to ever stop sharing my stories with you all!

Caz May

Friends Don't Say Goodbye

Book 2 of Always Only You (Austin's Story)

Coming Soon

Prologue | Dress in White

August 2018

It's absolutely freezing as I walk down Bridge Road, wearing only a tank top and trackies from leaving boxing. It has been such a sunny day, but as the sun is setting the cold sets in quick. Nearly at my ute, I'm about to unlock it when I see her.

Annika is struggling to carry a rather large suit bag towards a car parked just down from mine. My heart pounds in my chest seeing her again, as we've not spoken since she left to live with Jairus and we'd had a major fight. She looks absolutely stunning, having cut her hair a little shorter it frames her heart shaped face.
Rain is starting to pelt down, making her run awkwardly with the suit bag until she bumps straight into me. I could move, ignore her even but instead I ask, "Anni, is that you?"
She looks up, completely taken aback by my presence.

"Hi Austin," she replies, shaking her head as though she can't believe I'm actually standing in front of her.

I don't say 'hi' back, instead state, "So Bella wasn't lying then?"

"No Aust, I'm marrying Jairus in November and I'm sorry I didn't tell you."

Her words stab at my still broken heart and I speak with malice in my tone, "Yeah, you could have told me Annika. I...I..."

"I thought you'd not want to know," she says in an apologetic tone.

"How can you say that Annika?" I ask not waiting for her response when I continue, "You were my best friend. I still love you and the fact you're going to be wearing that white dress whilst you marry someone else really hurts...more than you'll ever know."

"I'm sorry Austin, I really am," she protests in the sweet innocent way that always makes my heart ache.

"Yeah so am I Annika," I spit at her a little meaner in tone than I feel, "but I hope you're happy."

Smiling wide at me she replies, "I am Aust...I really am but I gotta go. Take care."

She leans forward, closer to me, almost invading my personal space as though she's contemplating hugging me. I'm anticipating her hug and thinking about kissing her cheek, but instead I just smile as she walks away unlocking her car.

Getting in my ute, I watch her as she puts the suit bag in the back seat of her BMW and my heart shatters all over again just like the day she said goodbye when she moved out with Jairus.
I want her to be happy, but with me, not with him. It isn't that I hate the guy, he's good for her and it's clear her family loves him but I miss my best friend.

Reversing the ute out of the car park to drive home, my mind wanders, thinking of what I could do to be best friends with her again. It would hurt to be back in her life, and still be in love with her, but not being in her life at all hurts a hundred times more.

One | Pack it Up

Eight Months Earlier-January, 2018

I've barely spoken to Anni since our fight about her
confessing to being in love with Jairus. Her words stabbed
at my heart so bad, I'd snapped at her. Hurling words at
her, that I just didn't mean, I felt like a complete tool.
Honestly, I wanted to apologise, but every time I opened
my mouth nothing would come out or she'd give me a bad
case of dagger eyes that made me retreat like a wounded
dingo.

The tension in our apartment is like something out of a
horror movie, as we all tip toe around each other. Jairus
has been sleeping in her room since New Years, and Bella
has shifted in as my roomie. She's hardly ever
home, which at times I kinda like but at the same
time I like going to sleep thinking about her lying
in the bed across from me.

I'm still in love with Anni, but thinking about the
couple of times I'd fucked Bella always makes
me hard.

When she's lying across me I look over at her
whilst I sneakily jack off.

Watching the rise and fall of her chest oddly excites me.

I sometimes feel as though she's hiding something from me, that maybe she has feelings for me but I keep my trap shut. I'd rather keep the casual sex arrangement we have going on than talk about feelings.

Feelings were the enemy in my mind, as I always found it difficult to face mine. Telling Anni that I just wanted to be fuck buddies when I'd fallen in love with her was the stupidest decision I'd made in a long time, maybe in forever.

She's now packing up her stuff to move out, kneeling on her overly full suitcase trying to zip it up. I'm not going to let her walk out the door, out of my life without trying to make amends with her.

Stopping in the door jamb of her room, I laugh, "Need some help babe?"

"No Austin I don't. Leave me alone!" she snaps, sighing as she finally gets the zipper shut.

I can't tear my eyes away from her lean legs in the smallest denim shorts in existence.

Just that sight is enough to make my groin ache, "Anni, please. Don't be like that," I beg.

"Like what Austin?"

"I don't Anni...a bitch. I'm sorry ok."

"It's too late to be sorry Austin. You...you ruined us," she sighs, her words stabbing my heart.

"Anni, that's really harsh. I don't want to lose you."

"Yeah, well you should have thought about that before you opened your mouth Austin."

The way she's deliberately using my full name is vindictive, cruel and so not like her usual self.

"Are you sure about this Anni? Do you really love him?"

She smiles, coming to stand next to me. My heart is pounding in my chest, just hoping that maybe she's finally going to forgive me.

"With all my heart Austin...I can't explain it," she replies, her tone softer.

"Hmm, ok," I mutter walking out of her room, feeling as though nothing has changed since our fight.

She's leaving in two days, but I already feel like she's gone.

My heart is broken, shattered. Love is supposed to be amazing, but for me so far it's nothing but pain.

About the Author

Caz May is a librarian/teacher by trade, but was always destined to be an author from a young age. In her spare time, she can be found devouring books or writing her own stories with characters that may not be the typical romance heroes but are loveable just as much.

Caz is married to her own real-life bearded hero and has two fur babies.

She lives for Iced coffee, especially from Gloria Jeans or a Farmers Union but pretty much just loves food in general. When she's not writing, or reading a book most likely she can probably be found asleep or binge-watching shows on Netflix.

Check out her Instagram or other socials to get in touch.

Instagram- @cazmay25

Facebook- @CazMayAuthor

Wattpad- @Caz-May

Spotify- cazcat25

Website- https://cazcat25.wixsite.com/cazmay-author

Caz May

Roommates Don't Kiss & Tell

www.ingramcontent.com/pod-product-compliance
Lightning Source LLC
Chambersburg PA
CBHW020649110726
47901CB00001B/106

* 9 7 8 0 6 4 8 4 9 9 8 0 0 *